MW01138524

To Tempt an Earl

by

Kristin Vayden

BLUE TULIP
PUBLISHING

To Tempt an Earl
by Kristin Vayden
Published by Blue Tulip Publishing
www.bluetulippublishing.com

PROLOGUE

BETHANNY LAMONT CLOSED her deep brown eyes and sighed, knowing she'd never be able to sleep.

But she was trying to, nonetheless.

How could one partake of something as trivial as sleep when tomorrow was her debut? Every moment of training, every lady-like pursuit would come to a pinnacle tomorrow when she was announced at the ball held in her honor. Her skin felt feverish with excitement, her heart danced an excited rhythm, and her toes curled in anticipation for the final arrival of such a long-awaited night.

She sighed contentedly, secretively.

Because, well, she *did* have a secret after all.

It was entirely possible that she had subtly asked Lady Southridge — her self-declared grandmother — if Lord Graham — Lady Southridge's *much* younger brother — would, by chance, attend her ball.

Which he would!

And this knowledge was the true cause for her inability to sleep even a wink. But it wouldn't have mattered if she slept or stayed awake; her dreams would be the exact same variety and feature a very striking hero.

It had been two years since she'd last seen him, but every moment was etched in her mind as only a thousand remembrances can do. The slight curl of his hair, the exact golden hue of his skin, the way his cheeks dimpled when he flashed a smile.

She sighed. And relaxing into the soft comfort of her bed, she allowed her mind to wander into familiar territory; memories of Graham.

One of her favorites took place while only sixteen. She still hadn't *blossomed* — as Carlotta had called it — and already struggling with her awkward grace, she was striving to learn to waltz with some decorum.

She had *thought* she was alone. The library had certainly *seemed* empty, and she'd taken full advantage. With just enough space in the far corner of the room, she practiced a poised curtsey and began to waltz with an invisible partner. Whispering the count to keep from missing a step, she spun and swirled; keeping to her toes, her movements would be hopefully less clumsy. Unfortunately, all that keeping to her toes had done was to increase her lack of grace, and she tripped over her own feet and stumbled to the floor, arms flailing.

She swore.

After all, at sixteen one truly believes that the world does revolve around the ability to waltz. For if a debutant cannot waltz, how can a gentleman fall in love with her grace and beauty?

"I don't believe the duke would approve of such language from his ward." An amused voice shattered her irritation, replacing it with humiliation.

Bethanny glanced up, her eyes widening as dread chilled her heart.

Anyone but him. The Prince Regent, the worst gossipmonger. *Just not him.*

But as fate, or failure, would have it, it was the very handsome and dashing Lord Graham. His smile could warm her insides for days at a time, and, truth be told, he was the very person she hoped to waltz with someday.

Too bad that would never happen now.

Bloody waltz.

She never liked it anyway.

"I do find that perhaps my assistance is needed." He walked around the chaise and extended a gloved hand to her, his golden hair falling forward slightly as he bowed.

"Pardon?" Bethanny blinked.

"Come, let's try this again. I'm told I'm a wonderful teacher." He winked and then smiled when Bethanny placed a trembling hand in his. His amber-colored eyes danced with a mischief and merriment that immediately set her to ease, yet awakened some swirling emotion she couldn't name.

"You see, Miss Lamont. To waltz is about two people moving as one. So it's only natural that you'd find it exceedingly difficult to practice by yourself. Allow me the honor." He began to hum, his rich voice vibrating against her, melting her.

Unable to resist, and not wishing to, she delighted in the pleasurable sensation of his hand at her waist, radiating warmth. He was the perfect height, not towering over her, but tall enough to make her feel feminine, petite and… safe in his arms. He continued to hum and, exerting the slightest pressure, he led her in a waltz that, though was still somewhat lacking in grace, was far improved over her original attempt.

"See? You only needed an experienced partner." He glanced down and colored slightly.

Bethanny felt her brow furrow at his reaction, curious as to what secret meaning could have made him blush slightly.

"Well, you *did* say you were a good teacher. You have been proven correct in your assessment, my lord. I thank you," Bethanny replied, hoping she sounded more mature, more knowledgeable than her sixteen years.

"Thank you, Miss Lamont." He nodded. "Now, let us step this way." He tenderly led her to the left. "And you must remember that a gentleman will always keep a proper distance between himself and you. Don't let someone bully you into a more… intimate… embrace."

"Oh?" Bethanny swallowed then gathered her courage. "And how close would be too close, my lord?" she asked as she blinked innocently — or so she'd hoped.

"Hmm." Lord Graham's brow furrowed. "I'd think that anything closer than this would be considered too close, Miss Lamont."

Drat. He didn't pull her in closer. Thinking quickly, she tried again.

"Say some cad tried to pull me in. How would I extricate myself?" she asked.

"Clever question." He offered an approving grin. "Now, Miss Lamont, I'm going to attempt to pull you in, and you must resist. You see, a gentleman, or rake, will not want to draw attention to himself on the dance floor. He'd want to be secretive about his intentions, assuming your youth to make you easy prey."

"Am I?" Bethanny asked.

"Are you?"

"Easy prey," Bethanny asked, leaning slightly forward.

"Er…" Lord Graham blinked, then his gaze sharpened. He didn't answer right away but studied her for a moment, as if judging his answer.

"Actually, no. I don't believe you are."

"Good." Bethanny nodded, her toes tingling from his intense gaze.

"Do not let my answer give you a false sense of security. Rakes love a challenge." He raised an eyebrow.

"Oh." She glanced down to his shining Hessian boots.

"Now, if you feel that some scoundrel has pulled you in

too far, and you cannot extricate yourself…" Lord Graham pulled her in.

Bethanny felt her eyes widen as her lips parted in shock and wonder. He smelled of cloves and cinnamon with a hint of peppermint. She'd never forget that scent.

"Yes?" she whispered breathlessly.

"Simply step on the cad's toes. Hard." Lord Graham replied, grinning widely.

"Pardon?"

"Shove your heel into the cad's boot—"

Bethanny began to follow his advice and stomped her heel on his boot.

"Bloody — er, drat. Miss Lamont, I didn't intend for you to…" He took a deep breath and broke the frame of their waltz. "I didn't intend for you to practice on me." He placed his hands on his hips and shot her a longsuffering glare.

"Oh. Er, forgive me?" Bethanny felt her face heat with a deep blush.

Lord Graham shook his head and glared.

Bethanny gulped.

Then a grin broke through. "Of course!" He chuckled.

"Unfair! You had me frightened that I had severely offended you!" Bethanny scolded, and, before she could think, reached out and swatted his shoulder.

"You should have seen your face." Lord Graham laughed.

Bethanny glared.

"Hey, must I remind you that your foot inflicted serious damage on my highly polished boots? My valet is going to be livid! I'll be sure to place the blame on you."

"Afraid of your valet? Here I thought you were braver than that."

"You, miss, have never met my valet."

"True." Bethanny giggled, thrilled to be in such easy conversation. It was a dream. Ever since she had first seen him upon returning from Greenford Waters — the Duke's estate in Bath — Bethanny had harbored a secret obsession with Lord Graham.

"Miss Lamont, this has been a joy, but I'll now take my leave." He released her and stepped away, immediately rendering her chilled and craving his presence.

Bethanny shook her head at the fading of the memory. Time had been kind to her over the past two years, and she had finally bloomed — Carlotta's words — and now she actually had a chance to catch Lord Graham's attention and — God willing — his affection. The last time she had seen him was when he had bid them all farewell. She had cried for a fortnight afterward, knowing she'd not see him for at least two years. But now with her ball on the horizon, and with the good fortune of Lord Graham finally returning, there was finally hope.

She'd at least catch his eye. Though she had to admit that she'd catch everyone's eye. It was after all, *her* ball. But surely he'd see her as more of a woman than the child he'd been introduced to; at least she hoped for it.

Every fiber of her being hoped it.

Her governess-turned-guardian — who was actually more of an older sister — Carlotta Evermore, Duchess of Clairmont, was thankfully unaware of her secret. If she had any suspicion, she would have told her husband, the duke, who would have already taken it upon himself to have a long — or several long — lectures with her on the need to be extremely cautious in any sort of attachment. Bethanny found it very ironic, and, frankly, amusing that her guardian was so overly protective and overbearing, given his former reputation.

And she was quite sure that the information she'd been given concerning said reputation was of the *tamest* variety.

Also, the fact that Lord Graham was not much younger than the duke wouldn't help her cause either.

And quite the rake himself.

But rakes could be reformed, at least that's what always happened in the gossip, and, being a student of observation, she could readily attest to the truth of that gossip. The duke's intense love for his wife, Carlotta, was a testament of that fact.

And it wasn't an understatement when she said the man was reformed. Because if there ever had been a rake, it was he, and if there had ever been a man to make a complete about-face with his nature, it was also he.

For pity sake Bethanny and her sisters couldn't sneeze without him asking if they were catching cold. It was endearing, but also quite... smothering.

Bethanny's mind began to wander, and, as it usually did, found its way back to its favorite subject of pondering, Edward Greenly, Earl of Graham. And with a soft smile, she imagined what his hand would feel like at her waist as he led a waltz, and how soft his lips would feel pressed against hers in a kiss.

And Bethanny slept... and dreamed.

CHAPTER ONE

The day before.

"No." GRAHAM SUCCINCTLY enunciated the word once more, just in case his hoyden of an older sister, who had some misbegotten notion that she was his mother, hadn't understood the first three times he'd answered her question.

"You don't have a choice, Edward."

"Yes, I do."

"No. You clearly don't understand."

"I understand completely. I'm supposed to feel obligated to attend some chit's debut simply because you have a soft spot for the poor thing." He shook his head and narrowed his eyes. "I'm not daft, Dianna. You're on some forsaken, misbegotten, bloody mission to marry me off, and I'm not going to do it!"

"You don't remember." His sister, the meddlesome Lady Southridge, shook her head in startled amazement.

"Why should I remember? All you said was that someone named Betsy is having a ball, and I was expected there at eight sharp. What part of that conversation was supposed to be familiar?" he asked. He gestured impatiently to her, awaiting an answer.

"For heaven's sake, it's Bethanny, and *Bethanny* is Clairmont's ward!" She all but shouted, clearly aggravated. Of course, that was the dynamic of their relationship most times.

Loud and confusing.

It was moments like these he was exceedingly thankful for his estate near Edinburgh, for it provided the perfect escape.

From his sister.

"Clairmont's ward?" Graham furrowed his brow in confusion. "Why didn't you say so? Of course I'll be there. Wouldn't miss it for the world."

"I *did* say so. I simply assumed you to be intelligent enough to remember the poor girl's name. Believe me, I'll not give you so much credit next time, Edward."

"Hilarious, Dianna." He gave her a sarcastic expression, one he had often used toward her, even as a young lad.

"I wasn't teasing." She raised a daring eyebrow.

"Hurt, deeply." He rolled his eyes and flopped into a chair, earning a glare from his sister at his poor manners.

He propped his foot up on the table just to spite her further.

"If you had been here for more than a day or so in the past two years, you would have known exactly who I was speaking about when I said her name, but no. You've been gallivanting to Italy, Scotland, and heaven knows where else."

"I've been avoiding *you* actually." He shrugged.

"Edward!"

"Joking, er, mostly."

His sister placed her hands on her hips and narrowed her eyes.

He smirked, enjoying the sensation of provoking exactly the response he desired. "You know I had business to attend to."

"So why come back now?" she asked, and, honestly, he was surprised it had taken her as long as it had to ask that very specific question. Usually she was like an investigator at Scotland Yard. Though, he *had* only been back for a week and, well, he hadn't exactly told her he was in town until two days ago.

Though he'd assumed she'd already known he was in town. The woman had spies.

"Now that all my estate business is thoroughly established for the next generation of Grahams, I've decided it's time to marry." He leaned back, watching her expression with keen interest.

Her eyes widened then narrowed. Shaking her head, she shrugged. "No, honestly. Why?" His sister made a dismissive gesture with her hand, one that said, *Quit wasting my time and give me the real answer.*

"Er, I actually am." He felt chagrined. Was he that hopeless of a cause in his own sister's eyes?

"You are?" She blinked in disbelief.

"Indeed." He nodded once.

"It's about bloody time." Dianna stood and strode toward him, her eyes glancing heavenward as she mouthed a prayer. "I never thought I'd see the day."

Her eyes were glossy as she looked back to him. Was she crying? He stood up, confused.

Without hesitation, she pulled him into an embrace.

He heard her sniffle.

She *was* crying.

Bloody hell, he didn't realize he was *that* much of a lost cause.

"I, er, well." He patted her back awkwardly.

She took a deep breath and leaned back, her eyes glistening.

"It's wonderful! And I have the most perfect girl in mind—"

"No." *No, no, no, no!*

"What?"

"No. Dianna, listen to me. In fact, repeat after me everything that I'm going to say to you. Are you ready?" He reached down and grasped her hands, leaning forward till he was convinced he had her attention.

Her eyes narrowed, which he considered a *yes*.

"You are not to meddle." He waited then raised an eyebrow, lowering his chin while he speared her with a patient glare.

"You are not to meddle," she spoke through clenched teeth.

"Mature. You, as in… *you*. Try again."

"I am not to meddle," she repeated, though her cheeks were bright red and her teeth were still clenched.

"I knew you were smarter than they all claimed."

"Edward," she ground out.

"I, Edward, am the one who will be selecting the bride. Not you."

"I—" she began, intending to mock him.

"Dianna…"

"Very well. You are getting married. You'll pick the bride."

"Thank you. Was that so difficult?" He released her hands.

"Yes. In fact, I believe I'll rest all afternoon from the exertion of this very conversation." She rolled her eyes and backed away.

"Brilliant. I'll have the afternoon to myself."

"Not exactly."

"What do you mean?"

"Once you visited yesterday, I told the duchess and Bethanny of your arrival, and they immediately asked if you would attend the debut—"

"Which I've already agreed to, so I'm not seein—"

KRISTIN VAYDEN

"The point? Well, that's because you're interrupting me—"
"I'm not—"
His sister raised an eyebrow and waited.
He closed his mouth.
"Thank you. It would seem that your friend, Clairmont, is not dealing well with Bethanny's debut. His experience being of the darker variety, I imagine he's conjured up all sorts of evil men lurking in the corners having nefarious schemes." She shook her head.

"Clairmont?" he asked, just to make sure they were talking about the same person. He had kept in contact with his good friend but hadn't seen much of him since his marriage. Graham's travels kept him busy, and... well, he assumed Clairmont was busy with other... er... *things.*

"Yes... he's quite overprotective of the girls. And Bethanny, she's sure to attract the attention of all." His sister grinned, a strange expression lighting her gaze.

"How so?" he asked, curious and slightly concerned over his sister's expression.

He furrowed his brow as he thought about the slight-framed girl he remembered. Bethanny. *Miss Lamont.* Her eyes had taken up most of her face, deep brown and soulful, and far older and wiser than her young frame. There was nothing significant about her, save the eyes. She was thin, too thin, and had the figure of a boy rather than girl.

Poor thing. Clairmont was probably afraid he'd never find her a match.

She paused then tilted her head ever so slightly. "Never mind. The truth is that Carlotta rather thought that her husband might welcome your company to distract him from the stressful situation."

"Oh, was that it?" he asked, though he was sure he already knew.

"Yes."

"Not a problem. When did you say the debut was?"

"Tomorrow."

"Perfect. I'll stop by today and help the old man forget about his blossoming wards." He bowed.

His sister choked.

"Er, what?" he asked, confused.

"Nothing, nothing at all." She snickered, her eyes now dancing with some mysterious mirth.

But he never had understood his sister and didn't pretend to now. The truth was, he didn't really care either.

So, with a shrug and a bow to his sister, he quit the Southridge residence and made his way to Mayfair to catch up with his longtime friend, the Duke of Clairmont.

Bethanny studied herself in the mirror. The dress was perfect, utterly and devastatingly perfect. She spun slowly, taking in every drape of the rose-hued fabric and the pearl cream of the ribbon adorning it. The cut hugged her womanly shape, accentuating her curves, yet was still modest enough for the duke to allow her out of her room. And she knew full well that he'd have no reservations of locking her in her room if she were immodest, her come out or not.

He meant well, and Bethanny loved him, even if he was overprotective. She found it endearing rather than offensive. It reminded her of her parents, and that thought always brought her comfort, as if being reminded of them kept their memory, their legacy, alive, even when they were no longer. A pinch in her heart caused her to wince as she thought again about how her father wouldn't be there to watch her debut, nor would her mother kiss her on the cheek and encourage her. But it was enough to have her sisters, Beatrix and Berty, as well as the duchess and duke. Together, they made a family, Lady Southridge adding that final touch of random meddling that made everyone cringe. It might not be a perfect family, but it was hers, and she was thankful.

"Are you done admiring yourself?" Beatrix asked with amusement thick in her tone. Beatrix was sixteen, the very age of Bethanny when they had come to live with the duke. In two years Beatrix had grown from a girl to a woman, a keenly intelligent woman. Bethanny tried to keep her overprotective emotions in check, but in truth, she knew she was little better than the duke. But she couldn't help it. Since their mother and father died, Bethanny felt this... responsibility to be there, to be strong for her sisters.

"No." Bethanny glanced over to her sister and raised an eyebrow. "Perhaps you should come back later," she teased, hoping to lighten her own musings.

"If I did come back later, it would be tomorrow, and you'll spend the night in with a modiste rather than your nice warm bed back home." Beatrix quipped, a knowing smile bending her lips.

"Very well," Bethanny conceded. She *was* quite fond of her bed.

And morning chocolate.

And the newspaper.

"I knew you had some sense," Beatrix replied, a grin tugging at her lips.

Bethanny scrunched up her nose at her sister but smiled nonetheless. With a reluctant sigh, she signaled the modiste, Madame Beaulieu. She was a short woman, thin and petite, with chestnut hair strewn with silver.

"*Avez-vous terminé?*" she asked, her accent thick.

"Yes, I believe I'm finished," Bethanny answered.

"*Vous êtes une vision,* Miss Lamont. An utter vision. The gentlemen will fall to their knees at your beauty! *De l'avenir, les messieurs vont tomber à genoux autour de vous.*"

"Thank you, Madame Beaulieu." Bethanny felt her face flame at the compliment.

While she appreciated the sentiment, she would rather

prefer to simply draw the attention of one man, having *him* fall to his knees… now *that* would be perfect.

Shaking her head to dispel her daydream, she waited as Madame helped her out of the dress.

In short work, the dress was packaged up to take home. The servants at the duke's townhome in Mayfair would press it and have it perfect by tomorrow.

"Can we go now, please? I'm so hungry!" Berty whined.

"Yes, yes, we can leave now." Carlotta, Duchess of Clairmont placed her gloved hand over her mouth to stifle a giggle.

Bethanny indulged in an amused grin at her youngest sister's propensity for food, sweets in particular. If Berty wasn't eating, she was impatiently waiting till she was given the opportunity to do so again. At nine, the little girl was as opinionated as Lady Southridge and as stubborn as the duke. Her dark hair and feathery lashes made her appear innocent when the opposite was often far more accurate

"Berty, you cannot possibly be hungry." Beatrix speared her sister with a disbelieving glare.

"I am! It's been hours—"

"It's been perhaps one hour, Berty."

"One hour too long," Berty huffed, crossing her slightly pump arms in front of her slightly plumper frame.

Beatrix rolled her eyes and raised an eyebrow to Carlotta.

"We'll return shortly. I have faith that you'll survive until we do."

"But—"

"Berty…" Carlotta warned gently.

"Yes, Your Grace."

Bethanny noted the slight color in Carlotta's cheeks as Berty used the address *Your Grace* as they were to do when in public. Though it had been almost two years since their marriage, Bethanny doubted that Carlotta, or Lottie, as they usually called her, was accustomed to such a title. Her humility endeared her further to the girls.

"Come along, girls. Let's be off. We still have a few other places to stop before we head home," Carlotta spoke kindly.

"A few more places? Truly? I'm going to wither up and die!" Berty lamented.

Bethanny snickered then covered her mouth with her gloved hand as Carlotta shot Berty a silencing glare.

Beatrix snorted.

Berty stomped.

"It's not funny, Bea." She growled.

"Oh, it is. It wouldn't be nearly as amusing, however, if you didn't react so." Beatrix replied.

Berty glared and took a menacing step toward her sister.

"Girls?" Carlotta called, a slightly exasperated edge to her tone.

"Coming." Berty paused then raised her eyebrows toward Beatrix. Pointing to her eyes and then Beatrix's, she mouthed. "I'm watching you." Then, with a longing glance across the street at a pastry shop, she turned and followed Carlotta.

Bethanny swallowed her laughter and, rather, focused on all that needed to be done.

It was nearly one in the afternoon, and they still needed to visit the milliner and get back in time to prepare for Lady Hollyworth's small dinner party. Bethanny took in a deep breath, wincing at the smoky and stale scent that hung in the air. One more day.

One more day, but it felt like one million.

Graham followed Murray down the marble hall toward the library. Though the house looked the same as far as he could remember, the tone felt different. It wasn't noticeable, the change; rather, subtle enough that if he hadn't been away for so long, he likely would have missed it. But the atmosphere was lighter, freer, as if a weight had been removed from the very air. A weight he hadn't noticed till its presence had been removed. Pushing his strange observation to the back of his mind, he tugged on his gloves as he entered the library, a smile curling his lips as he saw his old friend.

"Clairmont!" he called out, immediately reaching for his friend's hand.

"I say, old man, how are you?"

He studied his friend. The cynical gleam in his eye was startlingly absent; rather, his expression was light, weightless even. A strange emotion stirred in Graham's belly, one with which he wasn't familiar.

Envy.

Shaking his head to dispel the horrid emotion, he focused back on his friend.

"Quite well, no worse for the wear." The duke chuckled.

Never before had Graham seen his friend so blissfully happy. It was almost frightening.

Yet the burning sensation of envy overpowered any other weaker emotion. Later he'd have to figure out why exactly he was feeling so out of sorts.

Or maybe he'd just forget it entirely.

"I can see that! You're positively tame! I never thought I'd see the day," Graham teased.

"Ah, I'm far from tame, my friend." Clairmont grinned wickedly.

Ah, there's my old friend.

"How is your governess these days?" Graham asked, earning a chuckle from the duke.

"Splendid. After all, she is married to *me.*" He raised an eyebrow, a very self-satisfied grin firmly in place.

"And here, that was the very reason I even asked the question." Graham shot back.

Clairmont glared.

Graham chuckled and rocked on his heels. How he missed teasing his friend. Perhaps the envy was simply a passing fancy.

"So I'm told that my presence is needed, with your ward's come out and all." Graham strode to a chair and sat, his gaze firmly on his friend, watching for his reaction.

"Who told you that rubbish?" Clairmont grumbled as he took the chair across from Graham.

"My sister."

"Your sister is nothing but a thorn in my side."

"Mine too."

"You haven't been around bloody long enough for her to even tickle you, let alone gouge out your flesh."

"My, my, we're macabre."

Clairmont glared.

"I can see why my presence is needed."

"I do not need you."

"Are you concerned that the girl won't make a suitable match?" Graham leaned forward, apprehension taking over from the earlier banter.

Clairmont's glare deepened.

"What?"

"I should be so lucky."

"Pardon? Isn't the whole reason for the season to find a husband?" Graham asked, perplexed.

"Yes, but—"

"You don't think she'll find a match?"

"No, but—"

"I'm failing to see—"

"Because you keep interrupting me! Damn, you're as bad as your sister!" Clairmont stood and stalked to the fireplace.

"Now, Clairmont, there's no reason to stoop so low," Graham grumbled.

"Forgive me. It's just..." He paused, his shoulders sagging slightly.

Graham stood and walked toward his friend, unaccustomed to seeing him in such a state of upheaval. It was awkward, and he didn't know how to react, or to help.

"Bethanny... she's beautiful," the duke spoke reverently, with pride and fear.

"I'm sure she's quite lovely," Graham spoke softly.

Clairmont turned toward him, an intolerant expression clouding his blue eyes. "No, you don't get it. She's not lovely, she's... she's... my nightmare. Every fortune hunter, dandy, rake, and decent fellow is going to be fawning all over her, and I will have to resort to beating them off with a large stick if they think they can gain entrance into my home. You know how men's minds work, Graham. They'll see her as nothing more than a fine face, a beautiful figure. They'll see her money, her connection to me and — and ah! I don't want some rake to ruin her." Clairmont was pacing furiously, his expression stormy, unsettled and wild.

"Heaven help your daughters, should you have any," Graham murmured to himself.

Clairmont stopped midstride.

Perhaps he'd spoken too loudly.

"Therein lies the issue. I'm responsible for my wards, but they have become my family. Bethanny, Beatrix, and Berty, they deserve love matches. Heaven knows how difficult marriage can be, and I'm married to a saint. I never understood the dynamic of marriage till I entered it myself, and, being ferociously in love with my wife, I do not want any less for the girls. They deserve to be cherished, adored, *wanted*. Not simply used to carry an heir and discarded. And for many men of the *ton*, that is exactly what they want from a wife. I refuse to sentence them to that fate. Not when it's in my power to protect them. As I said, marriage is difficult, and without any fondness, affection or love for the person you married, it's doomed."

Graham simply stared, gazing at his friend as if seeing

him for the first time. "I...don't quite know what to say."

Clairmont exhaled loudly, his gaze looking heavenward. "Your sister was right." He said after a moment. Then closed his eyes.

"No, I'm quite sure that's not what I was going to say." Graham teased.

Clairmont opened his eyes and glared, again. If Graham weren't so self-confident he would have wondered if his presence was even appreciated.

"No...and heaven help *you* if you dare repeat it to your sister. Bloody hell, I'd never hear the end of it."

"My lips are sealed." Graham made a show of pretending to lock them up.

"My heartfelt thanks."

"So, at the risk of hell freezing over... what exactly was my sister correct about?" Graham asked, once again taking his seat in his abandoned chair.

"I need help."

"With?" Graham leaned forward. Never before had the great Duke of Clairmont needed anything, let alone help.

Good Lord, what was the world coming to?

"I need you to help me keep an eye on Bethanny."

"Is that all?" Graham leaned back, his head tilting to the side. He was expecting something...more that babysitting a deb.

"All? You still don't bloody get it, do you? I swear I might have to agree with your sister on one more thing." Clairmont shook his head and paced a few steps more.

"Oh, and what is that?" Graham asked sarcastically.

"Your intelligence."

"There's not need to be insulting just because you're in a lather over your ward." Charles tugged on his coat sleeves, annoyed.

" Are you coming to the ball?"

"Am I invited?" Graham teased.

"You *were.*" Clairmont clipped.

"Yes, I'll be there. Wouldn't miss it for the world."

"Speaking of the world…why did you come back to London during The Season? You know your harridan of a sister will simply try to marry you off."

"Perhaps I'll let her." Graham studied the shine on his Hessian boots. After a moment he glanced up. Clairmont was studying him with an expression mixed between disbelief and horror.

"You can't be serious."

"You're quite right. The woman will be selected by myself, of course. Never can trust a sister. " Graham shrugged, a grin teasing at his lips.

"You… married." Clairmont pointed at Graham.

"Yes."

"*This* season?"

"I believe that is what I said, yes." Graham nodded.

Silence.

"Do you not believe me?" Graham asked, offended at his friend's cynical expression.

"I…do."

"You're bloody convincing." Graham grumbled.

"Why?" Clairmont asked, his brow furrowing.

"Why not?" Graham shot back.

Clairmont shrugged and walked toward him, sitting down in the chair directly across. "Why now, is a better question?"

"I'm not getting any younger."

"How sage."

Graham glared. Clairmont was wearing off on him apparently.

"I need to have an heir, and marriage cannot be as trying as you say. Look at you! Aside from the scowling, pacing, caged animal, you're positively beaming." Graham suppressed chuckle.

Clairmont didn't appear as amused.

"I'm one and thirty, I might as well get the whole business over and done with. Why not this season?" Graham shrugged and leaned back into the plush chair.

"You... are exactly what I'm afraid of." Clairmont stood abruptly. Truly it was as if the man could not sit still. It was bloody dizzying.

"Pardon?"

"You! Men like you are exactly why I am concerned about Bethanny's come out. Detached men, men who want heirs, spares, and a mistress on the side."

"I never said anything about a mistress." Graham felt the need to interject.

"Yes, but—"

"And if memory serves correctly, you have had scores more mistresses than I." He added further.

"Before Carlotta."

"Yes."

"So it's different."

"A mistress is—"

"No, and that, my friend, is exactly what I'm afraid of. A wife is not a mistress... and a mistress could never, ever take the place of a wife. The two are completely unrelated. I was once like you... an utter fool—"

"Why, thank you." Graham cut in, his eyes rolling in impatience. Clairmont was as emotional as a bloody woman. It was exhausting. Was this what marriage did to a man? Made him moody, emotional, and irrational? Heaven help him.

"I mean no disrespect."

"Because calling one a fool is generally taken as a compliment," Graham added.

"No, you nodcock."

"Ah, the compliments continue."

Clairmont cast his gaze upward as if in prayer.

"You look like my sister."

His prayer ended abruptly and was followed by a fierce scowl.

"What I'm trying to say is… unless your heart is invested in your wife, you'll never understand marriage, nor will you reap the amazing benefits of sharing your soul with another person. Carlotta isn't perfect, nor am I, but we're prefect for each other. She compliments where I lack and vice versa. It's a… waltz, our life together. Some give, some take, some crafty maneuvering, but never ever separated from the other. She's my lifeline, I'm her strength. I want that same… I don't know the word… I just want that for Bethanny, and quite honestly, I want it for you too…" Clairmont paused, his gaze piercing through Graham.

"Ah, old chap, I'm quite moved," Graham spoke softly. "I guess I never thought of it that way."

"So will you help me with Bethanny?" He took a step forward. "I just want her to be happy," Clairmont pleaded.

"Yes, I will. I'll be her bloody guardian angel if I need to be. There's nothing you have to fear." Graham stood and shook his friend's hand.

"Thank you, and in return, I'll ask Carlotta to give you the names of few good women of the *ton*. Your sister could do the same, but I'd trust Carlotta's taste over Dianna's."

"I agree wholeheartedly." Graham nodded.

"I thought you might." Clairmont grinned.

"Yes, well, I'd best be going. I will see you at the ball."

"Until the ball," echoed Clairmont.

Graham took his leave, his boots making short work of the stairs that led from the duke's resident to his awaiting carriage. Once inside, he released a pent-up breath.

Though the envy still stirred slightly, he felt a pinch of pity for his good friend. If his ward, Bethanny, was as beautiful as he'd said, then he had good reason to worry. But in Graham's experience, the father, or in his case, guardian, usually looked at the girl with a jaded view. While it was possible she was as perfect as Clairmont thought, it was very unlikely.

However, it mattered not. Because it wouldn't change his resolution to watch out for her this season. And who knew? Perhaps while watching out for her, he'd come across his future countess. It was entirely possible. So with a slight shrug, Graham glanced out across the flurry of passing buildings as he made his way back to his residence. An errant thought tickled his mind before dismissing it.

He hoped he recognized Bethanny. He wouldn't be much help unless he knew which debutant to keep an eye on. But, as soon as the thought passed through his mind, he dismissed it. After all, it was *her* ball. He'd have to be bloody blind to miss her.

CHAPTER TWO

Now that the whirlwind of activity had ebbed slightly, her eyes scanned the crowd, searching for his face. Hundreds of London's most elite were gathered in the duke's grand ballroom, but, of course, the one she was searching for was absent. He was late. Very late. If he were coming at all. But her heart whispered assurances that he would be there. After all, he had promised the duke.

And when one promised something to a duke, they followed through. Didn't they?

With a hopeful heart, she cast a final glance about the room then sighed heavily when her hope was met with defeat.

"Are you well, dear?" Carlotta, Duchess of Clairmont asked, her voice soft and kind, concern lacing the tone.

"Yes, I am. Simply… overwhelmed," Bethanny answered, and it was the truth.

Just simply not the *whole* truth.

"It is quite the crush." Carlotta gazed about the room, her eyes slightly wide.

Crush was an understatement. Of all the invitations they had sent out, not one had been refused. In fact, she was quite certain there were people here that most had only heard about, never actually seen.

Rumors, or ghosts of the *ton*.

Like the Viscount Neville.

It was well known among the *ton* that he had gone into seclusion after the death of his betrothed. Although the rumors abounded, no one seemed to know the full story. The speculation ranged from murder to a quick demise brought on by a broken heart in finding him with another woman.

Honestly, Bethanny hadn't paid much mind to the gossip surrounding him. But he was far more handsome than she'd anticipated. In a word, he was dark. Jet-black hair, olive skin, and, from this distance, even dark eyes shaded by severe eyebrows.

And a gaze that was met by her own. He lifted a dark brow as if questioning her.

Quickly, Bethanny glanced away. She was curious for heaven's sake, not *interested.*

After a moment she dared a glance back, curiosity overwhelming her good sense. Thankfully, he had turned his attention to Lord Benbrooke.

Indeed, everyone was in attendance save the one she wanted.

Suppressing the urge to sigh, she felt Carlotta grasp her hand lightly. "There is no reason to be anxious. You're a huge success," she whispered encouragingly.

Bethanny offered her a confident smile.

But her heart was anything but.

"I think I need some air," Bethanny spoke after a moment. Perhaps if she simply cleared her head, she'd be able to be more circumspect.

Carlotta glanced to her, her expression curious and distrusting.

"I'm in my own home. Honestly, I'm not going to wait in a darkened corner for some rake to assault me. I'll go around to the part of the house closed off from guests. I'll be perfectly safe," Bethanny assured.

Carlotta's eyes narrowed for a moment. "I'll go with you—"

"No, it will seem far less conspicuous if I'm alone. If you're with me..." Bethanny let her words drift. "Forgive my interruption," she added belatedly, abashed at her rudeness. After all, Carlotta *was* a duchess, and one did *not* interrupt someone of such high rank.

"I understand. " Carlotta regarded her then nodded. "I understand, but you must not be gone long."

"I'll only be gone a short time. I promise. I just... I just need a moment to myself." Without giving Carlotta a chance to change her mind, she spun on her slippers and walked away.

Bethanny felt Carlotta's gaze on her back as she meandered her way through the crush. She didn't want to appear in a hurry; she'd only draw attention. Slowly, she made her way to the edge of the ballroom, having only stopped for conversation twice. Each time it had been a gentleman, the wrong gentleman. Of course, it would be impossible for the *right* gentleman to speak to her, him being absent and all. Thankfully, all that had been needed was short polite conversation and a winning smile, and she'd been on her way.

Quietly, she walked down the hall, passing a few ladies and offering them a humble smile as they nodded in her direction. She placed her hand on the cool knob of the door to the powder room and cautiously glanced behind her. The women were just rounding the corner... and were out of sight. Quickly, she lifted her skirts and darted down the hall, passing three doors, till she came to the one she was looking for. Silently, she turned the knob and entered one of their many sitting rooms; however, this particular room had an adjoining door to another sitting room, which opened to a separate hall.

After making her way through both rooms and into the secluded hall, she exhaled a deep sigh.

It wasn't to be this way.

It was her debut; it was *her* night. It was to be perfect, and it… was not. Chiding herself for being so selfish, she'd rather focused on remembering her guardian's pride as she'd been announced. The duke and duchess had beamed, and the crowded ballroom had hushed as her moment arrived. Every eye had been on her, every gaze but the very one she was anticipating the most.

Irritated that she was back where she'd started, she strode down the hall, past the duke's study and out to a small balcony that few knew existed. The cool night air felt refreshing on her skin, prickling it with a chill that was welcome after being confined in the crush earlier. The night was full dark, the only light a half-moon arched in the sky, offering silver beams. Her skirts whispered against the marbled floor as she made her way to the rail. Resting her hands upon the cool stone, she gazed out into the garden, seeing nothing, but giving her mind freedom to wander. As a moment passed, her eyes adjusted to the darkness, and the world began to shimmer.

"I wasn't aware that this part of the house was open to the guests." A rich masculine voice startled her from her musing.

"Pardon?" Bethanny immediately stood, straightened her posture, and felt the wild gallop of her heart.

This couldn't be good.

She was alone, with a stranger, on a secluded balcony.

The duke was going to murder her.

If she made it out without being ruined.

Dear Lord.

"It is not. What, might I ask, are you doing here?" she asked in her firmest tone.

"I only just arrived, and, after the evening I've had, found

I needed a moment to regain my composure. I'm a friend of the duke and am quite certain I'm allowed on his private balcony. What about you?" he asked, a slightly teasing tone to his voice.

Bethanny narrowed her eyes. They had adjusted to the dim light, and as recognition dawned, her heart hammered in her chest.

Graham.

"I'm quite certain I'm permitted to be here as well," she responded, not quite knowing what to say. Did he recognize her? Was he simply teasing because he already had figured out who she was?

"Ah, a friend of the duchess then?" he asked lightly as he made his way toward her.

He definitely did not recognize her.

However, she couldn't determine if this was a bad thing or a good one. And it *was* rather dark. After a moment's deliberating, she decided to play along.

What could it hurt?

"You could say that." She shrugged. Then, feeling mischievous, she lowered her gaze and offered her most flirtations smile, hoping his eyes had adjusted to the dark, and he could perhaps notice it.

At least she *hoped* it was flirtatious.

After a moment, she risked a glance up to his shadowed features; a playful grin was tipping his lips and showed off the fairest hint of those beloved dimples she so fondly remembered.

She sighed... inwardly, of course.

"It's quite a nice view, peaceful, if I may say so." He came to stand beside her.

He was taller than she remembered, and possibly broader as well, but she couldn't be sure with the faint light.

"Exactly why I came to this very place."

"Is it quite the crush inside then?" he asked. There was a

slight lilt to his voice, not quite a brogue, but not the crisp English she was accustomed to hearing. He must spend quite a bit of time at his estate in Edinburgh to have taken on the faint accent.

She would have to thank Lady Southridge later for all the helpful information regarding her brother.

"Crush would be an understatement," she replied too quickly, her tone a bit wry.

"Not a fan of the crowds?" he asked, his tone light. "Or were there far too many gentlemen seeking the attentions of so beautiful a lady?"

Even in the darkness, his gaze was powerful, spearing right through her causing a myriad of strange sensations to swirl around in her belly.

"Or perhaps I simply wanted a moment to myself." she answered, her tone far more breathless than she would have liked.

"Perhaps." He shrugged.

"You don't believe me." She narrowed her eyes.

"No," he replied, unfazed.

"Why ever not?" Bethanny asked, turning to face him fully.

"In my experience, ladies do not visit deserted balconies unless they wish to be found."

Slightly shaking her head, Bethanny replied, "Which is exactly why I choose to use the private balcony? The one closed off from the party?" she asked in a disbelieving tone.

"Well…"

"I thought not." She shrugged her shoulder, a smile teasing her lips at besting him.

"You're a cheeky one," he replied, his tone holding a hint of awe.

"I prefer intelligent."

"Yes, I believe you would." He nodded, his grin widening.

"That sounded dangerously like an insult, my lord," she teased.

"No, no insult... simply... delayed respect."

"Respect?" Bethanny asked with a dubious tone.

"Indeed. Certainly a lovely lady such as yourself has to be aware that social functions can be quite... tedious."

"I'm sure the duke will be thrilled you think so highly of his party," she replied, a smile tugging at her lips.

"You mistake my meaning. People can be tedious. Petty even. It's simply... refreshing to speak with a woman who doesn't fall into those categories."

"I do believe that was a compliment."

"It was, and you should take it as such."

"Why, thank you." Bethanny stepped back and performed a deep curtsey, as if being presented at court.

"And a sense of humor to boot. I might have to actually find out your name." Graham chuckled, his dimples in full view.

"And ruin the mystery? I think not." Bethanny rose from her curtsey, her heart pounding.

"I do love a good mystery."

"Avid reader?" Bethanny asked.

"Yes... but that's not what I was referring to."

His posture changed, as did his expression, and at once, Bethanny's heart took flight because some instinct, some feminine awareness told her with all certainty that he was no longer simply teasing an innocent.

He was pursuing.

"Oh?" Her tone was breathless to her own ears, and she silently scolded herself for the betrayal of weakness.

"So, *mysterious miss* of the duke's balcony..." he teased, offering her a dramatic nickname.

"Is that the best you can come up with? Mysterious miss of the duke's balcony?" she asked, a laugh escaping her restraint.

"I thought it was quite clever myself." Graham paused his pursuit, his smile widening.

"It sounds like a Gothic novel."

"You know, you're quite right. I could have a future there if I ever so desire."

"Writing?"

"Gad, no. Offering my service for creating titles."

"I'm not sure that's a lucrative endeavor."

"Perhaps." He shrugged and took another step forward. "But you must admit, you'd be curious hearing that title. I know my curiosity is quite piqued."

Bethanny took a deep breath, as deep as her corset allowed, and drew up all her courage. "Perhaps. I might be curious… but there would have to be something more than a catchy title, my lord." She knew she was playing a dangerous game, but it was a game she had dreamed of playing since she'd first seen Lord Graham.

The memory of him trading banter with Berty over dinner one night flashed to her memory. Most lords wouldn't give a little girl the time of day, yet Lord Graham had traded wit with her, enjoying himself even. Bethanny had been envious of her little sister's ability to bait him. She'd sworn that someday she'd have her turn.

That day had finally come.

It didn't matter that he didn't recognize her. Regardless, he was still there speaking with her.

And for now, that was enough.

She opened her mouth to speak, but her nerves got the best of her and, rather than speak, she dropped her fan.

Likely because she had forgotten she had brought it in the first place.

It clattered to the floor lightly, and she closed her eyes in embarrassment at her own clumsiness.

"Allow me," Lord Graham spoke.

"No I've—" Bethanny's eyes flew open as she knelt down

to retrieve her fan.

As luck would have it, her elbow soundly clocked Lord Graham's head as he rose from retrieving the offending object.

"Ow!" He reached up to rub the surely sore area.

"I'm so sorry!" Bethanny spoke, horrified.

"Blo—er... ah, that... is fine, miss." He closed his eyes a moment, likely from the dull pain her elbow had needlessly inflicted on his person.

"I'm ever so sorry, my lord!" Bethanny felt her face heat with a scarlet blush that had to make her practically glow. She certainly felt like it. Without thinking, she reached up to his scalp and felt for the knot, her thumb grazing slightly over the skin as to not cause him discomfort, much like she had done a million times to her sisters.

But Lord Graham was most definitely *not* her sister...

Her hands stilled as she realized just what she was doing. "Forgive me, my lord." She quickly withdrew her hands and took a step back, belatedly realizing just how close she had been to him. The scent of cinnamon and cedar hung in the air, wrapping a spell of enticement around her, beckoning her to come closer. She started to take a step back, away from the temptation, but his hand at her back stopped her.

Practically burned through her, or so it felt.

"I'm quite well. However, I thank you for your concern," he whispered, his voice intimate.

"I—I'm usually not quite so... graceless," Bethanny answered, her thoughts muddled by the intense gaze with which he captivated her. In the moonlight, his amber eyes were silver, his golden-hued skin a soft buttery gold. He was beautiful..

"I'm quite thankful you are... you see, I was trying to find some excuse to hold you, and you neatly provided me with the perfect opportunity," he murmured, his gaze leaving hers and traveling down the line of her jaw and the curve of her nose before resting on her lips.

Dear Lord, he is going to kiss me.

"I do think you could have done without the knot I gave you at the top of your head," she replied, her words teasing but her tone far from it.

"A small price to pay." He shrugged. "However, I do believe there is a custom, when one gets an injury."

"Oh?"

"Indeed, usually, the injured party is given a kiss."

"Is that so? Silly me. I thought that was only practiced in the nursery." Bethanny raised a challenging eyebrow as her heart raced, beating an excited rhythm that hoped he would make good on his word and, indeed, kiss her. However, it would never do to appear *too* eager.

"I have it on good authority that it is still practiced outside of the nursery as well... so, being with tradition and all, I would appreciate a kiss." His dimples deepened as his smile widened then relaxed as his gaze once again became deep and soulful, searching hers.

"I cannot see the harm in upholding tradition. If you'll simply bow your head—" Bethanny began, knowing full well that was not his intention.

"Of course."

And before Bethanny could even close her eyes, his lips caressed hers. The touch was soft, lingering and velvety. His warm breath tickled as he drew back slightly. Her eyes, which hadn't closed, gazed directly at his. As if spoken out loud, his gaze asked for permission to kiss her again. At her slight nod, his lips met hers once more; however, this time, Bethanny closed her eyes, not wanting anything to distract from her first kiss, and as she had always hoped, it was from Lord Graham.

Graham was trying to not show his surprise that the mysterious miss on the duke's balcony — he still thought it was a clever title — was an innocent. Though, it wasn't a bad surprise, it was still quite shocking to him. He rather thought she was at least experienced beyond a first kiss. However, as she gazed at him just before he met her lips, he saw the uncertainty, the unsophistication in her expression that told him to tread carefully. And so he did, pressing the softest, most harmless kiss to her lips that he had ever given. Normally innocents didn't attract him, but... she was different. From the first moment when he'd seen her on the balcony, her very presence had called to him, challenged him; rather, he enjoyed her company. He wasn't accustomed to enjoying a woman's company, outside the bedroom, that is. But she was refreshing, witty, intelligent, and even in the pale light of the moon, she was breathtakingly beautiful.

As his lips caressed hers once more, he gave himself over to the feast of the senses she provided. The air surrounding her was fragrant like roses, heady and intoxicating. Her lips were soft, yielding, and eager, which created a response in his body that was much like a spark to tinder. Tentatively, she mimicked his movements, responding to and returning the kiss.

He wanted more, desperately desired to discover more of her flavor; so with care, he gently traced her lower lip with his tongue. His right hand, which was at her back, pressed gently, coaxing her into a closer embrace as his left hand reached around her back and rested on her shoulder. She willingly drew forward, her soft curves barely touching his frame, but it was enough to nearly cause him to toss caution to the wind.

But he didn't. Rather he forced himself to slow down, to teach, taste, and tease her. Anyone could take a kiss. But it took skill... it took effort... to *give* a kiss.

But that was before her tongue traced his lower lip, much like his had done moments before. Unable to deny her invitation, he opened his mouth and drew in her lower lip, teasing it before releasing. She gasped but didn't break the kiss, rather, pressed in further.

He was going to marry her.

That was all there was to it. He had to marry anyway, might as well be to an interesting woman with a delicious talent for the more passionate pursuits.

Heirs would be no problem. He'd have ten.

"I must know your name," he whispered against her lips.

"We've not been properly introduced." She smiled then pressed in for another scorching kiss.

If she did that again, he'd have no problem compromising her and making sure she was his.

Of course, if anyone happened upon them right now, she'd be just as compromised.

However, *thoroughly* compromised would be far more preferable as far as he was concerned.

Even in the thick haze of desire, his ears tuned into the slight sound of footsteps.

Which he promptly ignored.

However, she must have heard it as well because she paused mid-kiss and withdrew, her breath tickling his lips as she backed away.

He regarded her, a peaceful determination rising in his chest.

"I... I will see you later... won't I?" she asked, her tone breathless and her lips swollen and wet.

He loved that it was his kiss that had christened them, that lingered there still.

"Are you going back to the party?" he asked, praying she'd say yes. Either way he *would* find her.

Nodding, she took a step back, her gaze slightly unfocused and happy.

Which made him utterly *joyful*.

It was amazing how one person's happiness completed another's. And right then, he felt strangely complete.

It was unlike anything he'd ever felt, and he loved every

moment.

So caught up in his own revelations, he almost forgot to answer. But as her warm brown gaze — the precise color of rich earth — grew hesitant, he remembered himself.

"I'll find you."

He swore it.

"You will?" she asked, her face alight with hope.

And, oddly enough, he felt as if he had just slayed a dragon for her.

"I swear it." And he meant every word. He'd find her; he'd gain a proper introduction and then court her, only because it was required to follow the proper steps before he married her.

Compromising was looking promising, and quicker.

She smiled, a beautiful beaming grin that he was sure would haunt his dreams day and night, and then she disappeared.

CHAPTER THREE

BETHANNY FORCED HERSELF to walk sedately from the balcony, but she truly felt like flying. If that was possible.

Lord Graham.

Had. Kissed. Her.

And not a small kiss, but a real, deep and longing, everything-you-wish-you-could dream-about-but-are-too-innocent-to-understand kind of kiss!

It was a rotten shame that she had heard someone's footsteps. Though it was probably for the best. She would have continued kissing him for goodness knows how long! As she walked down the hall to the first parlor, she saw Carlotta.

"There you are! I was so worried! You all but disappeared, darling! Charles is going to have your head after he gets over his worry," Carlotta scolded, even as she rushed forward and pulled Bethanny into a gentle hug so as not to rumple their dresses.

"I'm fine, forgive me. I... lost track of time." Bethanny answered, thanking the heavens that the light was just dim enough that Carlotta couldn't regard her too closely.

Because she was sure her appearance gave something

away.

As if reading her mind, Carlotta's gaze dropped to her lips as her brow furrowed.

Bethanny had to think fast.

"We should return." Bethanny stepped back from her watchful gaze and went through the two parlors and into the hall that would lead them back to the ball.

Carlotta didn't say anything, which was disconcerting. Bethanny knew she was following by the quiet whisper of her skirts as she walked behind, but other than that, silence.

And all Bethanny could think of was that somehow, she *knew*.

She supposed there were worse things, but right now she couldn't think of any.

Carlotta caught up with her as the ballroom doors came into sight.

"I know you're hiding something," she whispered, her tone light but slightly dangerous.

It was the tone of a governess... and Bethanny tried not to give away her anxiety.

"Oh?" Bethanny answered.

"Yes... you have that same look about you... when you and your sisters tried to... never mind. Just know I'm watching you, young lady." She lowered her chin and speared Bethanny with a very pointed gaze.

"Very well."

The ballroom was every bit as crowded as before, perhaps more so. As Bethanny made her way through the crowd, Carlotta gently grasped her elbow and nodded toward the left. The duke was speaking in low tones to a few footmen, his expression grave.

This was not going to end well.

He paused and scanned the room as if sensing Carlotta's gaze. Once he saw her, his gaze directly cut to Bethanny.

And narrowed.

Bethanny swallowed, dread clenching her stomach.

The duke's normally light blue eyes were stormy. Bethanny struggled to maintain her carefree demeanor. The last thing she wanted to do was give the idea that there was more to the story than what she had said.

"Bethanny." His tone was filled with both relief and irritation.

"Your Grace." Bethanny nodded.

"Carlotta?" He turned to his wife, waiting for an explanation.

"She lost track of time." Carlotta spoke, her tone perfectly normal.

"She bloo—"He began, only to take a deep breath and gaze heavenward as if asking — begging really — for patience.

"Forgive me." Bethanny cast her gaze to the marbled floor, thankful that they were slightly away from the sea of humanity, in a far corner.

"You and I, we will have words later..." the duke threatened, his tone stern. But his blue eyes were softening, relief evident, and Bethanny knew that whatever scolding she would receive was surely deserved and would be administered in love.

"We need to begin the dancing," Carlotta murmured to her husband, her eyes darting from his to the crowded ballroom.

"Indeed. If only for the reason of keeping *you* here." He lifted an irritated eyebrow at Bethanny.

"I'll not disappear again," she replied, barely resisting the urge to sigh in exasperation.

"See that you don't," he replied sternly, then his eyes shifted slightly from her to just behind her. "It's about bloody time," he muttered, followed by, "Excuse me." He made it two steps before he turned back. "Carlotta, the dancing will begin in a moment. And I believe the first one belongs to me..." With a slightly irritated glare to Bethanny, he shifted his gaze to his wife, softening the frown. Clearing his throat, he made his way across the ballroom to inform the musicians to begin.

Bethanny followed his retreat for a moment before Carlotta touched her shoulder. Sure enough, the music had started, and the mass of humanity had begun to part to make room for the dance floor. At the sweet strains of the music, Bethanny grinned. How she loved to dance. She wasn't particularly graceful, not like her sister, Beatrix, who almost floated whenever they practiced, but she loved the joy dancing provoked. With music as a background, life seemed almost like a fairytale, hinting that perhaps anything could happen.

And with that thought, her wandering gaze searched for her heart's desire. But before she could find him, she noticed the approach of her guardian. He was a handsome man, a kind and generous sort, and Bethanny was proud to take her first dance with him.

He gently grasped her hand and led her to the middle of the room. She felt every eye following her movements. Was Lord Graham watching? Before she could finish the thought, the duke grinned playfully, and they began to dance. The minuet didn't leave much time for talk, for which she was thankful. Her heart was hammering as the full implications of what was taking place finally settled in her mind. She was officially *available.*

Though her heart was already stolen. Rather, given away.

Other couples lined up and joined the dance, easing her tension. The duke offered a reassuring smile, his eyes kind and proud.

She smiled back, thankful to have the first dance with him.

No doubt she'd dance with countless partners this night, but nothing would compare with what she had experienced only a few minutes ago on a deserted balcony with a certain lord.

And now that she knew what kind of bliss could be

experienced at the hand of one's heart's desire, she'd not settle for anything less.

Was he in the ballroom now?

Had he figured out who she was?

Bethanny tried to stomp out the anxiety in her belly at the question. Surely it wouldn't make a difference. True, he was one and thirty and therefore a bit older than she, but that hardly mattered.

It wasn't unheard of for a debutant to marry a lord who was old enough to be her father, grandfather even.

However, Bethanny was quite comforted to know that she wouldn't be in a position to marry out of necessity; for wealth or title. She might only be the daughter of a deceased baron, but her guardian was the Duke of Clairmont. And her parents had been wealthy and wise, putting measures in place so that she and her sisters now shared in that wealth.

Which was why the duke and duchess had constantly reminded her before her debut of the need to use caution and discernment. A beautiful heiress was a powerful draw, and there were a few unsavory characters who would not hesitate to ruin a lady in efforts to secure her fortune.

Shivering at the unwelcome thought, Bethanny glanced to the duke, who was grinning at her as they met and spun.

When the dance was finished, she scarcely had a moment to catch her breath before her next partner came to escort her back to the dance floor.

With a delighted smile, the duke bowed slightly and returned to his wife.

And once again, her gaze strayed to the many faces at the edge of the ballroom, searching for Lord Graham.

"Graham!" the Duke of Clairmont called none too quietly, causing the people around Graham to halt their conversations and glance up. He was striding toward him, his expression annoyed and impatient.

Join the club, Graham thought. He had been back in the bloody ballroom for ten minutes, and the vixen who had stolen his attention on the deserted balcony was nowhere.

It was as if she'd vanished, but he knew that she had to be *somewhere.* It was simply too damn crowded, and it didn't help that when he had encountered her, it had been in the moonlight, not the bright glow of the ballroom. He shook his head as his instincts told him that the higher illumination would only reveal a deeper, more radiant beauty that the moonlight ever could.

"I say, old chap, what's got you in a dither? It's quite the crush! Your little ward will be a success, I'm sure." Graham nodded, making eye contact before once again searching the sea of faces.

"Why am I in such a dither? Your sister and I have been searching for you. Between you and Bethanny..." The duke shook his head. "I thought you said you'd watch out for her! How then do you plan on watching out for Bethanny if you are not bloody present?" Clairmont bit out, his expression irritated.

"I was here earlier, but, if you'll excuse me, I'd had quite the evening and needed a moment to myself," Graham replied testily.

"That seems to be the common excuse tonight," Clairmont grumbled.

"Pardon?"

"Never mind. Why was your evening so bloody miserable?"

Graham exhaled, his shoulders slumping slightly before he straightened them once more. "One of my estates, the one in Oxfordshire, had a terrible fire. I just received word on the damages to both the building and those inside. Thankfully, no one was killed, but a few are suffering from minor injuries."

KRISTIN VAYDEN

"Oh, sorry to hear that." Clairmont's expression softened considerably. "Was the manor a total loss, or were they able to contain it?"

"The fire destroyed the kitchens and a few other rooms, but it will be fixed without too much trouble."

"I see."

"That's enough of the melancholy. Tell me, how is your lovely wife? I'm sure the two of you are quite pleased with the turnout tonight. I think I even saw Lord Neville."

"Indeed. Didn't I tell you that Bethanny would be a success?"

"Yes... yet I'm not sensing that you're pleased." Graham's brow furrowed.

"Must we truly have this conversation again?" Clairmont asked in a lament.

"No, I'm only nearly recovering from out last conversation."

Clairmont raised an irritated eyebrow and gazed back over the crowd. "I'd like to introduce you to Bethanny in a moment. Will you meet us in the far alcove after this set?" Clairmont asked, his gaze turning back to Graham.

"I'd be delighted. However, I'm concerned about your memory... I do believe I've had the pleasure of meeting Miss Lamont before."

Again he remembered the mousy-brown-haired, slight-framed young girl. For her sake — and the duke's — he hoped she'd grown into herself, at least somewhat.

"You're interest in my welfare is appreciated," Clairmont replied dryly. "However, I doubt you'd recognize her. She..." The duke raised his hand as if trying to pluck the correct word from thin air.

"She's changed?" Graham offered.

"You might say that." Clairmont furrowed his brow as if not fully convinced.

"Grown?"

44

"In a way…"

"Bloody hell, what in creation *did* she do, then? Sprout a second arm? Grow wings? You're no more help than my sister, and for me to compare you to Lady Southridge, I—"

"That is the second time you've insulted—"

"Because it's the second time I thought it! Just introduce the chit — pardon — young lady to me, if you please. I promise not to be intimidated by her third leg."

Clairmont shook his head then paused, tilting it slightly. "Exquisite."

"Pardon?" Graham leaned forward, completely confused. He glanced to the side then behind himself.

"Bethanny simply became… exquisite. That was the word I was searching for. You'll see for yourself in a few moments. Now, if you'll excuse me, I see your sister and promised her that she'd be in attendance when you two were reintroduced. I can't bloody well figure out why she'd care. Regardless." The duke turned and walked away.

Graham's mind whirled at his friend's comment. Why would his sister take such an interest in wanting to be there? It didn't make sense. But, knowing his sister, for something to make sense wasn't usually a requirement. Rather, he had learned to expect the completely senseless.

Already slightly irritated at his sister, he turned to head toward the alcove. As he walked along the edge of the ballroom, his eyes continued to scan the crowd for her face, wishing he had a name to go with it. His gaze drifted past the dancers, only to snap back to a beauty with the most beautiful, rich, coffee-colored hair. From this angle, he could only see the slight rise of the apple of her cheek and the slender line of her neck as it curved gracefully down the body of a goddess.

It had to be her.

In the moonlight, he wasn't able to determine what color her dress truly was, but he assumed it was slightly darker than the pale pastels usually worn by debutants. It had been one of the reasons he hadn't thought her an innocent. But as he watched the graceful flow of the rose-colored gown, he realized that it had to be the same woman. The cut was similar, though that could be said of many of the women of attendance. However, her shape…

That was most assuredly, not common.

At that moment, she spun, her eyes sparkling with delight as an enchanting grin lit up her exquisite features.

Exquisite. It seemed the perfect word. He'd have to thank the duke later for providing such a great adjective; too bad it was meant for another.

But Graham was sure that there was no one in the room who could compare with this beauty, his mysterious miss of the duke's balcony. He had been correct; the moonlight didn't do her features justice. Graham turned fully toward the dance floor, his gaze hardly blinking as he watched the young lady dance with a sense of abandonment. She was glorious, and her lack of grace was an endearing addiction to the mystery. A simple flaw that surprisingly made her even more perfect. It was apparent she was enjoying herself, and Graham felt the first flame of jealousy ignite in his chest, choking him. Never the possessive sort, Graham was shocked when he found himself narrowing his eyes at the lady's partner. He recognized him as Viscount Dwell. Affable fellow. Graham might even call him a friend, but in that moment he was anything but. Amusement broke through his jealous emotion as he momentarily wondered what would happen if he stormed out onto the ballroom floor and pulled his mysterious miss into a scandalous kiss.

He'd never do it.

But it was a delightful thought.

However, it would be prudent to find out some information first… like her name.

The set ended, and Graham cleared his throat and headed to the alcove, hoping to get the blasted introduction over and done with as soon as possible so that he could find his mysterious miss.

Clairmont was already waiting for him, as was his sister.

"Graham, I'm quite disappointed in your tardiness. To think, of all the events you choose to be quite unfashionably late to attend, you choose Bethanny's debut!" Lady Southridge scolded.

"There were… extenuating circumstances."

"Your bloody castle is burnt… not *burning*," she clipped.

"I only just learned… how did you know?" Graham's irritation at his sister evaporated into suspicion.

Rather than answer, she simply shook her head as if saying, *Must we discuss this again?*

Which, in all honestly, was the truth. The blasted woman was practically clairvoyant for all the information she seemed to uncover.

Or she simply had very-well-paid servants.

"Ah! Here she is!" Lady Southridge's face transformed from irritation to absolute rapture as Graham could only assume the *exquisite* Miss Lamont made her way toward them. He cast a final irritated glace to his sister before turning around.

And his heart stopped.

Then stuttered.

Of course, that he'd stopped breathing at the same time didn't help matters.

In fact, he was quite certain that he was having an out-of-body experience as he seemed to watch himself as the whole catastrophic scene unfolded.

No. No, no, no.

Bloody hell. The duke is going to kill me.

And if he did, that would be a kindness, because Graham was quite sure the only other option was burning alive with desire.

The exquisite Bethanny Lamont was none other than his

mysterious miss from the duke's balcony.

The very young lady he was supposed to protect… from men like him. And, even though he wasn't aware of who she was, he had already compromised her to an extent, and in doing that, confirmed every single one of the duke's fears.

The very fears he'd been enlisted to help prevent from coming true.

This was a bloody massacre, and he had no idea what to do. As the edges of the ballroom began to grow fuzzy, the duke thumped him on the back.

"Are you well, Graham?" the duke asked, his tone concerned.

And Graham gasped, finally remembering to breathe.

Which was another mistake — adding to his lengthy list this evening — for the air was already permeated with seductive scent of her, reminding him of the softness of her lips, the press of her soft body…

And heaven help him, he could have damned the consequences and all but ravished her right then, if not for the hesitant expression in her eyes.

Hesitation and… guilt?

And at once, Graham felt as if run over by a carriage with six horses and weighed down by bricks. Because Miss Lamont was not shocked at all to see him.

Which could only mean one thing…

While he hadn't recognized her, she had most assuredly recognized him.

Bethanny tried to keep her breathing even as she approached the circle of her family and Lord Graham. His expression would have been amusing had the implications not been so severe. To say he was shocked would have been a gross understatement. She was quite sure the man had stopped breathing, if his gasps at the duke's patting of his back were any indication. Which didn't bode well for her. He was even more handsome than when they had met on the balcony. His golden hair was slightly tousled, adding a bit of a devilish delight to his perfectly chiseled face. His jaw was set, as if angry, but his expression was void of that emotion.

His evening kit was dark and cut to perfection, accentuating his masculine frame. Her earlier assessment had indeed been correct, for he was broader than she remembered. His amber gaze was burning through her, creating the now named sensation of desire she had only just experienced earlier at his hand. It was intoxicating, it was tempting, it was... altogether frightening, because Bethanny knew that Lord Graham was beginning to piece things together. His gaze sharpened, narrowed, and then lit with awareness.

After all, as shocked as he was to see her, she hadn't the slightest surprise in seeing him, which obviously had led him to only one conclusion.

She'd known it was him all along.

But of course she would have remembered him! It was insupportable to think that a man, who had clearly matured already, would change so dramatically in a few years to make him unrecognizable. He looked just the same as he had in all her dreams: golden locks unwilling to bow to conventional style, amber eyes flashing with charm, and dimples that could make a girl melt. That his evening kit accentuated his broad shoulders and the musculature of his legs only heightened the memory.

However, a young lady could easily undergo such a transformation, such is the way of maturity, and Bethanny had blossomed late.

"Bethanny! Aren't you delighted that I reserved that fabric for you? No one will dare wear it after you are shining so brilliantly this evening!" Lady Southridge gushed and strode forward, her expression full of delight and mischief.

Bethanny felt some of her anxiety melt as she looked to her self-declared grandmother. "Yes, you always do have the best eye for color."

"She did have help, you know." Carlotta raised a playful eyebrow and joined their little circle, blocking the view of Lord Graham.

She wasn't quite sure if that was a good or bad thing.

"The gentlemen cannot keep their eyes off of you." Lady Southridge commented, tapping Bethanny lightly on the shoulder with her gloved hand.

"I'm sure His Grace is pleased with such a smashing debut." Lord Graham's voice penetrated the circle as he strode forward, his eyes cold.

Bethanny suppressed a shiver. Perhaps it was better when she couldn't see him.

"Thank you, my lord," Bethanny replied, her heart hammering as she searched his gaze for any warmth, anything that might give her hope.

"Graham, allow me to present my ward, Miss Bethanny Lamont." The duke made a sweeping gesture, and Lord Graham reached out his hand. Bethanny placed her gloved hand in his, her whole body trembling.

"A pleasure, Miss Lamont." He bowed crisply and kissed the air above her hand.

His accusing gaze bore into her, causing her heart to beat with guilt and trepidation. One thing was for certain: he wasn't happy to find out his mysterious miss wasn't so mysterious after all.

But why?

His gaze never left hers. She tilted her head, studying him, searching his gaze for her unspoken questions. His eyes remained distant, cool. One would think they would fairly dance with their secret. After all, if she could see herself, no doubt her eyes would be all but burning with it; however, that spark was snuffed with the ice in his gaze.

Drat the man. Everything was going so well, and he had to go and ruin it.

"Graham, isn't Bethanny lovely?" Lady Southridge asked, her face beaming.

"Yes, I must say I didn't recognize you, Miss Lamont." Lord Graham raised a challenging eyebrow as he continued to gaze at her.

"Ah, time has a way of changing us all, Lord Graham. I do hope that I make a lasting impression this time, however," Bethanny replied, biting back a grin as his eyes narrowed.

"Of course, my dear! How could Graham forget an exquisite vision such as yourself?"

"Indeed," Graham replied dryly.

The duke cleared his throat. "A moment, Graham?"

Lord Graham bowed and stepped away, following the duke a few paces away.

"Graham positively couldn't keep his eyes off of you, my dear," Lady Southridge whispered, pulling Bethanny's attention from the duke and Lord Graham's conversation.

"Oh, I'm sure it's simply that I've changed so much since he last saw me," Bethanny replied, her neck and face flushing with the depth of truth to her statement.

"Though I must say he appeared quite unsettled," Lady Southridge added.

To say the least… though I can't exactly blame him.

"He did seem to grow pale when he saw you, dear. Perhaps you remind him of someone," Carlotta added, her expression curious and watchful.

Far too watchful.

"What!"

All three ladies turned to the loud exclamation from Lord Graham who was quite upset about something.

What Bethanny wouldn't give to be three feet closer to overhear *that* conversation.

The duke appeared confused, yet determined, adding to

the mystery.

"I say, what could they be discussing to create such a stir?" Lady Southridge murmured.

"Heaven only knows," Carlotta replied with an amused grin.

"True."

The gentlemen made their way the short distance back to the ladies. The duke was grinning; Lord Graham was… *not.*

Without preamble, Lord Graham addressed Bethanny, "Miss Lamont, I'd be delighted if you'd reserve the supper waltz for me." His expression was anything but delighted, as he'd claimed to be.

Bethanny glanced to the duke who appeared pleased with himself, and then to Carlotta, who was studying Lord Graham with an open skepticism.

"Of course." She nodded slowly.

"If you'll excuse me." He bowed, turned, and left.

Bethanny watched his retreating back with a heavy heart. It was difficult gaining everything she'd wanted, only to have it stolen only a short time after.

She'd wait for the waltz, and then she'd find her answers.

Hopefully he'd be inclined to share.

CHAPTER FOUR

EVEN AS HE WALKED away from Bethanny, he could feel her gaze on his back. He was too close, and being that near to her was already wreaking havoc on his mind. As angry as he was with her, her berry-red lips kept reminding him of her taste; the smooth texture of her skin was then brought to the forefront of his mind as he mentally replayed their kiss over and over.

A kiss he wanted to experience again.

But it was not meant to be.

As if he'd needed another reminder, the duke had pulled him aside and all but forced him to dance the supper set with his ward. Of course, that wouldn't have been an issue, but the *reason* he wanted Graham to do it, *that* was the problem.

He wanted Graham to dance with her so that her first waltz would be with someone he trusted, someone he knew wouldn't take advantage.

Ha.

Advantage.

Because kissing her on a deserted balcony was a supreme idea for protecting.

Of course, he hadn't spilled his secret to his friend. He had no desire to be hung, maimed, or called out on a duel.

However, his guilt had caused him to lose his composure slightly.

But hopefully, no one had paid attention to his loud question.

At least no one who didn't already question his sanity, i.e., his sister and, now included in that exclusive club, Bethanny Lamont.

"Bloody hell," he whispered to himself. The evening was a disaster. And as if it couldn't get worse, he heard the first strains of the supper waltz.

"Better get this over with," he murmured again, closing his eyes for a moment, simply to gather his wits. He'd need them.

As he strode over to where Bethanny waited, his eyes narrowed. Already she was surrounded with suitors, no doubt all vying for her attention. The hot stir of jealousy reared its ugly head once again. Against his better judgment, he straightened his shoulders and went into the fray.

"Miss Lamont? I believe this is our waltz." Graham offered her his most charming smile. Just as he'd intended, the group of young bucks began to back away, their expression crestfallen.

Had he ever been that green? Dear Lord, he hoped not.

"Of course, my lord," Bethanny spoke softly, her brown eyes glancing down so that her dark lashes brushed against her cheeks, which were now tinged with a becoming shade of rose.

She was far too beautiful for her own good.

And he was far too much of a rake to be put in a position where he had to be honorable.

Self-control had never been so difficult.

She was silent as he led her to the dance floor. He turned to face her and slowly placed his hand on her hip. Even through the folds of her dress, he could feel the warmth of her skin. He immediately remembered teaching her to waltz, but there was no similarity to the girl she had been and the woman before him.

Except the eyes.

Her brown depths were the same rich color yet full of experience that belied her youth. Her form was perfection, a dream in his arms. Even the slight lack of grace with which she danced didn't lighten the atmosphere about them. Everything about her pulled him in. The entire waltz was a creation of torture; it unmanned him yet created the most arousing sensation of pleasure he'd experienced in some time, possibly ever.

Needing to distract himself, he grasped her hand and began leading.

Then promptly stepped on her toe.

"My apologies," he whispered, croaked actually, because he wasn't exactly in command of himself at the moment.

Bloody hell, it could only get worse.

"Of course," she murmured, her gaze fixed on his cravat.

Graham continued the attempt to pull himself together and was failing miserably when she spoke.

"I… forgive me, my lord. It's quite apparent that you did not recognize me from earlier. I am sorry for any discomfort that may have caused you," she said softly.

"I must say, I was indeed… surprised." Graham cleared his throat. Surprised? He was bloody well shocked to the point of suffocation.

She was silent then, her gaze shifting to the dancers surrounding them.

"You didn't… seem surprised, that is?" he asked, voicing the question plaguing him.

"I wasn't," she answered immediately, her gaze meeting his. Her chin tilted up defiantly.

"Oh." Because what else could one say? "But then that

would mean that…"

Her eyebrow arched in challenge for him to finish his thought.

Good Lord.

She'd known *who* he was and kissed him anyway!

Or had she kissed him *because* of it?

"Miss Lamont—"

"Bethanny, if you don't mind, my lord." Her voice was as exquisite as her body, melodic and alluring, a siren call if he ever had heard one.

"Beth — no, Miss Lamont. You mustn't let gentlemen be so familiar with you." He shook his head and scolded, aiming the chastisement at himself as well. He could not call her by her first name. It would be foolish and punishing. A first name implied certain intimacies… and in his current state of desire, he couldn't help but imagine those *intimacies* in bright detail.

"But it's you." She shrugged, calling his attention back to the conversation.

"Yes but—"

"And I believe, if I may be so bold to say, *I am* familiar with you, my lord." She smiled flirtatiously.

Blast it all, the chit had a point. But he was *not* going to admit that.

"But that doesn't mean…" He sighed in exasperation. "You still shouldn't let me call you by your name."

"But I like it." Her grin widened as her eyes danced.

"Good Lord, Bethanny — Miss Lamont — you cannot… you cannot say such things!"

Why was the ballroom so hot! His cravat was all but choking him, and for the second time that evening, he was struggling to breathe.

One thing was for certain, Bethanny Lamont was not good for his health.

She sincerely might be the death of him.

But oh, what a way to go.

"Why?" She shrugged delicately.

"Because the gentleman in question might take that as an invitation." Graham cleared his throat. He certainly would take it as an invitation, and if she were anyone else, he would *run* with that invitation… preferably to a very dark and deserted corner.

"Then the *gentleman* in question would finally be getting the point," she shot back, a smile teasing her lips.

"Pardon?" He almost choked on the word. Was she *that* bold?

"You. You are the gentleman in question, in case I wasn't clear enough."

"You were bloo — acutely clear. I say, are you always this bold?"

"No." She shook her head slightly, causing the coffee-colored curls to bounce delicately.

"I should hope not. No wonder your guardian was having a fit about your come out," Graham mostly said to himself.

"Oh, yes… he can be quite protective. But it's all done with a good heart, you understand. He was quite the rake, you know."

Graham felt his jaw drop.

"Er, yes… and in case you haven't heard, I have been known to be one myself."

"I'm aware." She shrugged.

"And yet you still bait me?" Graham felt his eyes narrow.

"I'm not baiting you, as you say. I'm simply being honest."

"Yes, well, perhaps it would be wise for you to not be so honest."

"Because you're a rake?"

"Yes."

"And you'll take shameless advantage of my inexperience?" she asked with a knowing grin, her gaze dancing with delight over knowing she'd bested him.

"Er…"

"Yes, because we simply couldn't have that happen… again. No, I'm quite sure I did not enjoy that kiss." As if to punctuate her point, she bit her lower lip then licked it as her gaze dropped to her slippers.

If her cheeks hadn't bloomed with color at her daring statement, Graham would have thought her a shameless flirt, the worst kind. Yet his instinct told him that she was doing exactly as she'd said, being honest.

Lord knew he could only take so much honesty before he went mad with it and did something brash.

Like kiss her again… in the middle of the crowded ballroom.

"Enjoyment doesn't equal affection," he forced himself to say, knowing that it was a lie. No, if this conversation was any indicator, he could very easily have more than attraction for the young lady.

"No, but it doesn't mean it isn't possible," she spoke bravely, her gaze once more meeting his.

"Miss Lamont, I cannot. You must understand. I… no. I made a mistake, one I am lamenting—" Graham forced himself to say it, knowing it would hurt her, but he saw no other way.

"Let me ask you a question. Would you have compromised me?"

"Pardon?" He sounded like an idiot.

"Well, would you have?"

"No," he answered, trying to figure out where she was going with the leading question.

"Because…" Her eyebrows rose.

"Because you're an innocent!" He spoke in exasperation, too loudly, for another couple waltzing with them shot him an irritated glance.

"Which is exactly why you sent me off on my way and

didn't ever want to see me again?" she spoke softly.

"No, but—"

"But all that changed when you found out who I was," she finished.

"YES." She finally understood!

"Why? And don't give your age as a reason."

"It is a good one — reason, that is. I am quite a bit older than you. But your guardian, the duke, would call me out. It would be pistols at dawn if he knew even the tamest version of what happened earlier this evening. For heaven's sake, Bethanny, he wanted me here to protect you!"

"From?"

"From men like me," he enunciated.

"Oh." Her lips held the shape of their word then slowly spread into a grin, which turned into a musical laughter that was even more alluring than he'd thought possible.

"You have to admit, that is quite amusing. Ironic, actually." Her face was lit up in a beatific smile.

"I do not see the humor."

"Pity, because it is indeed quite hilarious."

"I'm glad you're enjoying the moment."

Her face glowed with her restrained laughter, causing her to be even more breathtakingly beautiful. And then, unable to control himself, he grinned.

And that grin began to spread till it was dangerously close to a smile.

"Ah, see. It *is* amusing," she spoke through a small laugh.

Graham cleared his throat.

"Nevertheless." He glanced away, trying to control his wayward emotions.

"*Nevertheless*," she teased.

"Are you mocking me?"

"Yes." She nodded once.

"I — you're…"

"Enchanting," she finished, her gaze twinkling with

mischief. She was dazzling, captivating, and... no longer dancing.

Graham paused, his brow furrowed as he glanced around.

No one else was dancing either.

"I thought we should stop and not draw attention. You seemed to be... sensitive about that prospect," Bethanny whispered, her lips barely restraining her mirth.

When had the bloody music ended?

"Don't worry, my lord. We only danced a few moments longer than the music. I'm sure no one else noticed."

"No one else?" Graham asked, slightly panicked at his lack of attention to anything but the lovely woman — who was completely off-limits — in front of him.

"No, just... me." She raised a daring eyebrow and smiled.

Damn the girl.

He'd be angry if he weren't so intoxicated by the luscious tip of her lips and the desire it provoked.

Of course, that was what got him in this mess in the first place.

Because if there was one thing he was certain of, it was the absolute desirability of Miss Bethanny Lamont.

Now if he could only be so certain of his ability to resist that temptation.

CHAPTER FIVE

BETHANNY'S GRIN CONTINUED to grow as she lay on her bed and relived the evening of her debut. It had been a smashing success, but more importantly, Lord Graham had most assuredly noticed her.

And had kissed her.

She touched her lips, still in a wide grin, and closed her eyes, remembering the exact flavor of his kiss, the slight abrasion of his barely discernable beard against her skin, and the masculine scent of spice mixed with soap. If she breathed softly, she could almost smell it again.

She sighed.

The only other time she had been close enough to bask in the masculine scent that was Lord Graham had happened inadvertently and quite some time ago. Berty — being Berty — had stolen one of her ribbons and run off with it. Bethany had caught her red-handed and pursued her, chasing her down the hall, past the stairs and to the front door. Of course Berty had known that Bethanny wouldn't dare burst through the front door as she had. It simply wasn't done, for a young lady to behave in such a way, especially one living in one of the most sought-after addresses in Mayfair.

But just before Berty had made her escape, she had glanced over her shoulder at Bethanny and stuck out her tongue.

The hoyden.

Bethanny remembered the anger that had simmered at her sister's brazen behavior, and simply, the audacity of Berty sneaking into her room — again — and stealing a ribbon when she had millions — or at least close to that amount — of her own...

Enough was enough, so Bethanny narrowed her eyes and raced to the front door, peeking out through the side window. Sure enough, Berty was skipping along merrily, no longer concerned about her irate older sister. She began walking around the side of the block.

With a sinister laugh, Bethanny rushed to the servants' entrance out back. Quickly, she passed the startled servants and burst through the heavy wooden back door — after all, back doors were an entirely different variety and very acceptable to burst through — and turned the corner in hot pursuit of her sister, sure she'd intercept her readily and before anyone saw her outlandish behavior.

Of course, the only person she intercepted was Lord Graham, who was coming to visit her guardian, the duke.

Bethanny didn't have a moment to react; rather, she plowed into a black coat covering a very firm back and landed on her seat with a loud groan.

She leaned back and closed her eyes.

Perhaps if she pretended to faint, whomever she'd just accosted would forgive her for such a blunder.

But then she heard a familiar chuckle. "You might as well open those brown eyes of yours, Miss Lamont. I know you're quite awake," Lord Graham's voice called softly.

Inwardly Bethanny sighed with both humiliation yet delight in hearing his voice.

At least she could count on him not to hold her behavior

against her... though it certainly wouldn't assist her efforts in helping him see her as more than a little girl.

"Bethanny! Are you hurt! Oh Bethanny!" Berty's voice called a moment later, shrill and afraid. "Oh, Lord Graham, this is all my fault! I stole her ribbon, and she was surely looking for me! Oh, why did I do it! Blasted thing." Berty choked.

Bethanny continued to keep her eyes closed. At least her humiliation had one silver lining: revenge on her sister.

"Ah, so you're the culprit," Lord Graham scolded in a stern manner.

Bethanny almost opened her eyes at his tone, then caught herself, curious as to what he was up to.

"Bethanny? Please answer me! I'll never take your ribbons again. I swear it." Berty was kneeling over her now, patting her forehead and grasping her hands.

"She's quite injured, I'm afraid," Lord Graham added solemnly.

Bethanny wanted to roll her eyes but didn't; rather, taking secret delight in his playing along.

"Is she? What are we to do?" Berty lamented then gasped. "I know! In my picture books, the prince always kisses the beautiful girl to wake her! You're not a prince, but..." she paused, as if regarding him, "but you are a lord, so perhaps that is similar enough for it to work! You must kiss her!"

"Pardon?" Lord Graham asked in a confused tone. Bethanny could hardly blame him; it was a rare day that Berty didn't confuse her, and she was her sister!

"Kiss her! Oh, please kiss her, and I know she'll wake up, and then she can forgive me, and I'll never take her ribbons," Berty explained succinctly, as her young mind saw all the puzzle pieces fitting together perfectly.

"Er, I'm quite certain that is not how it works," Lord Graham argued.

"How would you know? Have you tried it?" Berty asked impatiently.

"Actually… no," Lord Graham answered.

"Then you have no experience from which to draw a conclusion. Or at least that's what Carlotta tells me… frequently," Berty grumbled.

"Ah, a wise woman."

"You're wasting time! Kiss her!" she demanded.

"I cannot simply kiss—"

"Yes, you can! Kiss her! There's no one around, and I'll not tell a soul. After all, this is—"

"Your fault, I know."

"Yes."

Lord Graham sighed.

Bethanny secretly bit the inside of her lip to keep from grinning. She'd have to thank her sister later.

"What if we just ask her—"

"No! That will never work!"

"You're quite opinionated for one so young," Lord Graham added.

"So I've been told. Now kiss her!"

"Very well, keep a sharp eye out, though. I'll not have some fop say I'm accosting your sister."

"Yes, sir," Berty immediately agreed.

Lord Graham's breath tickled her ear as he bent down. "I do hope that ribbon was made of gold, Miss Lamont." He chuckled then kissed her cheek. His lips were warm and soft, just brushing the corner of her cheekbone. It was lovely, sweet, and, at the same time, so melancholy, because though he was close enough to share the scent he wore of warm spice and peppermint, he was only there out of coercion of her sister.

Then and there she swore that one day he'd kiss her because he wanted to.

Like a fairy princess, Bethanny fluttered her eyelashes dramatically and gasped softly for effect, then rose.

Berty was beside herself with delight and a constant beg of pardon was forthcoming for some time after.

Lord Graham simply winked at her and left, surely to meet up with his friend, the duke, but Bethanny was forever changed...

It was amazing to compare the past and the recent happenings just the night before. They were so different. Yet sadly, they carried one similarity: the melancholy spirit. While Lord Graham had certainly kissed her of his own will, he hadn't realized it was her. And once he had, he'd regretted it.

But that didn't mean that Bethanny had to.

Rolling over on her bed, she rose and padded across the wooden floors to her low-burning fire. Holding her hands out, she let the warmth seep into her skin. A knock on the door alerted her that Molly, her maid, was bringing the newspaper and warm chocolate she'd requested each morning.

Warm chocolate with heaps and heaps of sugar.

And a splash of milk.

It was more of a dessert than anything else, but Bethanny could think of no better way to begin the day than with something sweet.

"Miss? You're awake early. Did you not sleep well, then?" Molly asked kindly as she laid down the tray.

"Actually, I slept quite well." Bethanny offered her maid a welcoming smile and reached for her chocolate.

When the first hint of flavor touched her lips, she closed her eyes, relishing the texture and sweetness.

"Since today is your at-home day, miss, which dress would you prefer? The blue or green?" Molly asked as she withdrew two garments from the wardrobe.

"The blue... I think." Bethanny's eyes darted from dress to dress as she peeked over her cup of chocolate.

"Very good, miss. You're sure to have quite a few callers today, it being the day after your debut and all. I heard it was quite smashing!" Molly's hazel eyes danced with excitement.

"It *was* quite the crush," Bethanny answered kindly.

"And would a certain lord have asked you to dance, miss?" Molly's eyebrow arched in question, a teasing grin at her lips.

"Perhaps."

"Oh! I knew he would, miss! You're far too lovely for any gentleman to not be begging for a dance! Was it all you were wishing?" Molly turned aside from the dresses and happily strode to her mistress, beaming with joy.

"Oh, Molly!" Bethanny grinned. Placing her chocolate on the small table just past the fire, she spun in a small circle. "We waltzed, Molly! A waltz! Can you believe it? It was delightful! Even now, I break out in gooseflesh simply thinking about it!"

"A waltz!" Molly echoed with delight.

"Yes! But..." Bethanny's joy was quickly turning to a worry. "However, we... did meet earlier... and he didn't recognize me."

"Well, you have done your fair share of growing up, you have." Molly nodded.

"Yes, well... I don't think he was pleased that it was me." Bethanny bit her lip.

"Oh? And why are you thinking that, miss? I'm sure he was thrilled!"

"No, you see... he... he seemed quite... shocked actually, when he discovered who I was."

"Shocked by your beauty, miss." Molly spoke confidently.

Bethanny shook her head then bit her lip. How she loved Molly; her fierce loyalty was a rarity and all the more reason for Bethanny's friendship with her maid. That loyalty also made Molly utterly trustworthy, but Bethanny dared not speak about the kiss out loud. She wanted it to be a delicious secret, one that was only shared by one other person. Graham.

"I do believe he found me... pleasing to behold. However, I *think*, no, I *know* he was unhappy because... well... you see, while he didn't know he was speaking with me earlier, I knew it was him. And I didn't say anything about who I was, even though I knew he didn't recognize me,"

Bethanny confessed.

"Oh." Molly furrowed her brow and quirked her lips. "Then we'll just have to change his heart a bit, won't we?" She grinned mischievously. "Your cap's still set on the gentleman, is it not?"

"Oh yes," Bethanny spoke reverently.

"You're a smart one, miss. He might have gotten his manly pride prickled a bit when he realized you were quicker than he, but I suspect that he'll come around, given the proper encouragement." Molly shrugged and went back to the dresses.

"Encouragement?"

"Well, yes, miss. With your beautiful coffee-colored hair and those bottomless brown eyes, I doubt he's missed what a beauty you are. Add to that your kind heart and smart wit, he'll not be able to resist. Besides," Molly smirked a bit before schooling her features into a polite smile, "he's not going to forget you, that's for sure. And that, miss, is half the battle already won."

"Why in the bloody hell do I have to call on her?" Graham was not in the mood to argue with his sister. In fact, he wasn't in the mood for anything other than swiping the French brandy from his study and drinking till sleep found him.

Because he hadn't slept a wink last night.

Not even a bloody minute.

Because each time he'd closed his eyes, she was there. Her deep brown gaze seared through him, igniting a passion he really wished would remain inexperienced. So, he'd open his eyes and stare at his ceiling, or the wall, or the fire — anything that would get his mind off her. Yet everywhere he looked, he'd grown bored with whatever it was he been gazing at — though it wasn't shocking. How interesting was a wall, really? He'd relived their kiss, which in turn, had reminded him of the soft press of her body against his, the warmth of her lips caressing his own, and the *flavor*.

Heaven help him, he couldn't forget the flavor.

It was honey and champagne.

It was desire and surrender.

It was unlike anything he had ever sampled before, and like an addict he was already craving more.

But that was exactly why calling on Miss Bethanny Lamont was a very bad idea.

"Bloody hell."

"You've already said that... much as I wish you wouldn't. What is it that has you in such a foul mood this morning?" his sister commented sternly, her gaze scrutinizing him in a way that made his feet itch with guilt.

That was the rub. He *did* feel guilty. Guilty, because he hadn't recognized her. Guilty, because even after he had realized just who she was, it hadn't changed the fact that he'd wanted her.

Badly. And still did.

And finally, he felt guilty because he'd been asked by his best friend to look out for her. When, in actuality, all he'd wanted to do was compromise her so that she'd be his. Which, in turn, would betray his best friend. And possibly cause a duel, and he'd be the one who deserved the bullet.

"Edward?" his menace of a sister asked impatiently.

"I'm tired."

"You're not *that* old."

"I *feel* that old," Graham replied, sitting and resting his head against the back of the chair.

"All the more reason for you to marry this season then. Am I correct? I never thought I'd see the day when my baby brother was too tired to chase a skirt."

"See here!" Graham's eyes blinked open rapidly, and he

stood.

"No, no, you're right. You're simply getting on in years. Why, to be honest, I was thinking the very same thing last night."

"Pardon?" Graham asked skeptically, his expression turning to a deep frown.

"Last night," his sister hitched a shoulder, "when you were dancing with Bethanny. You did seem quite... fatherly."

"WHAT?" Graham felt his jaw drop.

"You were quite... stoic. I've never seen you act in such a way with such a beautiful woman. My only answer was that you felt decidedly paternal."

"Damnation."

"You're quite vulgar this morning. I'd thank you not to curse any more, my—"

"If you say *ladylike sensibilities*, I might lose what breakfast I ate." Graham rolled his eyes. "Father-like? Paternal? I don't even know what to say."

"I was simply offering my observations." His sister shrugged slightly then raised her hand and examined her gloves.

"Paternal."

"You're repeating yourself again."

"I can't quite believe you said it."

"Of all the things I've said in my life... *this* is what you cannot get over? Truly?" Her eyebrows shot up in shock and derision.

"Actually... yes," Graham grumbled.

"Then one must deduct from your response that your inclinations toward the girl went an opposite direction." A grin began to tip the upper corners of her mouth, a grin all too familiar to Graham.

He had been played. By his sister.

And he didn't think the morning could get worse.

"I have no idea what you're implying." He strode to the

fire and tugged on his cravat.

"You might be dense, but you're not stupid, Edward. She *is* a very beautiful young lady."

"Who I supposedly have paternal feelings for," he mocked, his face twisting in a sneer as he glanced to her.

"Or decidedly unpaternal feelings... perhaps the feelings of a potential suitor?" she asked, a delighted gleam in her eye.

Graham wanted to poke her in that blasted eye.

"Have you lost your mind?" Graham spun and faced her, calling her bluff and hoping he hadn't exposed just how close to the truth she was.

"No, I'm quite certain I'm in full possession of my faculties. You, dear brother, are the one I'm questioning."

"I, how could, why..." Graham took a deep breath and turned away from his sister.

"Sputtering always implicates you, Graham. You might as well admit it." His sister shrugged.

Shrugged, as if what she was implying wasn't damning. Or potentially ruining of a lifelong friendship.

"I admit nothing," Graham spoke through clenched teeth.

"Admission is not necessary for it to be true."

"I still do not see why I must pay a call on her this morning," he replied after a moment.

"Uncomfortable with the topic at hand? Is a change in conversation necessary? Hmm?" His sister's gaze narrowed in delight as her lips bent into a knowing grin.

"Actually, if you remember, that very question was the first that began this whole demented conversation."

"Demented? I fail to see how that adjective applies." She raised her chin a notch.

"Demented. Dear sister, most conversations I partake of that include you often include that very adjective."

"I'm insulted," she huffed.

"But not shocked." Graham grinned.

His sister's eyes narrowed, and if the two siblings had

been younger, he no doubt would have seen her stomp her foot and growl. However, her irritated expression fazed into a knowing one.

Graham knew that expression. Whatever she was thinking was not good.

At least, not good for him.

"You're afraid," she challenged.

"Of what?" Graham scoffed.

"A deb."

"That's... you mean to say... I cannot... won't dignify that statement with a response." Graham sneered and turned away.

But stopped when his sister began clapping.

"Pardon?"

"I'm applauding you," she replied as he turned an annoyed glare to her.

"For? Or dare I ask?" he replied tightly.

"You finished an entire sentence after your stammering. You've come quite a long ways. I know how difficult it must be for you to lie about something so... delicate."

"I—I—" Graham sputtered, fully exasperated and furious.

"Don't choke, Graham. After all, if you're *not* afraid, why so adamant? And yes, I do believe delicate is the correct word for this subject, or *woman*." She took a few steps forward, her smile fading into concerned pinch in her brow.

Bloody hell, it was the look of pity.

Anything but pity.

"I want to see you settled. You yourself even said this was the season. There's no way you didn't notice the girl, Edward. I watched you. I saw your expression. Don't let a little bit of age difference and an irritable duke stand in the way of what could be life-changing."

"I have no idea as to what you are referring," Graham replied succinctly, biting the words as they came from his mouth.

Wishing that it truly was as simple as his sister had said. But she hadn't been there when Clairmont had confided in him. And even though his sister knew him well, she didn't know him *that* well, and if she did, she certainly wouldn't be suggesting that he pursue the purity of Bethanny Lamont. No, she'd be protecting her *from* him. That knowledge alone was enough to remind him of his place, of his necessity in staying away from her.

But oh, if she didn't tempt him, then nothing in this world ever would.

"I appreciate your sentiment. Truly. However, all is not as you expect, dear sister. You might think differently, but you are not omnipotent, and in this, you are mistaken." Graham bowed, turned on his heel, and left.

His sister's silence echoed louder than anything she could have ever said. She'd known he was lying, just as easily as he'd known the lie himself. And if he'd known she'd never believe him, why had he done it?

The truth was far more frightening than the possibility of admitting his feelings. Because the truth was, he *wanted* to lie to himself, but the problem with lying to oneself is that one never truly believed it.

Even if one wanted to.

CHAPTER SIX

GRAHAM CALLED HIMSELF ten kinds of fool as he handed his card to the butler while he waited outside the duke's residence. He hadn't even planned to make a call. It all had started out as a walk to clear his head, and being near Hyde Park had necessitated that very park be the one he'd ambled through. However, after that amble, his clarity of mind had not improved, so he'd continued walking, and had found himself across the street from the duke's residence.

Just as Lord Neville was allowed entrance.

It was well-known that Neville was a recluse, and if he was visiting the residence of the duke, he had a bloody purpose in mind.

And all Graham could think of was that the purpose in mind was to court Bethanny.

Which was a wretched idea. She'd never be happy with the likes of someone like him. Of course he didn't rationalize *why*. Simply *thinking* it was enough, and soon he found himself knocking on that very door, swearing in Italian as he waited for the butler to return.

"Lord Graham, please follow me," Murray spoke in his

mild manner.

Graham nodded and soon was led to the red salon. Upon entering, all other details faded into the background as searched for her.

"Lord Graham." Her melodic voice reached his ears a fraction of a second before his gaze found hers. She was a queen holding court with a room full of suitors, all vying for her attentions.

"Miss Lamont." He bowed crisply.

"Would you care for some tea?" Standing, she walked over to him, her gaze illuminated as if harboring a secret.

A secret he shared.

Immediately his irritation melted like a spring snow, and he felt himself grinning.

"Not at the moment, but I thank you," he offered, his tone dropping slightly.

As if realizing the intention of his tone, her cheeks blossomed with color, adding to her already-staggering beauty.

Graham's grin widened.

"Won't you please…" She paused, glancing around. Every chair was occupied with a hopeful swain. "Excuse me a moment. I'll have Murray fetch a chair." She rallied quickly.

"No, there's no need, Miss Lamont. I'm needing to speak with His Grace. However…" he paused and leaned in slightly, thrilled when she followed suit and leaned in as well, "I will return when all the… children… leave." He glanced over to a few hopeful men seated on a couch, each wearing disgruntled expressions, which pleased him greatly. With a wink, he reached for her hand. Without breaking eye contact, he kissed the soft flesh on her wrist, hanging propriety, and let his greedy lips partake of her lavender-scented skin.

Her breath caught, her eyes widened, and just when he thought he had rendered her senseless, one of her delicate brows rose in challenge, as if she was humored by his display.

Like a peacock displaying his feathers for the rest of the suitors to stand by and envy.

"Oh, well, thank you for stopping by," she murmured, her tone provocative and low, meant for his ears only.

His blood stirred, and a devilish grin played at his lips. With another wink, he bowed and turned to leave but not before noticing a suppressed grin from Lord Neville. Graham paused and regarded him. Lord Neville raised his chin defiantly, though his lips were pressed together as if suppressing some merriment of sorts.

Graham nodded then left, curious as to what was so entertaining to the reclusive lord. It truly was an odd reaction to have, considering the circumstances. Unless the gentleman thought Graham was not a threat; if so, Neville was sorely mistaken.

Shaking his head, he made his way to Clairmont's study. As he strode down the hall, his mind wandered back to Bethanny. Her hair had been pulled up prim and proper, but the mass of hair had seemed to strain the pins, as if only needing the slightest encouragement to break free and tumble down unconfined. A wall of desire hit him, unforgiving as he tried to overcome the intense craving to see her in such a state. Because if her hair were down, then certainly she wouldn't be wearing such a proper day dress, which would mean she were wearing something softer, something easier to—

"Graham?" The duke's voice shattered his immoral daydream like a mirror dropping from a balcony.

A very tall balcony.

"Er, hello." Graham cleared his throat and pulled on his cravat.

Dear Lord, it was times like these he was thankful God had seen fit that no one could read another's mind.

"Good to see you. Are you quite well? You seem a bit... unsettled," Clairmont said as he studied Graham.

"Between you and my sister, I feel as though I'm back in

short pants," Graham grumbled, feeling more of himself.

"Apologies…" The duke glanced about for a moment. "I assume you were searching for me?"

"Yes, I had a question about…" Graham glanced behind him. "Could we continue this conversation in your study, perhaps?"

"That type of question, eh?" The duke's eyes narrowed slightly.

"Indeed."

Clairmont nodded and went back into his study, standing to the side as Graham entered. Graham closed the door, and took a step toward Clairmont's mammoth desk. Pausing, he turned back and locked the door. Nodding once, he resumed his course toward the duke's desk and took a seat, facing his friend.

"Very well. What was your question?"

Bethanny couldn't focus on Lord Somter's voice, nor could she recall exactly what they'd been conversing about. However, with Lord Somter, one rarely had to follow the topic closely; all that was needed was a nod or a well-placed *Yes, my lord,* and he'd continue to prattle on.

And on.

And on.

And Bethanny was far too distracted to pay attention when she kept checking to see if Lord Graham had shown up once again.

I'll return when all the children leave.

A smile struggled to break free as she remembered his verbal challenge. She was delighted with it, with him and his playful manner. It was the brightest spot of her day.

"Wouldn't you agree, Miss Lamont?" Lord Somter asked.

Bethanny's gaze met his, but before she could offer her

agreement, or disagreement — though either would have been a blind guess, seeming as she still wasn't sure of their topic of discourse — he continued on, speaking about his estate's landscaping.

At least she knew the topic of conversation now. Not that it was particularly interesting.

She offered the middle-aged lord a polite smile as he continued. It wasn't that Lord Somter wasn't handsome enough to tempt her — if one could get past the endless prattle — it was just that neither he, nor anyone else in attendance, was Lord Graham. And that alone was enough to disqualify him. She glanced about for a moment, searching for a polite excuse to extricate herself from his one-sided conversation, and her eye caught Lord Neville's.

He was watching her with amusement softening his dark features. As if enjoying her torture, his eyes danced with merriment. Unable to ignore it, Bethanny raised an eyebrow of challenge.

To which Lord Neville simply smiled.

Never before had she seen him smile, and good Lord, if she weren't so attached to Graham, she'd have set her cap for him.

His smile was glorious, masculine but dark, brooding somehow. Deeper than a simply expression of the face, it was an expression of his soul.

A moment later, he stood and walked toward her. Quickly, Bethanny turned back to Lord Somter, who was, of course, still talking, and waited, curious as to what Lord Neville was planning.

"Somter? I'm about to take my leave, but before I go, would you allow me to give my regards to the lady?" Lord Neville bowed graciously.

"Oh, well… of course." Lord Somter seemed reluctant to let his captive audience go, but politely excused himself and took a biscuit from the tray.

After two steps, he wheeled back around and grabbed three more.

Bethanny suppressed a smile as she turned to Lord Neville.

"My lord."

"Miss Lamont." His lips twisted into a small grin.

"I thank you."

"For saving you?"

"Whatever do you mean?" Bethanny teased.

"Nothing, apparently." His grin grew.

"Are you indeed leaving?"

"I must, now that I've stated as much."

"But it wasn't your intention before you saw my plight," she stated.

"No, not necessarily." He shrugged.

"Then, I thank you for your sacrifice on my behalf." Bethanny grinned.

"Ah, but it is not sacrifice when in service to such a lovely lady. Though I suspect all of us are but distractions from someone else." His gaze was piercing and dark, but not disappointed, simply amused.

"Whatever could you mean by such a cryptic comment?" Bethanny glanced to the floor, not willing to inadvertently give away the truth of his statement by the honesty in her eyes.

"I'm simply... observant. One should always take care not to have one's heart broken," he offered while still grinning. But this time, the amusement faded from his eyes, a hint of torture, or pain lurking beneath.

"Indeed," Bethanny agreed. After all, she was too aware of the implications for herself, as well.

"I wish you a lovely afternoon, miss."

"Thank you. I offer you the same," Bethanny spoke softly.

With a single nod, Lord Neville quit the room, but not

before he walked far too close to Lord Somter. In a slight misstep, he jolted the gentleman's knee where his tea was resting in his hand, spilling the contents on his breeches.

"Bloo— er, ah," Lord Somter sputtered, his face turning an unattractive shade of pink.

"Apologies! How clumsy of me!" Lord Neville replied at the humiliated gentleman. And as Lord Somter began to wipe at the tea, Lord Neville glanced back to Bethanny, meeting her gaze, and winked.

Winked, because his actions had been no accident.

She'd have to thank him later.

"Well, old chap, I guess you're leaving with me. Allow me to—"

"You've done quite enough, thank you," Lord Somter replied tightly. With a highly disgruntled expression, he turned to Bethanny. "Forgive me, Miss Lamont, but I must depart as well."

Bethanny nodded.

Lord Neville took a step behind Lord Somter and grinned.

"I understand," Bethanny replied graciously.

After a curt bow, Lord Somter turned, glared at Lord Neville, then left.

Lord Neville bowed again, this time with a slight flourish, and took his leave as well.

Bethanny turned to her other suitors. Their rapt attention had been focused on Somter and Neville, each offering delighted expressions of… gratitude?

"Would anyone care for more tea?" Bethanny offered, regaining control of her parlor.

"Indeed." The remaining men offered her polite grins and empty cups.

Now, if only there were a few more Lord Nevilles to help her remove the remaining, then perhaps Lord Graham would return.

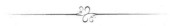

"Miss Lamont seems to have attracted quite a bevy of suitors," Graham offered as he sipped his brandy.

Clairmont growled then took a sip of his own. "Indeed. Bloody mess."

"I thought the goal was to marry her off." Graham almost choked on the words. The thought of her belonging to any of the peacocks in the red parlor made him, well... see red. A blistering, bloody shade of it that was causing his fists to flex and his jaw to clench. But now was not the time to display his attraction.

Anytime but now.

"It is, but... men are like starving wolves," Clairmont mumbled.

"Pardon?" Graham felt his brow furrow.

"Bethany is exceptional in beauty, exceptional in pocket, and exceptional in her connections."

"By connections you mean, yourself, of course," Graham teased.

Clairmont simply shot him an exasperated expression.

"What I'm saying is that she'll attract them all, *all!*"

"As opposed to... none?" Graham offered. He was quite fond of the *none* theory himself.

Then he could easily sweep in and—

"No, I don't want none, I just want... I want the right one."

"So you want one?"

"Yes."

Could he volunteer? That would make it simple.

"But he has to be good enough for her."

Perhaps he shouldn't volunteer...

"Someone with morals, a clean past, someone who won't see her as a means to an end."

"Noble attributes." Graham nodded, hating that most of

them excluded him.

"What does the duchess say?" Graham asked.

"To stop worrying."

"A wise woman."

"Shut up."

"I was simply agreeing with your wife." Graham shrugged and took another sip of brandy. He needed it.

"She doesn't need anyone else to be on her side."

"I didn't realize we were taking sides."

"There's always sides."

"I wasn't aware—"

"And you must always be on my side."

"Why?"

"Because..." He paused.

"You're outnumbered?" Graham offered, a grin bending his lips as he watched his friend's expression turn irritated.

"No, I'm most certainly—"

"You are, admit it."

"No."

"Admission doesn't mean it's not true," Graham replied before thinking. Then cursed.

"What was that?"

"Nothing," he bit out. Of all the times to be thinking of *that* conversation with his sister.

Bloody hell.

"As I was saying, I need you on my side."

"But what if I disagree?" Graham asked.

"You won't." Clairmont nodded assertively.

"Confident, eh?" Graham replied.

"Completely."

"Must be nice," Graham murmured over his glass.

"What?"

"Ah, nothing of importance."

Clairmont walked a few paces to his window and gazed out.

"Neville and Somter have taken their leave," he commented, no doubt seeing their departure from his window as it faced the street.

"About bloody time," Graham whispered lowly.

"I say you're bloody talking to yourself all the time. Should I be concerned?" Clairmont spoke snidely.

Graham offered him a bland smile and took a lingering sip of brandy—

"What did *you* think of Bethanny?"

And promptly choked.

"Graham?"

It was a ring of fire in his throat, burning as it descended into his stomach and scorching his lungs as he coughed and sputtered.

"Damn it all, don't waste my good brandy by breathing it in." The duke shook his head as Graham tried to gain a semblance of composure.

"It wasn't that difficult of a question."

"No, no I simply…" Graham began to explain but another fit of coughing overtook him.

"Are you going to live through it, then?" Clairmont spoke sardonically.

"Through sheer force of will," Graham ground out, his throat still on fire.

Clairmont laughed.

"You're a lot of bloody help."

"I'm not the one who breathes brandy."

Graham glared; after all, what could he say? Clairmont was right. At least he didn't know *why* he'd breathed in the brandy.

"Now, if you're once again in control of yourself, I'd like to know the answer to my question." Clairmont rocked on his heels.

"What question?" Graham asked, though he knew the question full well.

"What did you think of Bethanny?"

"Ah." Graham stood and took a few steps toward the fire. Shrugging slightly, he replied, "I am in agreement with you."

"Oh?"

"Yes, I was just told a few moments ago that I was only allowed to be on *your* side. So therefore, my opinion must align with yours," Graham teased.

"Nodcock."

"Why, thank you."

"Honestly, though."

"I appreciate your sentimental name calling."

"Not that. Damn, you're damn irritating. You know that?"

"I know."

"So?"

"So what?"

"I swear, I feel as though I'm talking with Berty, when she was *seven!*"

"Delightful child."

"Pain in my... er... yes. Delightful child," Clairmont amended, a wry grin teasing his features as he shook his head. "If you please." He exhaled.

Graham sighed in defeat. So much for trying to distract him from the question. It was a simple enough answer, but he didn't know if he could keep the truth, the raw honesty of it, from leaking through his tone and being noticed.

"She's... exquisite." Graham breathed, turning to the fire lest the Duke see the longing in his eyes.

"She is. You didn't recognize her, did you?" Clairmont offered lightly.

"No."

Graham heard Clairmont's footsteps till he saw him out of the corner of his eye, standing beside him as he gazed into the fire as well.

"Tell me the truth, no sides, no sarcasm. Are my fears

founded?" Clairmont asked with sincerity to his tone that pierced through Graham.

Because Graham was the wolf that Clairmont was concerned about.

He was exactly everything the duke wanted to protect Bethanny from.

But Clairmont was his friend, his best friend. And he'd not betray that, regardless of how much he wanted to.

"Your fears are most assuredly founded, my friend," Graham replied, closing his eyes.

"That's what I'm afraid of," Clairmont murmured.

Me too.

CHAPTER SEVEN

"ARE THEY GONE, then? Beatrix poked her head into the salon, asking the question only after making certain that she was only asking the obvious.

"Indeed." Bethanny sighed, exhausted. Who knew entertaining could be so tiring?

"Anything interesting happen?" Beatrix asked, her face alight with curiosity and wonder.

"Ah, no. Wait. Yes!" Bethanny leaned forward and watched her sister's smile grow as she hurried to sit next to her.

"What happened?"

"You've heard of Lord Neville, correct?"

"The recluse?"

"Yes!"

"Was he here?" Beatrix asked.

"Yes, and he was by far my favorite."

"But I thought—"

Bethanny reached out and covered her sister's mouth with her hand.

"Hush!"

Beatrix nodded, and Bethanny removed her hand. "Sorry."

"Not like *that*."

"That?" Beatrix's brow furrowed in confusion.

"He rescued me." Bethanny shrugged, watching closely as her sister's expression became shocked and brimmed with expectation.

"How so?"

"Well, Lord Somter was quite determined to converse the entire afternoon away. And when I say converse, I mean he was the one talking, the *only* one talking."

"What a bother." Beatrix rolled her eyes.

"Indeed. Well…" Bethanny went on to explain the whole fiasco to Beatrix, who giggled with delight.

"He sounds perfect." Beatrix sighed.

"For someone, but not me," Bethanny replied honestly.

"Did you happen to see… Mr. Perfect?" Beatrix asked, her expression teasing.

"Yes… in fact, I did. And he was quite improper." Bethanny bit her lip.

"What?" Beatrix's eyes widened.

"Don't fuss. It was all in fun. In fact, I was waiting in here because he said he'd return. But it's getting late, and I don't think he's going to make good on his word."

"Perhaps he's simply speaking with the duke."

"He said as much."

"Carlotta says that those two together chatter like old dowagers." Beatrix shook her head and giggled.

"She does not." Bethanny gently pushed her sister's shoulder, grinning.

"Yes, she said it to me earlier when she saw them disappear into the duke's study."

"Hmm… is he still there?"

"I'm not sure… but I'm certain we can find out." Beatrix smiled wickedly and stood. "Well, are you coming?" she challenged, her eyes dark and mischievous.

Bethanny exhaled, debating. "Yes," she answered hesitantly. The last thing she wanted was to be caught searching for him.

Even if it was the truth. A lady had her pride.

"Berty is with Carlotta, so we can be ever so quiet," Beatrix whispered as she eased the door open and glanced out.

"I say, that girl is louder than elephants," Bethanny whispered.

Beatrix shot her a look of complete agreement and gasped.

Without warning, Bethanny was shoved into the hall.

Directly in front of the duke and Lord Graham.

Wide-eyed, she simply blinked at the gentlemen, who were now regarding her with a mix of alarm and puzzlement.

She was going to murder her sister.

"Bethanny, didn't see you there, er, have all your swains left then?" the duke began, his expression no longer surprised.

That she was able to shock him at all was quite impressive.

"Y-yes, Your Grace." Bethanny stammered, her eyes darting between the duke and Lord Graham.

"Ah, the little boys all went home, did they?" Graham's eyes gleamed with amusement, adding to the already enticing dimpling grin he was displaying.

"What the devil are you talking about, Graham? You honestly can't think that she'd want to marry someone as old as you, can you?" the duke huffed, his expression intolerant.

Graham's dimples disappeared.

Bethanny grinned.

"There is something to be said about maturity, Your Grace," Bethanny offered, dipping her gaze to the floor with a flutter of her lashes.

"There's a distinct difference between maturity and age, darling. Many gentlemen may have one, but not necessarily the other," the duke corrected kindly.

Bethanny glanced up, first meeting Lord Graham's gaze, which was heavy with awareness. His amber-colored eyes were warm, yet restless, as if fighting some internal battle.

Not wanting to betray her affections, she turned to the duke and his warm blue gaze that bespoke the affection he harbored for her and her sisters.

"Indeed," she agreed.

"However, I would have to say that Graham has exceeded my expectations and has reached a level of maturity I did not anticipate." The duke turned to his friend, a wry grin tipping his lips.

"Your kind words set my heart to fluttering," Graham replied sarcastically.

"I'm sure it's more of a compliment than you'd hear from your sister," the duke dared.

"In saying that, you're implying that my sister has something important of which to notify me, and I find that exceedingly unlikely."

"For shame!" Bethanny scolded before she thought better of herself.

Both gentlemen turned to her with surprised expressions.

"Forgive me," she paused, then soldiered through, "but your sister is a dear woman who loves you, and you as well, Your Grace. Her attempts to display that affection are oft times..." She tried to think of the correct word.

"Ludicrous?" the duke offered in a helpful tone.

"Fraught with terror?" Graham added a moment later.

"Abhorrent?" the duke tried again.

"Meddlesome," Bethanny ground out, her tone impatient.

Lord Graham snorted.

"However, the end result is not a testament of the depth, the intention is," Bethanny finished.

"Ah, well said, my dear." the duke nodded sagely.

"Er, yes," Lord Graham agreed, somewhat reluctantly.

Bethanny smothered a grin.

"Oh, don't let propriety steal your amusement at my expense, Miss Lamont." Graham held out his hand in a welcoming gesture. "By all means, dazzle us with your beautiful smile," he challenged in a teasing tone.

Unable to restrain herself, Bethanny allowed her smile to break free, along with a small spell of laughter.

"I say, are all your wards this outspoken?" Graham mock-whispered to the duke.

"Yes, I blame Carlotta."

Graham nodded sagely.

"And your sister."

"Quite right," Graham agreed

A moment of silence descended in the hall, a stalemate.

"I do believe I will bid you farewell." Graham bowed then turned to his friend, grasping his hand and shaking it.

"Very well," the duke replied. "You will be at the Symores' rout later this week?"

"Er, yes." Graham responded, but not before cutting a quick glance to Bethanny. It was far too quick for her to read its possible meaning.

Drat.

"Until then." The duke nodded and strode down the hall then paused. "Beatrix? Am I mistaken, or do you have studies to attend to?" He didn't even turn around, simply spoke aloud.

Bethanny turned and watched a very flushed Beatrix step out from the large fern and make her way down the hall. "Yes, Your Grace," she murmured, turned around and winked at Bethanny, then carried on behind the duke.

"Minx of a little sister you have there," Graham commented.

"You have no idea." Bethanny shook her head.

"Did you enjoy your afternoon?" Lord Graham asked, his

golden eyes drawing her in.

"Some moments more than others," Bethanny offered with what she hoped was a flirtatious grin.

"Ah, I suppose a lady is entitled to selecting her amusements."

"Indeed. I must say, though…" she leaned in slightly, overjoyed when his eyes glinted in merriment and he leaned in as well, "Lord Neville is quite the unexpected hero," she teased, hoping to provoke a reaction.

"Neville?" Graham repeated, his tone tight.

"Yes. Perhaps later this week at the Symores' rout I'll share my diverting tale." Bethanny gave him a saucy grin, turned and walked away.

As she took a few steps, she bit her lip in anxiety, praying that her ploy had worked.

She had only made it seven steps before she felt a tug on her hand. Her heart racing and her skin feverish with awareness, she turned. Lord Graham's dimples were in full force, adding to the captivating smile and straight white teeth he boasted. The cut of his jaw somehow accentuated the shape of his eyes.

Bethanny tried not to hold her breath—

But failed.

"You cannot say such things and expect for me to be patient." He shook his head and tugged her hand till she followed him. He glanced down the hall and pulled her into a room, one she knew wasn't used as often. The pale yellow parlor was small, and therefore remained unoccupied most of the time, making it the perfect place for a bit of privacy.

"I choose to keep my diverting tales till a later time," Bethanny teased. "And I fear there is nothing you can do, Lord Graham, that will change my mind. Consider this fair warning." She raised a daring eyebrow.

"A challenge? I accept." Lord Graham released her hand and bowed. "I've uncovered a fair share of secrets, Miss

Lamont. Consider this *my* warning." He reached down and grasped her hand once more and pulled her in toward him. "Some secrets are worth more than others. Just how much should I risk in trying to uncover yours?" he whispered, his eyes roaming her face, sending shivers of anticipation through her.

"I don't know many secrets, I hate to waste your valuable time," Bethanny responded, thankful her tone wasn't as breathless as she felt.

"Hmm... tell me about Neville," he murmured, and reached up and traced the lines of her neck with his gloved hand. The smooth texture of his glove felt like silk against her skin, cool yet leaving her feverish.

"What about him?" Bethanny asked, curling her hands into fists till her nails bit into her flesh, hoping it would help keep her wits about her.

"Did he rescue you? That's what I've been told."

"Perhaps. I do believe you've also been told that you'll learn the full story later. Are you so impatient?" she asked, then felt a daring grin tug at her lips. Slowly she reached up and ran her palms across his shoulder and down his arm, tracing his form.

Lord Graham's teeth clenched.

Bethanny grinned wider.

"Two can play, Miss Lamont."

"Undoubtedly." She shrugged and bit her lip, glancing down at her own boldness.

"I never expected you'd grow into someone so stubborn," he spoke after a moment, his caramel-colored eyes searching hers as she raised her gaze to meet his.

"We all change."

"Indeed."

"Some more than others," she added with a grin.

"Yes... well." Lord Graham appeared uncomfortable and took a step back, clearing his throat.

"Lord Graham, I do believe you're blushing," she teased.

"I am not." He looked offended.

Bethanny didn't believe him. "You must know that I do not hold the fact that you did not recognize me against you. Don't you? I'm quite aware that I don't look very similar to the young girl you left behind."

Lord Graham cleared his throat." Dear Lord, what am I doing?" he murmured softly and turned.

"Wait," Bethanny called out as he started for the door.

He paused but didn't turn, his head hanging as if berating himself.

Bethanny strode forward and placed a hand at his back, encouraging him to turn. He obeyed, his eyes tormented.

"Yes?" he asked hesitantly.

"Don't," Bethanny commanded softly.

"Pardon?" His golden brows furrowed, giving him the expression of a confused Greek god.

"Just… don't. Because all the things you're berating yourself for are the very things I'll be dreaming about tonight," she whispered, praying her confession of bold truths wouldn't leave her brokenhearted.

"You don't know me." He shook his head.

She reached up and cradled his face in her hands. "Yes, Lord Graham, I do. I know you, I know your family, I know your friends, and, more so, I know you deeper because of how I've come to know you *through* them." Softly she reached up and kissed his cheek. "And for me, that is enough."

Lord Graham was still as she whispered her final words. She backed away a step and waited.

He regarded her softly, as if unsure yet hoping, wanting to believe her. Then, just as she was afraid he'd leave without another word, he reached out and grasped her hand.

"Until later," he murmured. Tugging on each individual finger of her glove, he slowly removed the soft leather from her hand, never once breaking eye contact.

The soft halo of light gold in the middle of his amber gaze was illuminated with a delicious seduction that held her captive. She gasped softly, remembering the life-giving breath she was so desperately in need of, and struggled to continue her rhythmic intake. Slowly, feeding the already swirling anticipation, he raised her hand and kissed her wrist, allowing his soft lips to graze along the sensitive flesh before pressing another warm and alluring kiss. His nose drew a lazy circle as his warm breath tickled her skin.

Straightening his posture, he gently handed her back the removed glove and winked then walked away.

Bethanny's gaze greedily took in the strong shape of his shoulders and how they tapered to a trim waist. The soft thump of his boots on the floor helped slow the rapid cadence of her heartbeat.

Later couldn't arrive soon enough.

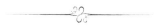

Graham tapped his boot on the wooden floor. Though the sound was of his own making, it annoyed him all the same. So he stood and paced.

Bloody hell.

It had been two days since he had last seen Bethanny, and he was acting like a caged tiger, so desperate was he for the sight of her. He had fought back and forth, a civil war within himself, over the reasons he should or shouldn't pursue the consuming attraction toward the girl.

Because she was a *girl*, young, untainted, pure.

Honestly, his antithesis. She deserved far better than he, yet he found that he wanted her all the same.

Which was only proof of the depravity of his soul.

Oh, he hadn't been too bad…

Or perhaps he had, but regardless, he never thought a deb would ever wield such power over him. It was…

unsettling.

Yet he was powerless to stop it.

He needed to clear his head. But so far nothing had worked — not brandy, not cards at White's, nor riding breakneck speed through Hyde Park. He desired no woman save the one he shouldn't want. And he wasn't a fool enough to think a quick tumble with another would solve anything; rather, he was quite certain it would make matters worse.

Graham paused in front of the low-burning fire, inhaling the faint scent of smoke.

He could visit the duke again.

But he didn't truly have a reason to visit… and he wasn't of the habit of dropping by anyone's residence simply to… chat.

He wasn't a woman.

He glanced at the clock and noticed the hour. It would be quite fashionable to take ride through the park. Perhaps if Bethanny…

Before he could finish the thought or consider the repercussions, he was striding toward the door.

"Please have the curricle readied," he asked of his aged butler.

"Of course, my lord." He bowed with practiced ease.

Graham turned and bounded up the stairs. After changing into a finer coat, he made his way to the curricle. Snapping the whip, the bays charged forward, pulling the stylish carriage into the street. Graham refused to think about his actions, rather focusing on the slight breeze that alleviated the air of some of the London stench. The trees were green, and the air warmer than yesterday. The sun hung in the lower western sky, and the clouds seemed friendly, rather than threatening rain.

Truly London was beautiful when the weather allowed.

He guided his bays to the duke's residence and pulled them up just before the house. The stately stone structure boasted several floors and impeccably manicured boxwoods. Graham knocked and withdrew a card, waiting.

"Yes, Lord Graham?" Murray answered, his face the usual unreadable mask.

"I'm here to see…" he cleared his throat, "I'm here to see Miss Lamont."

"I see." The butler accepted the card and disappeared into the house.

He was impatient and anxious, curious as to what was taking Murray so long. Had the duke rejected his request? Was Bethanny out already?

Was she with another gentleman?

Graham began to clench his fist.

"Right this way, my lord." Murray appeared and guided him to the usual receiving parlor. "Miss Lamont will be down directly."

Graham nodded.

"And His Grace will also be here shortly," Murray added.

Graham nodded tersely. *What's done is done,* he thought, *but how to—*

"Graham! I saw your curricle, and Murray said you're here to speak with Bethanny? No doubt you'll wish to take her out for a ride — a brilliant idea. Wish I would have thought of it myself. She can get her practice in with you rather than I."

"Practice?" Graham asked, his elation at the duke neatly taking care of his predicament taking a nosedive as he considered the reason.

"Why yes! She's been invited by several gentlemen for turns about the park, but she declined. I'm assuming it's nerves. I imagine it would be quite tedious the first time. You're a good egg to consider her. Surely she'll feel quite relaxed with you. Take the pressure off, so to say." The duke rocked on his heels, a very self-satisfied smile on his face.

One that Graham wanted to remove with bodily force.

"Indeed," Graham replied, because what else could he

say? *Actually I'm here as one of those lovesick swains hoping to steal a few precious moments of her undivided attention...*

"Ah, here she is." The duke held out his hand to Bethanny as she entered.

Graham was thankful Clairmont was preoccupied, for surely he would have seen the truth written clearly across his face in that moment. Like a man starved, he feasted upon the sight of her in the neat green dress as it darted in at her hips and rounded her curves in the most delicious fashion possible. It was as if the dressmaker had designed the dress to tempt a man, to lure his thoughts into forbidden territory, all with the guise of modesty, as it covered all the areas it also deliciously highlighted.

Fashion be damned.

"Miss Lamont." Graham bowed and forced his thoughts into submission. Taking a deep breath, he flashed her one of his most charming grins.

Her color deepened with an innocent blush, causing his blood to simmer with unfulfilled desire.

Forbidden desire.

"Lord Graham." Bethanny nodded, her eyes sparkling with secrets that Graham shared.

And heaven only knew how many *more* secrets he wanted to share.

"Isn't this grand?" the duke commented.

"Indeed," Graham murmured, his gaze trained on Bethanny. "Shall we, Miss Lamont?" He offered his arm.

Softly, she placed her hand on him. The comfort of her touch was as peaceful as it was alarming. Who was this woman who could provoke such strong sentiment and emotion? What was it about her that caused him to react so? Graham prided himself in his self-control. He made women swoon.

Not the other way around.

Graham led her to the curricle and glanced to the sky.

Puffy clouds were swept across the late spring horizon, outlined in silver and far too lightly colored for rain. Sending up a prayer of thanks, he helped Bethanny in and then entered as well. The carriage was well-sprung, and Graham couldn't help but feel the elation of pride as he took in hand the reins.

"So, I find myself curious as to why you are here. Not that I object, mind you," Bethanny asked in her honest manner, her brown eyes clear.

"Can I not enjoy a turn about the park with a lovely lady for company?" Graham asked back smoothly. He resisted the urge to clear his throat as Bethanny's gaze sharpened as if trying to lift the reason from his mind.

"You are indeed free to do so, as I am free to be flattered by your compliment. However, we both know that you do not wish to draw the attention of my guardian. So my curiosity isn't exactly satisfied, Lord Graham." She grinned lightly, leaned over, and bumped his shoulder playfully.

"Minx. Must you always be so curious?" he grumbled, though a grin broke through.

"Indeed. It's why you like me so," she replied cheekily.

"Is that so? And here I was simply taking you out so you'd not be nervous for the other more... suitable... gentlemen who wish to bask in the glow of your company," Graham replied, then watched as her brow furrowed. He hadn't meant to hurt her tender feelings, yet she had a way of putting him on the defensive, as if he needed to take extra measure to protect himself.

To protect his heart.

A grin tipped her lips. "Lord Neville *did* mention an outing. How kind of you to take me out so that I may rid myself of all anxiety." She hitched a shoulder.

"Neville?" Graham asked lightly, though his grasp on the leather straps tightened considerably.

"Indeed. Amicable fellow."

"Amicable," he muttered.

"That is precisely what I said." She shrugged. "Oh, look! There's Lady Symore! Her rout is in a few days. Will you be attending?"

Graham nodded to the gentle lady as they passed her and a companion. "I believe so."

"Then I shall save a dance for you." Bethanny beamed at him a charming grin.

"How kind of you to read my mind and give me the true desire of my heart," Graham teased.

"You are most welcome. But back to our original conversation—"

"Good Lord, you're like an elephant."

"I hope you are referring to my intelligence rather than the size of my nose, Lord Graham." Bethanny gave him a stern glare, though her eyes danced.

"Of course!" He waved impatiently.

"Then I'll accept your compliment. Now, at the risk of causing you to think that perhaps your attentions are unwanted, because I believe I've make myself quite clear on that particular subject—"

"Honesty and all—"

"Indeed." She shot him a glare and waited, as if making sure he'd not interrupt.

Graham gestured for her to continue.

"What I mean to ask is… Do you like me, Lord Graham?" She asked the pointed question and shifted to face him.

Graham exhaled a frustrated breath. Did he like her? She was a borderline obsession! Against everything he knew to be safe or wise, she had vaulted every barrier, boundary, and taken up residence in his heart without any invitation.

And he wouldn't have it any other way.

Yet the issue with the duke was a continual douse of cold water over the burning embers of desire that smoldered, carefully restrained, within him. It was no small matter.

"A direct question."

"I do not like to beat around the bush. I could be coy, flirtatious—"

"You do not think yourself flirtatious?" Graham interrupted, shocked.

"Er... no. Why? Do *you* think I'm flirtatious?" she asked, a question in her gaze.

"Well... yes. Quite."

"Oh, well. That's because it's you."

"I see. But wouldn't that mean that you did know you were flirting—"

"I suppose... yes. You are correct. I have been flirting. I don't think I truly was trying, though. It's more of a... natural reaction."

"Natural reaction?"

"Yes. To you. Because whether or not you like me, Lord Graham, I do like you." She lowered her gaze, a rosy blush highlighting her cheekbones and making her beauty appear even more exquisite.

Graham's throat went dry; all he could do was stare, memorize the exact color of her blush. He'd find roses that same color and deliver them to her house tomorrow.

Of course, he'd not add a note.

But she'd know.

And that was enough.

"I quite like you too, Miss Lamont," he whispered softly, hesitantly, as if saying the words out loud would damage the truth, the fragility of the emotion.

"I am very... thankful to hear that, Lord Graham," Bethanny replied then glanced up to meet his gaze. Her brown eyes were smoldering with a passionate acceptance of his words.

There was a *but* on the tip of his tongue, yet he held it, restrained the intense desire to preserve his emotional pride. Because if there was one thing that Bethanny Lamont had taught him, it was that learning to love meant eliminating pride of any sort.

It was a bloody difficult lesson.

Yet as he glanced to the road and then back to her unflinching gaze, he realized he knew the cost was minimal compared to the reward.

"There's a question in your eyes, Lord Graham. Rather, a obstruction. You wish to tell me that what you feel isn't license to act upon it," Bethanny replied, her brow pinching slightly as a bit of the light faded from her eyes, like the sun slipping behind a cloud, still present, yet dimmed.

"I…" He took a deep breath and exhaled, focusing on the road ahead.

"Tell me about yourself as a boy," Bethanny questioned suddenly.

"Pardon?" Graham asked, turning to face her again.

"Your boyhood. You see, Lord Graham, I'm quite aware of your adult life, credit being applied to your sister. However, your childhood I know little about. I suppose I never asked that of Lady Southridge, and I find I'm curious," Bethanny asked, a kind smile fixed on her face.

"Oh, I suppose it was average."

"I sincerely doubt that." Bethanny shook her head and smoothed her skirt.

"Why? Is it so difficult to imagine my average tutor? My average growth? My average adventures…" he trailed off, grinning.

"Yes. It is. Rather, I see you as exceedingly mischievous, haltingly rebellious, and far too charming."

"And you said you didn't know about my childhood," he scolded good-naturedly.

"I don't. However, I assume the man before me had to have grown from a similar boy." She grinned.

"Oh? So I'm a — what did you say — exceedingly mischievous, haltingly rebellious, and far-too-charming gentleman?"

"Precisely." She laughed, the sound like chimes.

"Very well." He chuckled. "Now tell me about your childhood."

"It was..." She paused, glancing ahead.

The pause lingered till Graham felt a furrow in his brow

"Lovely," she whispered.

"Forgive me, but your reaction doesn't match your description," Graham said quietly.

"Lord Graham, we are opposites in some ways, and some ways we are alike. We are alike in the aspect that we have both lost our parents." She glanced back, a small smile in place. "I say my childhood was lovely because it indeed was. I had love, security, warm embraces, and hot chocolate by the fireplace where my sisters and I all gathered around our mother, who would read to us. Yet my heart grieves that those lovely times shall never be had again. It is possible to feel joy and pain. The important part is to let the joy in through the pain, and to never lose hope." She reached out and placed her gloved hand on his as it held the leather straps, then she removed it.

"Well said, Miss Lamont."

Bethanny studied the man that she had secretly loved for so many years. Exhaling a soft breath, she glanced away and watched the scenery of Hyde Park pass her by. A comfortable silence hung in the air as the soft clipping of the matched bays carried them onward.

"I wish I knew them better," Graham spoke softly.

"Your parents?" Bethanny asked as she turned toward him once more. His golden hair was glistening in the rare sunshine, yet his topaz eyes were troubled, lonely.

"Yes." He nodded once then turned to directing the team. "I was quite young, so I don't remember much. What I do remember is hard to distinguish between my own memories and the stories I've been told by my sister."

"I see. It is a blessing to have your sister, though, for her to remember so much and share that gift with you."

"My sister does have a gift for speaking endlessly on subjects. I'm quite thankful one of those subjects was my parents." Graham chuckled, the mischievous light returning to his eyes.

Bethanny laughed. "How fortunate."

"If we were talking about any other subject, I'd be disinclined to agree with you, but since we are referring to my parents, I must agree."

"Sounds painful."

"Indeed it is." Graham winked.

Bethanny shook her head.

"Tell me about Neville," Graham asked abruptly.

"Pardon?" Bethanny felt her brow furrow at the quick change in conversation.

"Neville." Graham spoke the word like it tasted foul. "You said he championed you, or something of the sort. You also promised to tell me what happened." He speared her with an impatient gaze.

"Do you normally charm your female companions with such sparkling conversation?" Bethanny crossed her arms, her ire raised by his suddenly surly demeanor.

"No. I'm not nearly so emotional around other women."

"You mean moody."

"I mean emotional. Women are moody. Not men."

"Says the moody man."

"I'm brooding," he replied.

"Brooding?" Bethanny asked, her eyebrows shot up in surprise. No. Neville was dark and brooding. Graham was flirtation and charm all rolled into a shockingly handsome gentleman with secrets behind every gaze.

Bethanny felt overly warm simply thinking about it.

"You, Lord Graham, are not brooding. Or dark, or... whatever other adjective you were conjuring up to futilely name yourself."

"Conjure?" He grinned and shook his head. "You are overly efficient at changing the subject, Miss Lamont."

"You are overly efficient at distracting me, Lord Graham."

"It's the smile." He winked and grinned, showing off every dimple.

Bethanny sighed then scolded herself for being so easily melted. Squaring her shoulders, she met his gaze. "It's certainly *not* the personality."

"You wound me!" He grasped his heart and gasped.

Bethanny rolled her eyes. "Neville neatly dispatched Lord Somter There may or may not have been tea involved... on offending gentleman's clothes. It was quite an entertaining few moments, I must say."

"Somter? That windbag?" His golden eyebrows arched in surprise.

"Yes."

"Oh."

"Oh?"

"Well... yes. I rather thought it was some sort of heroic act. Not the outwitting of a fool." Graham snorted dismissively.

"Pardon me, but what he did *was* heroic! The way Somter was carrying on, I'd likely still be there listening to his prattling on and on about some forsaken horse, flesh or... maybe it was his garden? I'm not sure. I lost interest." Bethanny waved dismissively as Lord Graham chuckled. "However, the point is, he noticed my plight. And acted." Bethanny nodded firmly and waited.

"I'm exceedingly grateful that your threshold for heroic acts is so incredibly low. It bodes well for all your swains."

"True heroism is kindness, Lord Graham," Bethanny

KRISTIN VAYDEN

spoke directly. "Noticing someone else and putting their comfort, their needs, before your own... It's an act of selflessness, the first trait a woman should look for in any gentleman. Love could never grow where there is no kindness."

Graham watched his team intently, but Bethanny could see by the slight squinting of his eyes that he was considering her words carefully.

"Wisdom and beauty." He turned toward her, a soft glowing in his gaze. "Rare traits indeed. I have been properly chastened, Miss Lamont." He bowed his head and glanced back to her. "As much as I resent that Lord Neville was your hero of the moment, I'm indebted to his actions as they were surely a blessing to you."

Bethanny smiled. "Thank you, Lord Graham. I'll be sure to pass along your sentiments—"

"Minx."

Bethanny laughed loudly, covering her mouth to muffle the sound.

Graham shot her a sideways glance, his eyes full of mischief. "Never muffle such a glorious sound, Miss Lamont. A laugh such as yours should echo through the park."

"Flattery." Bethanny teasingly tapped his shoulder.

"No, Miss Lamont. Honesty."

"Ah, that I can accept, then. I thank you for the compliment."

"You are quite welcome. Now, I must confess to the sins in my blackened heart because I have been silently searching for a small shred of privacy in this blasted park, and I have found none." He exhaled in an exasperated manner.

"Privacy? What sort of secrets were you planning on disclosing?" Bethanny asked, suspecting his intentions but wanting confirmation, praying for it.

"My secret was that I was searching at all, Miss Lamont. Because we both know what would happen if I had found it."

104

He turned his gaze to her. It smoldered with restrained desire, with promised affection.

"It is a pity, then. And I'll lament the loss. For surely..." Bethanny leaned forward just enough to inhale the spicy scent coming from his fine coat, "I would have loved nothing more."

Graham's eyes widened slightly and then shifted to frantically glance about the park. "There." He urged his horses at a faster gait as they rounded a corner. A grove of trees stood close together, yet far enough apart for a curricle to enter into the grove. He slowed the horses and maneuvered them into the trees.

Bethanny's heart hammered with anticipation and fear.

Fear because the last time he'd kissed her, it had been followed by astounding rejection. Of course, he hadn't been aware of her identity then.

Now he was.

And he wanted to kiss her anyway.

The idea made the moment even sweeter.

"Miss Lamont." Graham toyed with the leather reins, his brow furrowed and uncertain.

Bethanny's heartbeat stuttered.

"I find I'm now questioning my impulsive nature—"

Not letting another moment pass, Bethanny gently reached up and ran her finger down his jawline and softly encouraged him to turn his head. His eyes were tortured, uncertain. She only hoped it was because he was trying to be more honorable than he ought... not because he didn't want her.

Yet he had said he liked her earlier; in fact, implied far more than that. So without any more hesitation, she slowly leaned forward, gaging his reaction. His expression changed from uncertainty to a smoldering passionate gaze that warmed her from her toes to the tip of her head.

Slowly, he leaned forward. Bethanny closed her eyes and memorized the soft press of his lips to hers. The kiss was so light, so soft that it was over almost before it began. Bethanny waited, eyes closed and her heart hammering with anticipation and hope.

He kissed her again, just as light as before. His lips molded to hers, lightly nipping and teasing, but he backed away before she could fully give herself to the sensation.

"I'll not break, my lord," she whispered, a smile teasing her lips as she opened her eyes.

"Are you so sure?" Graham asked just before he teased her lips once more, this time slightly more demanding.

"Hmm. Indeed. Why don't you find out for yourself?" Bethanny whispered boldly, her heart hammering with her wanton request.

Graham chuckled. "Says the lamb to the lion."

He leaned down and nudged her jaw with his nose till she tilted her head slightly, offering him unhindered access to her neck. "What a foolish lamb."

"Sometimes risk is worth the reward," she replied breathlessly. His tongue swirled against her flesh, creating a heat that welled within her.

"Indeed it is," Graham agreed and all but attacked her lips. His kiss was immediately demanding. Gone was the gentle coaxing, the teasing nipping. He reached out and held her tightly. "This will not do." Graham growled.

For a moment Bethanny's heart stopped.

Was he referring to kissing her? Had he changed his mind?

But before her mind could wander far, he stood and pulled her up as well. A moment later, he leaped from the curricle. After adjusting his jacket, he turned and wrapped his hands around her hips, lowering her to the soft grass. Immediately, he pressed her against the curricle, his hands grasping her back and then tracing down to her hips. His kiss was hot as he teased her lips open with his tongue and then groaned when she met his passion with her own as she pressed into the kiss, mimicking every movement he made. He tasted of mint; his kiss was both playful and passionate, a perfect combination that sent her heart racing.

The passionate spell around Bethanny was shattered when Graham broke the seal of their lips and then covered her mouth with his hand as she began to speak. Then she heard it.

Laughter.

Graham shook his head and removed his hand slowly after she nodded in understanding.

The laughter continued, and Graham began to glance about the grove of trees, then paused. Without a word, held out his hand for her to grasp as she alighted into the curricle. He hopped up and gazed at her, his expression one of annoyance at the interruption of their burning desire.

She understood the sentiment.

With a sigh, he coaxed the horses to leave the grove. Bethanny glanced back to their private haven as they left, wishing they could have stayed longer.

Wishing she could stay forever in his warm embrace.

"I thought it wise to not tempt fate, Miss Lamont," Lord Graham murmured. "Though I sorely wished to do so." He turned and offered her a small smile, his eyes still smoldering with passion.

"I understand," Bethanny replied as she smoothed her skirt.

"Though I think I might have been mistaken in one thing," he commented lightly.

"Oh?" Bethanny turned to look at him.

He nodded, and a slightly worried expression crossed his handsome features. "You, Miss Lamont, are the lion. And I am nothing more than a foolish lamb," he replied. He smiled then, but the gesture didn't reach his eyes.

Bethanny didn't know what to say. After all, how does one lay to rest all the worries upon men's shoulders?

Especially when they have the makings of potentially

ruining a lifelong friendship.

Though she didn't *think* the duke would object so severely to Graham, if he were to officially pursue her, she wasn't sure.

And if *she* wasn't sure...

Then Graham was not either.

"Perhaps we are both lambs," Bethanny whispered.

"Indeed, Miss Lamont. Indeed."

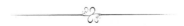

Graham waited silently as he surveyed the Symores' rout. It was a smaller affair than Bethanny's debut; however, it was still well-attended. After the amazingly confusing interlude in the park with Bethanny, he had avoided the duke's residence like the bloody plague. He had already failed in keeping his distance; he couldn't afford any further slip-ups. Not till he was sure.

Not till he was certain he wouldn't break her heart... or the duke wouldn't break his neck. But, in avoiding the residence, his insatiable craving for even a small glimpse of Bethanny had multiplied one-hundred fold. Like a man starved, he scanned the sea of people, knowing that once he found her, he'd be powerless to stop approaching her, dancing with her, stealing away with her to taste her kiss once more.

Already Graham had spotted Lord Neville, who he detested on the principle that Bethanny had a diverting tale of which he was the unlikely hero. Reluctantly, he admitted to himself that he was fully anticipating that her disclosure of earlier would involve him, but to discover it was Neville? His blood boiled hot with jealousy in simply thinking of it.

Damn the man for adding to the thick pea soup of emotions brewing within him. For that very purpose, Graham had been keeping an eye on the reclusive lord, evaluating his competition.

Competition, as if Graham was in the running in the first place.

He was a man divided. Half of him was insistent on the honorable behavior of a gentleman that necessitated his loyalty to the duke. Which, in turn, meant that he was unable to pursue Bethanny.

The other half of him said *to hell with it* and *take her anyway*.

He was quite in agreement with the second half. But couldn't get his bloody conscience to agree.

As if his thoughts conjured her, the object of his desire appeared. She was clothed in a light blue velvet gown that displayed just a hint of her luscious curves. Her creamy white skin was luminescent, angelic almost in its beauty. Her thick mane was intricately styled in a manner than drove Graham wild with the distinct desire to unwind it and unwrap the present beneath.

Her gaze searched the room, as if simply observing, then she paused and tilted her head slightly, like a bird. A breath later, her gaze found his and locked, a smile flirting on her alluring visage.

Graham nodded, forcing himself to grin in response, though there was nothing amusing about her beauty, her allure. Rather it was acute torture.

Bethanny's attention was then captured by Carlotta, who touched her lightly on her shoulder.

The very shoulder that would haunt Graham's feverish dreams that night.

She turned.

Graham followed her gaze then swore.

Neville.

Narrowing his eyes, he swore again for good measure. He was unable to see Bethanny's expression, but judging from the grin on Neville's face, she wasn't exactly telling him to jump in the Thames.

Pity.

It was a capital idea.

Bethanny was nodding and her shoulders — bloody hell, he loved her shoulders — shook slightly as if she were laughing.

Devil take the man for making her laugh!

Unable to stand aside while Neville charmed his way into Bethanny's good graces, Graham strode forward, silencing his conscience and gagging it.

Lord Neville stepped back and took his leave as Graham stepped forward, bowing crisply.

"Lord Graham." Bethanny's eyes danced with delight. How he loved that he was the cause!

"Miss Lamont, beautiful as ever." He placed a very proper air kiss to her wrist, but not before he winked scandalously, just to remind her of their earlier flirtation.

She blushed, and he felt exceedingly pleased.

"Always the flatterer." Bethanny sighed, teasingly.

"I'm an honest man, Miss Lamont. Don't impugn my integrity by implying my compliment was not utterly sincere."

"Very well." She chuckled softly.

"May I have the supper waltz?" Graham asked, praying that Neville hadn't asked for that particular honor.

"Of course."

Graham exhaled the breath he hadn't realized he was holding. "Delightful."

He seized the ripe opportunity to linger in gazing at her, offering his most winning smile, one that had caused many a woman to fall under his spell.

Judging by the color rising in Bethanny's cheeks, she was no exception.

"There's no need to use your excessive charm on me, my lord," Bethanny demurred.

"Oh?" Graham asked, a wicked grin teasing his lips.

"No. You see, I'm already quite aware of your dimpling

grin that drives us ladies mad. In fact, I remember it from quite a long time ago. Its... potency hasn't faded with time," she confessed, her rosy color heightening.

"I shall have to remember that. However, if I must not use my charm, what device is left to me?"

"Device?"

"Indeed. What allurement shall I use?"

"Ah, Lord Graham, I thought you far keener of mind than to ask such a simple question."

"Simple? You think my inquiry a simple one?" He pretended to be affronted.

"Indeed. For if my memory serves correctly, which it almost always does," she said with a sly wink, "then you have already the answer. Of course, when you employed it first, you were not aware of my identity," she added, somewhat reluctantly.

Good Lord, was she asking for another kiss?

Her confident gaze faltered slightly then lingered on his lips

The possibilities... The temptations were overwhelming, slamming into him with a force that caused him to catch his breath. Quickly he glanced about, further silencing his nagging conscience and searching for a private balcony or alcove where he might taste the delights of her mouth once more.

Of course, that was when the first strains of the quadrille began.

As if restraining a smile, she bit her lip then glanced away, taking the heat of her gaze and its implications with it.

"If you'll excuse me, I do believe I... ah, Lord Neville!" Bethanny beamed a welcoming grin.

And all the pulsing of desire that flooded his veins switched to the fury of jealousy.

With effort, Graham suppressed a growl.

Substantial effort.

"The breathtaking Miss Lamont," Neville murmured, bowing crisply and holding her gaze.

Unable to suppress his immature reaction, Graham cleared his throat.

"Ah, Graham, pleasure to see you this evening. I must say, Miss Lamont must find your presence quite comforting."

"Comforting?" Graham questioned, his eyes narrowing slightly.

Neville had the audacity to shrug. "Indeed! It's well known you are chums with His Grace. To know you are looking out for Miss Lamont's best interest would most assuredly qualify as comforting, I would assume." His expression was far too innocent.

Graham felt mocked.

And old.

Bethanny turned to him, offering a smile.

And Lord Neville arched a brow, grinning wickedly.

He *was* being mocked!

"Perhaps, I must say that I'm very thankful for the relationship I have with Miss Lamont's family. It provides the most diverting opportunities," Graham replied coolly.

"Indeed." Lord Neville's lips quirked in a sly and knowing grin.

"Indeed," Graham clipped.

"Er, Lord Neville, I believe this is our dance?" Bethanny offered as her gaze darted between himself and Lord Neville. Her tone was confused, yet amused as well.

"Of course, I shall enjoy it above all things." He grinned devilishly and led her away toward the growing crowd.

Graham kept his eyes trained on her form as he walked around the perimeter of the dance floor. As the music began, Bethanny's gaze darted to his, meeting for only a fraction of a moment. The quadrille began, and his eyes savored her imperfect grace, the slight tilt of her head as she took pleasure in the flow of the music. Lord Neville was an attentive partner, and again the fire of jealousy burned within him.

"Just what are you staring at?"

Graham startled and then turned a withering glare at his sister.

"I'm... keeping an eye on Neville," Graham answered then cleared his throat.

"Neville? Why in heaven's name are you watching—?" She waved her hand dismissively as she turned and scanned the dancers, but paused.

As fate — cruel beast that it was — would have it, she glanced at the dancers just as Neville and Bethanny were dancing in a circle, his hands holding hers as they promenaded, his expression full of interest and a dash of desire.

"Oh," she stated flatly then, "Oh!" Her eyes widened as she glanced to Graham then back to Bethanny.

"No. It's not, I assure you..."

"Complete sentences, Graham."

"No! You must cease your thinking."

"I assure you that your request is entirely impossible."

"No."

"Yes, and what's so wrong with it? She's a lovely girl!"

"That's just it! She's a girl!"

"As opposed to...?" She let the question linger, pregnant with implications, her eyebrow arching in question and devilish delight as she awaited his answer.

"Ah! This, *this* is why I leave for Scotland, why I travel!"

"Because of a girl? Wait—"

"No." Graham spoke with too much volume and glanced about, waiting till the few curious stares he'd attracted were cast elsewhere. "No," he continued, much softer but through gritted teeth. "I travel to get away from you, from your assumptions, your meddling nature, and the extreme irritation with which it vexes me! And the fact that Bethanny is a female is entirely different than the fact that she's a girl, as in very young. Besides, have you even thought to consider what Clairmont would do if he thought I was casting eyes at his ward? The man's in knots as it is, asking *me* of all people to help keep an eye on her!" Graham finished, congratulating himself on not only perfect complete sentences, but finishing the entire explanation without raising his voice... or unclenching his teeth.

He slowly relaxed his aching jaw.

"Ah, I see."

With that, she simply blinked, watching him.

As if his long explanation was nothing more than a comment on the weather.

Bloody hell. His sister was going to be the cause of his early demise. He was sure of it.

Death by vexation.

He waited, and because he was never able to claim an exceeding amount of patience, he reverted to his juvenile nature. "What?"

"Hmm?" She shrugged, a decidedly feminine action that bespoke a calm disinterest.

If she didn't kill him by vexation, *he* might kill *her* for that same reason.

"I find it remarkably difficult to comprehend that you have so little to add to the conversation."

"Graham, I find that sometimes it is far more telling to watch rather than speak." She leaned forward slightly and waved her fan, hitting him with a stale breeze. "In case you didn't gather my meaning, *now* is one of those times."

"Hmm," he replied, knowing that anything he said would be held against him as evidence of whatever she was trying to prove.

"Yes. You protest too much."

"Because you are insisting on—"

"You having remarkably superior taste in women than you have had in the past," Lady Southridge finished, a sweet smile softening her features.

"I—"

"Graham, I might be quite a bit older than you, but those years have given me something you cannot claim."

"And what is that? An uncanny ability to vex me?"

"No, experience. And," she paused and tilted her head slightly, "just to make sure I'm clear, I cannot think of a better man for Bethanny than you." She nodded then leaned back.

"Pardon?"

"You heard me."

"Clairmont is insistent that she keep away from—"

"Rakes and jaded libertines, fortune hunters and scoundrels of every sort?"

"Yes!"

"And you, dear brother, do not fall into those categories."

"Oh? When did I acquire such a pristine reputation? I was quite under the impression that I was still considered a rake by most standards."

"Oh, you're not perfect. If anyone knows that, it is I." She fluttered her fingers dismissively.

"And... you are very adequately contradicting yourself, dear sister."

"No, you might be a rake, but you're not jaded. You're not a scoundrel or even a rogue. You're a... *charmer*."

"Charmer... I don't know if that's a compliment or an insult." Graham shook his head; this conversation was going beyond the pale of absurd.

"Indeed. Your dimples make the ladies swoon, and I *will* say you are an opportunist."

"Rake. The word you're looking for is *rake*."

"No, rakes take and never give. You, Graham, when you find the right woman, will give everything. Which is also why you're so scared."

"I'm not scared."

"You're also a terrible liar, but that's beside the point.

You're scared because what if your affections aren't returned with the same fervor as given? What if you're not acceptable—"

"I'm not."

"Have you even considered the possibility that you might be?"

"No, because I'm not, I'm not going to give myself bloo — er, wretched hope when I know there is none. I'll not delude myself."

"Then that, my dear brother, is your loss. Your deep and immense loss." Lady Southridge's expression turned to pity, causing Graham's stomach to clench.

Pity. How he hated it.

Especially from his sister.

Without another word, she walked away shaking her head slightly.

Graham released a silent sigh of exasperation and frustration. Lady Southridge was his sister and, as such, was required to have allegiance to him, to think of him better than anyone else. He was family, after all, and blood ran deep. But Graham didn't want to give himself the permission to hope.

Yet that's exactly what he found himself doing.

Hoping.

Because what if she was right.

Wasn't it worth finding out?

CHAPTER EIGHT

BETHANNY WAITED ANXIOUSLY for the supper waltz. She had danced each set, each with a calf-eyed suitor who complimented on her dress, eyes and the grace with which she danced.

One even compared her to a swan.

She was quite certain she could tread the boards and be an actress for all the composure and acting she'd done to accept *that* compliment with social grace.

It would have been easier if she hadn't just stepped on his toe.

Twice.

Yet still the gentleman insisted on her grace.

It was dreadfully amusing and far less true.

The first strains of the supper waltz began, and Bethanny's gaze darted about, searching for Graham. This was the dance she was waiting for, and as she glanced about the room and didn't see his face, her heart grew heavy with disappointment.

"I believe I am the fortunate recipient of this dance." Graham's honeyed tones breathed softly into her ear from directly behind her.

Barely resisting the temptation to lean into his strong frame, she simply closed her eyes and focused on the nearness of him. As she did, she could feel the slight heat from his body permeating her back, her neck tickling with the softest breeze from his words and the slight smile to his tone.

"And to think I had begun to anticipate the need to search for a different partner," she murmured softly as she turned.

"Never." Graham swore softly. His gaze was deeper, richly filled with something she couldn't quite name. It was captivating, intoxicating, and welcomed her into its secret depths.

"I'll keep that in mind," she whispered.

He held out his hand, and she placed her gloved fingers within reach. With a caressing touch, he closed his fingers over hers, his gaze never leaving her face as it caressed her features.

"Shall we?" he asked, one of his dimples coming into view from the small quirk of his lips.

"Indeed."

Graham led her to the ballroom floor, and with the practiced ease of a thousand waltzes, he led them into the swirling mix of dancers. But it was different than the last time he had waltzed with her. His hand at her waist was firmer in his touch, as if holding her with purpose, without the intention of ever letting go. His arm, outstretched along hers, was perfectly respectable, except his fingers were grasping hers tightly, not painfully so, simply... possessive. And then, he squeezed slightly, running a finger in a soft swirl against the back of her hand.

It was delicious.

And distracting.

She stumbled, earning a grin from her partner.

"Your fault," Bethanny challenged.

"Indeed. Shall I try it again?" he whispered, his eyes

taking on a devilish light.

Leaning forward slightly, Bethanny answered, "Yes."

"You'd think I'd be accustomed to your forward nature," Graham remarked with a grin.

"I'd think you'd expect it, given my relationship with your sister," she shot back cheekily.

"Ah, but dear Miss Lamont, that would imply that I thought you in the same context as my sister. And that, I can assure you, is not the case," he whispered meaningfully.

"That is exceedingly good news, my lord."

"Is it?"

"Yes, though I did surmise that information," she replied.

"Oh? Did you now?" he asked with an entertained grin.

"Indeed." She leaned in slightly, as if imparting a great secret. "I don't imagine you kiss your sister like you kissed me."

Graham leaned back, his gaze shocked.

And then he misstepped.

"Now, we're even, my lord."

"Remind me never to enter into a wager with you." He shook his head, though a delighted grin showed off both glorious dimples.

Bethanny barely resisted the urge to sigh. "Ladies do not wager."

"Ah, but didn't you say you were quite close with my sister?" he shot back.

"Yes, but a lady simply guesses, and if she happens to be right, well..." Bethanny shrugged.

"Ah, but that is where you and my beloved sister differ, Miss Lamont."

"Oh?"

"Yes. You see, you said that if a lady *happens* to be correct, whereas my sister would simply assume she was correct in the first place."

"Ah, I believe you're correct. It seems I have much to

learn," she teased.

"Heavens, no. I beg of you." He shot a heavenward glance of desperation then grinned.

The waltz ended, leaving Bethanny with a pang of disappointment. Graham would now take her to Carlotta, bow, and then take his leave. If she were lucky, he'd ask for another dance, but to do so would certainly cause talk.

If only.

Graham released her waist and guided her along the marbled floor, just as she'd anticipated, in the direction of Carlotta. Desperate to keep him for just a few precious moments longer, she glanced about, searching for a reason — valid or not — to keep him close.

But then he turned slightly, leading her toward the balcony.

Her heart soared then beat double-time as she tried to anticipate his reasons. Did he *want* to kiss her again? *Would* he kiss her again? Was there any possible way to — aside from brazenly kissing him herself, but her bravery had its limits — get him to consider that option?

"I thought you might enjoy some air."

"Yes, thank you. It's quite a lovely evening, is it not?" Bethanny asked, her tone light in contrast with her rapidly beating heart.

"I have yet to see anything lovelier," Graham spoke softly, and she turned, seeing his gaze focused on her.

Against her better judgment, a bubble of laughter broke through her tense state. "Forgive me." She covered her mouth with her gloved hand, her eyes still smiling with amusement.

"I will do no such thing," Graham rallied, his gaze stern yet slightly taken aback.

"My lord, forgive me, I beg of you. It was poor manners on my part."

"Indeed. However, I must know *why* you chose to laugh at my sincere compliment," he challenged, his gaze turning warm with amusement.

"Ah, shouldn't a lady have her secrets?"

"No. A *lady* wouldn't have laughed."

"Are you implying then that I'm no lady?" she shot back in challenge, her lips bending in a teasing grin.

"Yes. Indeed."

"Well, a *gentleman* wouldn't dare imply such a thing."

"I am no gentleman, it appears. And now that we have successfully ascertained that neither you nor I have any manners or breeding," he challenged then took a step closer, "I demand you tell me why you were laughing at my expense."

"Demand?" Bethanny replied archly.

"Request," Graham amended with a mocking bow.

"Ah, much better." Bethanny spoke through a small laugh. "If you must know, my lord—"

"Edward."

"Excuse me?" Bethanny stilled, her eyes wide with wonder, and her mind racing with the implications of such an informal address.

"Edward, my name. Since we've already dispatched the idea that I'm a gentleman, I insist that you call me by my Christian name."

"Ah." Bethanny swallowed. After taking a fortifying breath, she felt an adventurous grin take over her previous astonishment. "Then, to be fair, you must address me as Bethanny." She hitched a shoulder.

"To be fair." Graham tilted his head.

"Yes."

"Right then, Bethanny. Do your sisters call you Beth?"

"No, actually." She felt her brow furrow at the tangent their conversation had taken.

"Ah, good. You don't look like a Beth. Bethanny suits you perfectly."

"I'm pleased to know that my parents' decision in regard to my name meets your standard, *Edward*," she replied, though her heart skipped a beat as she said his name aloud.

"Now, then, Bethanny, you were saying?" Graham asked, taking a slow step forward, his gaze locking with hers so that her mouth went dry, yet her lips trembled with the desire to taste his once more.

Without apology, he tugged her into a darker shadow in a slight alcove on the balcony, away from gossiping eyes. The view was open and vibrant with the last remaining hues of sunset. He stepped away, giving her room to breathe and think.

"I was saying?" she replied breathlessly.

"Yes, the original conversation, on why you found my compliment entertaining. You see, Bethanny, a gentleman takes such an action from a lady to heart. It's impugning to his integrity."

At once she remembered the gentleman who'd compared her to a swan.

And laughed again.

She truly should learn to control her emotions better. But being with Graham, calling him Edward, and teasing him so openly was crumbling every proper behavior in her well-educated social wall.

Graham shook his head in a scolding fashion; his gaze continued to scorch her.

All amusement vanished as she lost herself in his amber gaze.

"Because it... you see, my lord," she took a calming breath then continued, "compliments are wonderful when spoken from the heart, not simply recited pieces of trite prose meant to provoke a response in a lady." Bethanny released a nervous breath, her eyes searching his.

"Oh." His expression was indifferent, yet the lines around his eyes appeared deeper.

The silence continued, so she filled it with nervous chatter. "It was earlier that a gentleman compared my dancing to the grace of a swan in flight. Anyone can see that I'm not particularly graceful. Such a compliment was an insult to my own intelligence and awareness of my personal attributes. I'm not so vain to think myself as perfect or without fault. And I'll admit that your compliment, while I hope, was utterly sincere, sounds like a line from a Gothic novel." She bit her lip and turned to the panoramic line of the London horizon etched in the bright purple and orange hues of sunset.

"I... see."

"It was never my intention to offend you, my lord," Bethanny quickly apologized. She glanced down but didn't turn to face him.

"So, we're back to *my lord*?" Graham's voice sounded closer, deeper, and she turned, her eyes widening as she saw he had taken two silent steps and brought them practically touching. The fabric of her gown was brushing against the dark coal color of his evening jacket, creating a whisper of sound, a flash of heat crept into her very soul.

"I'm beginning to think you have a secret obsession with lurid novels, Bethanny," Graham teased, his eyes dark and full of mysterious secrets.

"As I've said, I'm not overly concerned with them," Bethanny responded breathlessly.

"You seem to have an unusual knowledge for one so uninterested," he commented. The corner of his lip tipped up slightly.

"Beatrix."

"Pardon?" His eyebrows rose in inquiry.

"My sister, Beatrix. I don't have to read the novels to know about them. My sister explains them in detail over breakfast," she explained, her heart pounding.

"Ah. And, just to alleviate any confusion, I was sincere." He tilted his head slightly as his gaze roamed her features then fixated on her lips.

His gaze was like a caress, and her mouth trembled in

response.

"I'm afraid you'll have to explain further," she replied, her own gaze darting about his handsome face. Just a slight step forward, and she'd meet him lip to lip, but desire wasn't a substitute for courage, and though she had been bold in the past, she was still an innocent.

"My compliment," he clarified with a slight grin.

"Then I thank you."

"However, I'll be sure to be more original in the future," he amended softly as he leaned forward.

"In the future?" she asked with a traitorous hope in her voice.

"Oh yes, the future... Bethanny," he whispered. Just as his lips touched hers, he retreated. His warm breath tickled her newly moistened lips and caused them to burn with desire.

"I shouldn't be doing this," he murmured, the movement of his lips brushing against her own in the slightest manner, like a butterfly's wings.

"Yes, yes you should," Bethanny replied boldly, then leaned forward and pressed her lips fully to his.

He groaned as if tortured, but he didn't resist her, rather, pressed deeper into the kiss, sweeping her away in the bliss of his affection. Gently, he guided her backward, small footstep after small footstep. The slight movement barely registered to her as Graham continued to taste, tease, and tutor her mouth to return his kiss. She startled when her back gently met a balustrade to the side of the balcony. Leaning back from the kiss, she glanced up to Graham then around, trying to gather her whereabouts. Somehow he had guided her into the shadow of the corner of the balcony, shielded by a large potted palm. Her gaze sought his.

"I'm not an exhibitionist." Graham shrugged. The simple movement was boyish, shy.

"Not to mention possibly damaging to my reputation,"

Bethanny added dryly, a grin quirking her swollen lips.

"Perhaps."

She raised a questioning eyebrow.

"However, since we have such a lovely and secluded place, let's not waste it, shall we?" Graham added with a devilish grin, his eyes dark with heated intentions.

"Waste not, want not." Bethanny grinned and met him halfway as he kissed her gently.

But she wanted more. So much more. Without hesitation, she pressed into him, winding her arms around his shoulders and reveling in the steel-like musculature of his back, felt even through his evening wear. His coat was fine wool, soft, and she allowed her greedy fingers to roam his back before settling on shoulders.

His teeth tugged her lower lip, pulling her slightly forward in a playful manner, and she felt herself smile as she continued to return his kiss. Each sensation was so fresh and exhilarating she was sure he could taste her excitement and devotion through their heated exchange, but she didn't have the experience necessary to practice restraint. Rather, she gave herself over to the swirling emotion of first love, of first desire as she began to tease the soft and slightly curling hair at the base of his neck. Tugging slightly, she grinned as he groaned softly, his warm breath fanning against her lips before he took them back with a driving possessive kiss. Emboldened by his reaction, she plunged her hands further into his hair, twisting slightly, feeling a strange empowerment as she felt his kiss grow ever more demanding, more possessive, causing her own heart to beat faster with the heady sensations he created. His hands, which were bracing himself against the stone balustrade, now roamed her arms, gently squeezing. He slipped them behind her back and pulled her in tighter till breathing became gasping with delight. He traced the lines of her back as his hand dipped lower—

"Ah-hem."

Graham released her quickly, his chest rising and falling in quick succession as he spun and hid Bethanny behind his back, protecting her.

And her reputation.

Even with scandal a breath away, she smiled, feeling protected, and dare she think it? Loved?

"Neville." Graham nodded then cleared his throat.

"Lovely evening, is it not?" Neville spoke in a disinterested tone.

"Indeed," Graham answered, his voice tight.

"Since there was a break in the dancing, I thought to take in the air... I'm sure that there will be many more to follow me in such an idea," Neville spoke pointedly.

Bless the man, Bethanny thought charitably. Quite expertly, he had saved her and Graham from greater danger as, no doubt, others would indeed follow and come to gather some fresh air. Neville was going to be discreet. Few others would have. And as much as the idea of Graham being trapped into marriage had its appeal — and after that kiss, she was as good as compromised — she wanted him to *want* to marry her, not be obligated to do so.

"Thank you." Graham nodded, his tone far softer.

Neville didn't respond, but the sound of his retreating footsteps let her know he was leaving.

Graham sighed heavily then turned, his shoulders slightly hunched from their proud position earlier.

"That... was far too close for comfort," Graham said, then ran his fingers through his hair, settling it from her earlier attentions. "However, I do not think he saw who you were, since you were in the shadows. You must take care, Bethanny." Graham's golden eyes grew concerned.

"I'm sure Lord Neville will not say—"

"It's not that. While I believe that Neville is a gentleman, I cannot claim a close acquaintance with the man. What I'm trying to say is... simply use caution. If Neville is a scoundrel, and he ascertained your identity, he will likely think that you share your... charms... liberally."

"Pardon?" Bethanny was aghast.

"Bethanny." Graham spoke softly and reached down to grasp her hands. The heat from his touch warmed the fear that had begun to grow within her. "Innocents do not kiss... like this," he finished. "And while it pleases me to no end that you are so passionate, someone else might mistake your... fervor... and try to use it to their advantage."

"Oh. So if I kiss one gentleman, some would think that I'd kiss *any* gentleman?"

"Precisely."

"That's rot." She pulled he hands out from his and fisted her palms.

Graham chuckled. "I couldn't agree more. But sadly, it's the truth."

"Just because I kiss you doesn't mean—"

"You know that, and I... hope... that..." he teased.

Bethanny swatted at him.

"Ouch."

"Liar."

"I wanted you to feel confident about your pathetic attempt."

"You!"

"Now there, little kitten, pull back those claws. Your quarrel is not with me." He grasped her wrists and pulled her in close.

Bethanny narrowed her eyes.

"I'm intimidated," Graham mocked.

"You should be," Bethanny ground out, still piqued.

"Then I simply must disarm you." He chuckled and kissed her lightly on the lips. "You were saying?" he whispered a moment later.

"It's not fair," Bethanny murmured. "I've only ever kissed you. For someone—"

"A hypothetical someone, mind you."

"Regardless—"

"You need to kiss me more."

Bethanny paused. "On that we utterly agree." She grinned and rose up slightly on her slippered toes and kissed him.

"However..." Graham pulled back, "the truth is that we do not have time to continue... arguing."

"Is that what we're doing? Remind me to provoke you more often."

"I? You were the one provoked. I'm the pacifist in this arrangement." He nibbled her lower lip.

"We need to return."

"I know... but that doesn't mean that I like the idea."

"I utterly agree," Graham whispered.

"But perhaps... I can arrange for us to argue again soon?" Graham took a step back, releasing her and giving them a respectable distance, perchance someone should come upon them.

"I would love that above all things," Bethanny answered, her heart swelling with joy.

"Then, *Miss Lamont*, dear Bethanny, I bid you adieu until later." He bowed crisply.

"Until later, *Lord Graham*, dear Edward." She grinned.

His eyes danced as he turned and strode out from the balcony, passing four debutants as they made their way out into the fresh air. Four sets of eyes followed his departure. Then the girls turned and sighed contentedly, till they saw Bethanny.

"My, my..." One of the debs eyed her meaningfully.

Bethanny recognized her, Doris Hawkes, a girl in her third season, who loved gossip.

Delightful, Bethanny thought with annoyance.

"Fancy meeting you *two* out here... alone." Doris made her way, the three other debutants following behind, eyeing each other meaningfully.

"It's a beautiful evening." Bethanny shrugged. "And it *is* quite the crush within." She nodded toward the exit.

"Indeed." Doris raised an eyebrow.

Bethanny offered an innocent smile. "Enjoy the sunset," she spoke politely as she made her way past the girls and to the exit.

"Oh we will," Doris responded then added lowly, "Though I'd imagine you hardly noticed it."

Bethanny pretended not to hear and made her way into the ballroom.

After all, what she'd said wasn't far from the truth!

CHAPTER NINE

GRAHAM COULDN'T WIPE the smile from his face. After his clandestine interlude with Bethanny, he was soaring on hope's wings. Surely, if he explained his intentions, Clairmont would agree to his suit.

Graham was a decisive man. Once his mind was made up, it was very difficult to alter it; and his mind was made up that he wanted Bethanny. It was the strangest of irony, that he would be asking his best friend for permission to court and marry her. Even stranger that he sincerely was anxious on the duke's answer to that very question. For a moment, he questioned his quick decision, his immediate and passionate attachment to her. Was it too quick? Would it fade with time, leaving him lamenting the fact that he'd chosen so quickly?

No.

While he hadn't been in her company for long, now that she was grown, he *had* been around her quite a bit when she was younger. People did change, but it was clear that all of Bethanny's metamorphosis happened on the outside. Her heart, passion, and lack of grace that she exerted in life remained true; it was evident in her candor and honesty; it was evident in her very ability to dance. Bethanny would continually challenge him, excite him, and remain fiercely loyal.

Was this love? He wasn't sure, yet he knew if he continued on this path, it would either lead him to love or madness.

Likely both.

And what a delight to find a woman capable of creating such emotion. Such… a profound reaction in him. Graham knew he'd have secured a rare treasure if the duke allowed his suit.

Perhaps he should approach him now? Patience never been his strong point, so with a determined air, Graham's gaze searched the ballroom for the duke's face, but couldn't locate him through the crush.

"Blast," Graham murmured.

"You!"

Graham turned at the sound of his friend's voice.

"Clairmont? Clairmont! Just the man I've been searching for." Graham began to grin a welcome to his friend but halted, a chill rushing up his spine as he took in the cool anger simmering below his friend's gaze.

"What happened?" Immediately Graham was on alert, his gaze darting about.

Bethanny!

"I believe that is the question *I* am to ask *you!*" Clairmont bit through clenched teeth. "Blessed providence is on your side that we're in a crowded ballroom." He fumed.

"Pardon? What in heaven's name are you speaking of?"

"You… come with me. Now," Clairmont ground out, then spun on his heel, heading out the main ballroom and down the hall.

Foreboding clenched his chest. Devotion, loyalty, honor — all words that were useless without action. He owed Clairmont; after all, he was the closest thing to a brother he'd ever had. So with his mouth set in a grim line, he followed his friend out.

"Get in," Clairmont ordered as he gestured to the closed carriage bearing the duke's crest.

Nodding, his lips pressed together, Graham entered the carriage, heart pounding with uncertainty.

The carriage lurched forward as the driver pulled them out of the Symores' residence and onto Curzon Street toward Berkley Square. The silence was thick and heavy as Graham folded his hands and watched his friend.

The duke was silent, brooding, and his gaze was searing as it attempted to bore a hole directly through Graham.

"Are you going to speak with me, or are we to make eyes at each other for the remainder of the evening," Graham spoke impatiently.

Clairmont remained silent.

"I don't know whether to question your sanity or to be afraid. You've never been this quiet," Graham drolled.

"That's because I'm trying to convince myself that I shouldn't call you out."

"A duel? What in the bloody hell—"

"Bethanny," the duke bit out, his eyes burning with barely suppressed anger.

"Bethanny," Graham repeated. It was amazing how one word could carry so many implications, so many emotions... so much potential.

"Yes, my *exquisite* ward, who I was under the misapprehension that you were to protect."

"I—"

"Don't speak!" Clairmont shouted.

Graham closed his mouth and silently fumed as his mind spun. He knew that the duke wouldn't take lightly his emotional attachment to his ward, but this was going too far.

"You... I trusted you. And what do I discover? That this evening you had her pinned to a wall, tangling with her like a common courtesan."

"You will not speak of her in such way," Graham bit out, his teeth clenched.

Clairmont gestured angrily to Graham. "I was referring to *your* dishonor, not hers. This is your fault. Yours. Damn it, Graham, we know how to charm women! We understand just what to say, how to say it, and are experts at executing a simple touch or kiss to create desire. We get what we want, when we want it. And damn it all to hell if you're going to take that from Bethanny!"

"What makes you think I'm simply sporting with her? Do you think so little of me that I'd greedily take what is not mine without a thought? Is my loyalty so thin? So weak that I'd forget our years of friendship and betray you in such a way?"

"I—"

"No, now it is your time to listen." Graham tugged on his cravat till it came completely loose. He tossed the silken scarf to the side of the bench and blew out hot breaths of frustration.

"Did it ever occur to you that I might possibly care for her? That my behavior is not selfish? How little do you think of me? In our friendship, our association, when have I ever corrupted an innocent? When?" Graham demanded.

"Well—"

"I have not ever! Nor would I! If you have a fraction of understanding of the frustration I have experienced knowing that the woman I am falling in love with is *your* ward? Have you any idea the sleepless nights I've endured, knowing that the very woman I'm charged with protecting from men like me, men like *you*, is, in fact, the very one who has slipped beneath my skin and captured me so utterly that I'm becoming much like those blasted dandies that go all mooncalf over a woman! And I don't care! Hang it all!"

"Graham—"

"I'm not finished!" Graham pointed a finger at the duke. "Don't begin to tell me I'm not up to scratch. I'm bloody well aware of it. I don't need your confirmation." Graham exhaled, his shoulders heavy, just like his heart. Because that was the searing truth. He knew it well enough himself. He'd be damned if he had to hear it confirmed by his best friend.

"May I speak now?"

"If you absolutely must," Graham replied tiredly.

"And—"

"Who do you think you are, condemning me? And just who informed you of my whereabouts?" Graham interrupted, his irritation surfacing once more.

The duke stilled, his eyes widening before softening into a hurt expression. "I saw it myself," Clairmont answered quietly, too quietly.

Graham's heart stilled.

Somehow, it was different, knowing that his friend had witnessed with his own eyes the heated exchange between himself and Bethanny. It shamed him. Because the truth was, he knew better. While Bethanny was passionate in a way that men only dream of, she was still an innocent. And regardless of how much she'd wanted the kiss, Graham had, in fact, taken advantage of her passionate nature and explored it more than any man ought — any man save her husband.

Husband.

The word haunted him, taunted him with a vision that disappeared like vapor. Because the sad truth, the one he had tried to bury with fantasies of hope, was that he was not worthy of her. At once, the anger, the frustration dissipated into hot shame, into the blackest pit of hopelessness.

It was suffocating.

"Stop the carriage," Graham spoke softly.

"Graham, no... perhaps I was... too impatient with my accus—"

"Stop the bloody carriage, *Your Grace.*" Graham locked gazes with his friend, knowing that such a formal address would gain his attention.

"Graham."

"Your Grace... the carriage. Now," Graham repeated, his tone grating on his ears as he heard his own desperation.

The duke rapped on the roof twice, and the horses slowed their pace.

Without another word, Graham opened the door and rushed into the night, feeling it swallow him, covering him in the bleak truth.

It could not be borne.

He had no other option other than to leave, to rusticate in Edinburgh where the temptation of Bethanny Lamont could only haunt him, where the visions of her beauty would be imagined, not touched.

Good Lord, not touched.

His body ached with unrequited desire.

Yes, he had no other option. Tomorrow. He'd leave tomorrow. He had work to do in Edinburgh as well; he'd pour himself into his assignment, leave behind all... hope. Because that was what was killing him now, softly, slowly, like poison. Hope. Because he knew it was a lie.

There was no hope.

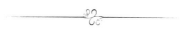

"And where have *you* been?" Lady Southridge's voice teased as Bethanny tried to subtly enter the crowded ballroom.

"Enjoying the evening," she replied offhandedly. However, she couldn't restrain her smile or the soft sigh that escaped her lips.

Good Lord, she'd never survive at a gambling table.

"Ah, you appear to have... thoroughly... enjoyed yourself," Lady Southridge remarked.

Bethanny spun to face her, eyes wide with worry. "What do you mean?"

"Ah, dear. I'm far too... mature... to be hoodwinked."

"Ah, mature…" Bethanny grinned.

"Yes, a nice way of saying old, dear. Though I'd not claim to less than four and forty years."

"You don't look a day over eight and thirty."

"Blessed child."

"Thank you," Bethanny demurred.

"However, you didn't succeed at changing the subject. Speaking of which, you haven't seen my wayward brother, have you?" Lady Southridge's eyes danced.

"Er, no, I don't see him."

"Ah, again, I'm not one to judge, but if you wish to keep your secrets, I suggest you get better at hiding them. Of course, you don't *see* him now… I asked if you had seen him… as in the past. Clever wording won't throw anyone off, dear." Lady Southridge patted Bethanny's shoulder lightly, shaking her head.

"I have not seen him recently," Bethanny amended.

"Which implies that you saw him at some time. Come, Bethanny. You can do better. Truly throw me off," Lady Southridge challenged, tapping Bethanny's shoulder playfully.

"Er… I haven't seen him?" Bethanny tried.

"Perfect. Vague," she tilted her head thoughtfully, "yet honest. Good girl. Now, I hear my brother is a delightful kisser. Are the rumors true, or were they grossly exaggerated?" She leaned forward, her grin wide and her gaze bright.

"Lady Southridge!" Bethanny scolded hoarsely as her gaze darted about the room, hoping no one else could have heard such a brazen question.

"Oh heavens, girl. You must trust me. I'd not ask such a question where it could be heard!" Lady Southridge rolled her eyes and shook her head.

Bethanny's gaze shot back to the people around them, noticing that they, indeed, were not paying the least bit attention.

"I…"

"Yes?"

"Yes."

"Yes…?" Lady Southridge leaned forward, waiting.

"Yes." Bethanny straightened, affixing a polite smile in place.

"You do realize you didn't actually answer my question." Lady Southridge cocked an eyebrow.

"Yes, I did."

"But — ah… clever girl. You're learning." Lady Southridge nodded her approval.

"I try." Bethanny shrugged offhandedly, a grin teasing her lips.

"Try harder. You're going to need it to get past that guardian of yours."

"The duke? Graham's his best friend —"

"Ah… see? You admitted everything I wanted to know with just a simple sentence." Lady Southridge clicked her tongue and shook her head.

Bethanny took a deep breath. "But I'm quite sure you already knew all of this information, so why the interrogation to begin with?" Bethanny asked impatiently, though with a grin.

"Because I'm preparing you."

"For?"

"Charles, the duke, Clairmont — whatever you wish to call him." She flipped her fingers dismissively.

"But Graham —"

"Graham is much like the duke *was* before Carlotta… and *that* is all your innocent ears need to hear on the subject."

"But —"

"No, you'll be fighting an uphill battle… your own Waterloo, if you must."

"How dramatic." Bethanny leaned back slightly and gave her best disbelieving expression.

"You doubt me? Have I ever been wrong?" Lady Southridge placed a dramatic hand to her chest.

"Yes."

"Aside from that one time."

"You told me that lemon would turn my hair blonder."

"It does."

"It was orange. Thankfully I was able to steal some of cook's coffee and stain it back. Heaven help me if I had used *all* the lemons you brought me!"

"That was one time—"

"And then with the powder—"

"It said on the bottle—"

"Must I continue?" Bethanny scarcely resisted the temptation to place her hand on her hip.

"I'm not wrong on this." Lady Southridge sighed theatrically.

"Very well, what do you suggest?"

Lady Southridge leaned in slightly, her eyes narrowing the smallest fraction. "Evasion."

"Pardon?"

"Evasion... don't answer any direct questions."

"You want me to *lie?*"

"No! Heavens, child. Not lie. Simply... don't offer any free information." Lady Southridge flipped open her fan and waved herself with it.

"How is that not lying?" Bethanny asked, disbelieving.

"It's exactly what we were practicing before. You can do it. And it might buy you some time."

"Time? Why do I need time?"

"Child, you're so innocent." Lady Southridge glanced about the room then pulled Bethanny around an alcove. "Graham... as much as you see the knight in shining armor... others simply see his past. Sadly, the duke is one of them. As his sister, I'm able to see past his unsavory history and see the potential, much like you, but I'd wager we see that *potential* quite differently." Lady Southridge winked. "Give the duke time. Give him a reason to trust your judgment, time to get accustomed to the idea of Graham not just being a friend." Lady Southridge nodded encouragingly.

"But as family." Goosebumps prickled along Bethanny's skin at the thought.

"A son-in-law, to be exact." A dangerous grin tipped Lady Southridge's lips.

"I see."

"Good girl. Now—"

"What about Carlotta?" Bethanny asked.

"Ah, if my instincts are correct…"

Bethanny glanced heavenward with an exasperated expression.

"Then Carlotta has… other things… on her mind."

"What things?"

"I'm sure you'll learn soon enough," Lady Southridge hedged, not answering, but her gaze alight with secret knowledge.

"Very well," Bethanny relented.

Lady Southridge opened her mouth slightly, as if to add one final word to their conversation, when she paused, her gaze sliding past Bethanny and lighting up with recognition. "Lady Symore! What a crush." Patting Bethanny's shoulder, she leaned in and whispered as she walked toward their hostess, "Remember our little conversation, ducky." She winked and caught up with the grinning Lady Symore.

Bethanny watched the older ladies titter and gossip as they locked arms and turned about the room. Without a thought, her gaze wandered, searching for Graham's form, his golden halo of slightly curly hair, his broad shoulders filling out his evening kit with masculine beauty. But he was nowhere to be seen. Was he in a gaming room? Had he left? The momentary disappointment fled as she remembered his promise.

He'd continue their... conversation... later.

And that thought alone would lend to the most delightful dreams for which a girl could wish.

CHAPTER TEN

"BETHANNY? BETHANNY!"

Slowly Lord Graham's voice changed pitch till it sounded identical to her sister Beatrix's.

"Bethanny, for pity sake, get up already!"

That was most assuredly *not* Lord Graham speaking.

"Ugh," Bethanny moaned, trying to roll over.

"I'll get the pitcher," Beatrix warned, her tone low and threatening.

"Why?" Bethanny whined, not caring that she sounded eleven, which, ironically, was the same age that Beatrix had learned about the effect of dumping a pitcher of cold water on her sister when she wasn't willing to rise from bed.

"Because you'll murder me if you find out from anyone else."

"Find out what?" Bethanny asked, her eyes unwilling to open. The soft comfort of her bed called to her with its inviting warmth. Her body relaxed, her mind drifted —

"You'll thank me later." Beatrix sighed.

A tepid deluge of water cascaded over Bethanny's hair, soaking her pillow and sheets.

"Ah! Ah! Beatrix! I'm going to—"

"He's gone, Bethanny."

Bethanny had just shot out of bed, her blurry vision searching for her sister's form so she could throttle her.

But her words halted her threatening advance.

"Who?" Bethanny asked, though she feared, dearly feared she knew the answer already.

No. No. No.

"He left for Edinburgh this morning," Beatrix whispered.

Bethanny stumbled backward and landed on her soggy bed. Rivulets of water dripped down her nose and cheeks from her wet hair, but she hardly noticed.

He left?

Why?

Hadn't he said, hadn't they made plans to see each other again soon?

So perhaps the plans weren't exactly set in stone, but *he had* said they would meet again soon.

It didn't make sense.

But that didn't stop the pain, the rejection, from piercing her heart with dread.

"I'm so sorry, Bethanny," Beatrix murmured.

Bethanny glanced up, through the wet strands of hair clinging to her face, and watched her sister place the miserably empty pitcher on the side table. Beatrix's expression was full of empathy, pain.

Beatrix had always been the most sympathizing of the sisters.

Also the most inventive — thus the pitcher of water.

"How did you find out?" Bethanny asked.

Beatrix walked toward her, reaching out she smoothed the hair out of Bethanny's face and sat beside her.

Then jumped up, patting her bum, casting an apologetic grin at her sister.

Serves you right, getting wet too. Try the whole pitcher over your head.

Beatrix kneeled in front of Bethanny, grasping her hands and holding them tightly. "I heard the duke and Carlotta talking over breakfast. They didn't know I was approaching, so I hid behind the wall and listened once I heard Lord Graham's name mentioned. Something about Lord Graham having business in Edinburgh. Carlotta questioned his sudden disappearance, and the duke didn't answer. I left soon after, knowing you'd want to be aware after..." Beatrix bit her lip.

"After?" Bethanny asked, her eyes trained on her sister's expression.

"After you two disappeared last night," Beatrix finished then proceeded to bite her lip.

"Oh no." Bethanny groaned and leaned back on the bed so that her legs still dangled off the side. "Where did you hear that?"

"Carlotta." But don't fret! I'm sure no one else noticed," Beatrix spoke then paused, "though I think Lady Southridge might suspect—"

"Oh, she is far past suspicion," Bethanny mumbled.

"Don't you find it odd that Carlotta hasn't questioned you?" Beatrix asked.

"Lady Southridge mentioned something of that. She implied that Carlotta has other things pulling at her attention... whatever that means."

"Hmm."

"Hmm?" Bethanny asked, propping herself up on her elbows.

"You don't suppose..." Beatrix stood and took a step around the bed.

"No. I don't," Bethanny replied, not caring. Not when everything in her wonderful world had simply gone topsy-turvy.

"You don't?" Beatrix asked, her expression curious.

"Hmm?" Bethanny glanced to her sister, quite lost in her

own misery.

"You're a lot of help."

"I'm the one still soaking wet and trying to mend my possibly broken heart," Bethanny shot back.

"You *know* it's the only way to get you awake quickly." Beatrix rolled her eyes.

"Regardless—"

"Regardless, you *are* grateful I told you. Now, when you hear the information from the duke, you can keep your wits about you." Beatrix nodded.

"I hadn't considered that perspective." Bethanny blinked.

"That's what sisters are for." Beatrix shrugged. "Goodness knows, the duke will have an apoplectic fit once he realizes that his *friend* is a candidate for son-in-law of sorts. Lord Graham does have a bit of a rakish past, you know." Beatrix spoke with brutal honesty.

"Yes, I'm quite aware. Though I've never been told the details. I'm not sure I *want* to know them either. I might be tempted to claw out some widow's eyes. Not exactly proper ballroom behavior, you know." Bethanny sighed.

"Wise." Beatrix nodded sagely.

"However... I must know why, in your opinion, the duke would be so against Graham's pursuit? Heaven knows, it's the only pursuit I'd even consider." Bethanny blew out an exasperated sigh and sat up.

"I think..." Beatrix narrowed her eyes, "that he is simply... afraid."

"Afraid? Of Graham?" Bethanny asked, confused.

"Afraid that Graham isn't up to scratch. As much as the duke blusters about us, he's quite fond of us girls. He won't simply marry us off to be rid of us."

"Goodness knows, Carlotta wouldn't let him entertain the thought," Bethanny added, a small smile lifting her lips.

Beatrix smiled back.

"Beatrix?" Bethanny felt her brow furrow. "What do *you*

think of Lord Graham?"

"Er, honestly? I don't know him well enough to form a positive or negative opinion. On one hand, anyone who is related to Lady Southridge must have a delightful sense of humor, patience, and deep family loyalty. I mean that in the best possibly way," Beatrix added quickly.

Bethanny chuckled.

"And he *is* close friends with the duke, and we know the duke well enough that he'd not surround himself with friends who had corrupt moral fiber."

"True." Bethanny nodded.

"I suppose my only fear… is that he simply wants you for your beauty. Because, make no mistake, as soon as I suspected something, I asked Lady Southridge, and she was quite adamant of how he looked at you. But attraction isn't love, Bethanny. You have so much more to offer than a pretty face." Beatrix hitched a shoulder.

Love for her sister overwhelmed Bethanny's heart.

And forgiveness for the pitcher incident.

"Thanks, Bea."

"It's just the truth." Beatrix patted the bed. Finding a dry spot, she sat.

"I'll not lie, I wished he'd find me beautiful, but when you consider just how many beautiful ladies there are amongst the *ton*, for him to single me out must at least *imply* that there is something more that he finds enticing about me, other than my beauty," Bethanny spoke softly.

"Forgive me for saying this, but I must ask. If I held my tongue and found out later that I should have said something—"

"Beatrix, just ask."

With a deep breath, Beatrix gazed directly at her sister, her eyes concerned. "But what… what if *because* you're the duke's ward, he sees you as an easy target?"

"I understand. But that would also compromise his

loyalty to his friend."

"Indeed, but have you considered that the duke perhaps wants to protect you from that very possibility? Think on it. Has Lord Clairmont ever sought to have you entertain any interest in his friend?"

"Er, no."

"Why? It's not as if Lord Graham is too old, not from a good family. If anything, the duke *would* be pushing you toward him," Beatrix completed softly.

"I never... that's an enlightening perspective," Bethanny allowed, "but I don't see its merit. My own instinct affirms Lord Graham's integrity."

"I hope you're correct." Beatrix nodded. "But perhaps..."

"Yes?"

"Simply keep your eyes open, Bethanny. Be wise."

Bethanny nodded. "I will."

Beatrix stood.

"Bea? One more question... I'm not sure I want to know the answer... but... if Lord Graham truly cared for me... why would he leave the country," *My, how dramatic,* "after being... singular with his affections to me?"

Beatrix took a deep breath, her brown eyes glancing to the floor then meeting her sister's. "I don't know... but it wasn't love, that much I know. Love fights, Bethanny. Love endures, suffers the fires of hades and beyond for the simple hope of completion. Love always thinks of the lover, rather than itself. And perhaps there *is* some selfless motivation behind Lord Graham's behavior. I simply can't fathom what it could be."

"Nor can I," Bethanny added, sharing a pained look with her sister.

Nor can I.

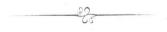

Graham rocked slightly with the swaying motion of his fine carriage as he made his way toward Scotland. Normally, the soft sea breeze and familiar landscape would be calling to him, beckoning him to the safe haven of his estate near Edinburgh.

This was anything but normal.

Rather with every turn of his carriage wheels, the acute sensation of leaving behind his beating heart grew stronger and more painful. Releasing a long sigh, he loosened his cravat and leaned against the plush upholstery. He *was* doing the right thing.

His firm conviction in that, was his only armor against the temptation to turn tail and head back to England; if only to see her face once more.

A humorless chuckle escaped his lips. The girl had reduced him to a lovesick sop. After pitying all the other fools who had fallen so utterly over the moon for a chit, he now found himself among their ranks.

Who was he fooling? He was their bloody general.

He ran his cool fingers down his face, swearing under his breath.

"This is the right thing. The honorable act," he mumbled, trying to remind himself of exactly why he was putting himself through such exquisite torture. Unbidden, the hurt and betrayal etched on Clairmont's features came to mind, reminding Graham of just what his affection toward Bethanny had cost.

She deserved better than the likes of him. It was the harsh, cold truth. Bitter like the north wind and just as severe.

Love was every bit as miserable as he'd feared. No wonder men dreaded the marriage mart. It surely was a man who'd thought of the first arranged marriage.

Bloody stroke of brilliance.

To be free of the laceration of a breaking heart when the woman you loved either didn't return your affection, or in his case, was simply out of reach. Horrible, miserable existence, this love.

Yet as miserable, as emotionally distraught as he was, he couldn't regret one moment. One kiss.

In fact, he'd do it all again.

Over and over, because as much as the pain was slowly maiming his heart, he had those precious — albeit stolen — memories to live within him.

Such a treasure was worth any pain.

It was because of that love that he knew he needed to leave. To give her the freedom to find a man with far more integrity, far more honor, and far less of a checkered past than himself.

Oh, he had never been *too* scandalous, but when compared to the purity of Bethanny, it made his history seem black. He wouldn't bind her purity to his sins, past or not. She deserved more.

He wanted her to have more.

Even if it meant it wasn't with him.

However, that was the very reason Scotland was a necessity. Being near her, he would never be strong enough to allow her the freedom to find that perfect man. He would push, fight, and veritably claw his way into her line of sight so that no other man would stand a chance. Because what Clairmont had also said was startlingly true. *He did* know how to charm her, how to speak in precisely the most honeyed of tones that would render a woman boneless and unable to resist the temptation of his advances. He wasn't arrogant. He simply knew and had used it to his selfish advantage more than his share.

And bloody hell, he knew that given the chance, he'd seduce Bethanny. And she needed, deserved more.

He needed more for her.

Thus, Scotland. Where he couldn't stand in her way, where the duke could pick out a blameless gent from the *ton* and marry her into the protective safety of innocents.

Damn it all if he wouldn't give his fortune to be that gent.

The carriage hit a pothole and jostled, shaking him from his melancholy stupor. Fisting his palms, he pressed them into the soft seat and clenched his jaw. Doing the right thing had never been so difficult.

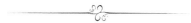

"Have you found out anything more?" Bethanny closed the door to her sister's room quietly before turning her questioning gaze to Beatrix.

"No. Believe me, I've tried as well."

"Bother."

"Agreed. What about Lady Southridge? Did you ask her?"

"I went to see her, but she wasn't available. She was out on Bond Street shopping."

"I'd ask the duke, but that would leave me in the suds."

"Quite right. He'd only demand you explained *why* you were interested, and we'd get nowhere." Bethanny heaved a dramatic sigh and flopped — very unladylike — onto the chaise next to the fire.

"How are you faring?" Beatrix asked quietly as she came and sat next to her sister.

"Aside from wanting to throttle him…" Bethanny tried to put on a brave face, but her throat began to ache as she held in her emotion.

Ennui, be damned.

A tear made its way past her determination and trailed down her nose.

"Bethanny." She sighed. Softly, Beatrix put her arm around her sister, pulling her into an embrace.

"I'm the eldest. I'm to be the one to take care of you, not the other way around."

"Dearest, you *have* taken care of us, you always will too, but that doesn't mean you have to always be strong. Sisters are here for when you are weak, when you need support. Is it so wrong for you to need us as much as we need you?" Beatrix asked softly.

"I suppose not, but—"

"No arguing. I'm right, and that's that." Beatrix smiled.

"You've grow quite bossy." Bethanny gave her sister a watery smile.

"I had a good teacher." Beatrix shrugged, laughing quietly.

"Beatrix? Bethanny? Are you in there?" Berty's voice called through the closed door.

"Yes, we're here," Beatrix called out, a rueful smile tipping her lips as the youngest sister barged through the door and slammed it shut.

Not on purpose, simply because that was Berty.

Loud.

Ungraceful.

And, because it was worth mentioning again — loud.

Of course, she was also still slightly round from her baby fat, with the largest and expressive brown eyes. She could charm the whiskers off a cat.

When she wanted to, that is.

"What are you two doing hiding in here? Wait." Berty paused, her eyes narrowing then widening with alarm. "Bethanny! You're crying! Why? I'll kill him. Who is it? Who broke your heart? Wait... is it Carlotta? I didn't think anything of it when she left breakfast a little green this morning. Was it—"

"Berty, dear... sit." Bethanny shook her head and sniffed delicately.

Berty paused then sat.

On the very edge of the chair, as if expecting to jump up and... do something.

Heaven only knows what.

"All is well. I'm sure Carlotta is well, as am I. I simply—"

"No. You are not well. I don't appreciate you keeping the truth from me. I'm not a child anymore."

"Of course not, Berty." Beatrix reached out and patted her sister's hand then glanced to Bethanny, raising her brows.

Bethanny sighed. "I'm simply… confused."

"About Lord Graham?" Berty asked in a hushed whisper.

"Pardon?" Beatrix and Bethanny asked in unison.

Berty rolled her eyes. "Honestly. You two…"She shook her head. "I'm not as dense as I look. I might be young, but I'm not bloody blind."

"Berty!"

"Sorry, sorry. I know, I know. I'll not say it again." Then she whispered, "It *was* an accurate sentiment—"

"Berty…" Bethanny warned.

"Very well," Berty huffed. "I might not be at all your parties, but I do have two eyes in my head. And two ears. Whenever the earl's name is mentioned, you bite your lip and look down at you lap, and your ears turn red."

"Oh heavens," Bethanny lamented, letting her head slightly thump the back of the chaise. Goodness, she couldn't be *that* transparent, could she? With a heavy sigh, she glanced up at her sisters.

"Don't worry, I don't think anyone else noticed." Berty shrugged.

"How comforting."

"I—"

"Girls?" Carlotta's voice called through the closed door.

"Honestly?" Bethanny whispered.

"We're here!" Beatrix called out as she and her sisters sat up straighter and smoothed their skirts.

"Ah, there you are. I've been looking — dear me! Bethanny, have you been crying?"

"Good Lord!" Bethanny whispered in a plea.

"Er—"

"Don't try." Carlotta held up her hand and turned to shut the door.

"I—"

"It's Lord Graham, isn't it?"

"I'm thinking I should simply announce this in the newspaper. I'm quite sure all of London knows!" Bethanny stood and huffed.

"A bit dramatic, are we?" Carlotta asked.

"You have no idea," Berty replied.

Bethanny turned and glared at her sister.

"It's the truth. After all, you're the one—"

"Berty, you're not helping," Beatrix interrupted. "Bethanny is simply concerned that someone will cry rope on her... you know, tell all her secrets?"

"It's not *that* much of a secret," Berty added.

"Again, *not* helping," Beatrix ground out.

"Girls? Let me speak with Bethanny alone, do you mind?" Carlotta asked with regal grace as she touched Berty's shoulder gently.

"Yes, of course." Beatrix stood.

When Berty opened her mouth, a defiant glint in her eye, Beatrix grabbed her hand and pulled her up from the chair.

"We'll be in the library." Beatrix spoke with a steely edge, daring her younger sister to argue.

"I'm coming, I'm coming. There's no need to cut off my circulation." Berty pulled her hand out of Beatrix's grasp. After pausing and sighing deeply, she turned to address Carlotta. "We shall be in the library." She nodded emphatically and breezed from the room, leaving Beatrix behind.

"As if you didn't hear me the first time." Beatrix shook her head at Carlotta.

Carlotta held up her hand to hide the wide smile Bethanny could see dancing in her eyes.

Berty was entertaining, if nothing else.

Beatrix nodded and closed the door as she left.

"Come, darling. Is your tender heart feeling broken from the earl's sudden departure? I had noticed him paying marked attention toward you, and I was going to speak with you concerning it, but I was... distracted. Forgive me."

Bethanny's heart pinched with longing for her own mother as she saw the care, the concern etched on her former governess's face. A tear welled up and escaped.

"Dear Bethanny, " Carlotta murmured and strode forward, pulling her it to a tight embrace, clearly not concerned that her dress would be wrinkled or stained with tears.

"Pardon me, I—"

"You're hurting. And I imagine you wish you had your mother here," Carlotta whispered, her kindness releasing a new torrent of tears from Bethanny.

"Yes, I feel like such a ninny." She sniffed, leaning back to look at Carlotta.

"Don't. I cannot tell you how many times I have wished for advice from my own mother, to simply feel her arms around me, to smell her rose water." Carlotta inhaled deeply, as if smelling it from memory alone.

"I miss her."

"As you should."

"But you and the duke—"

"Are not your parents. I understand. But I hope you know, beyond all doubt, how much we love you. You might not have your parents, but you do have love, dear."

Bethanny smiled through her tears. "I know. Thank you."

"Now..." Carlotta led them back to the chaise and sat beside her, "Lord Graham left for Scotland. I take it you weren't expecting this."

"No."

"Can you tell me why?" Carlotta asked, her green gaze

sharp and patient.

"No."

"Can't or do not wish to?" Carlotta tilted her head slightly.

"Don't wish to?" Bethanny added softly.

"I see… was there an understanding between you and the earl?"

"No," Bethanny answered, her heart calling her a fool for wishing so desperately to answer differently. "However," Bethanny felt her shoulders slump in a very unladylike manner, "he did imply that he… enjoyed my company."

"Has he kissed you?" Carlotta asked directly.

"Er—" Bethanny stammered.

"Yes then." She nodded. "You really shouldn't let gentlemen kiss you, dear. But I happen to know someone quite like the earl," she winked conspiratorially, "and those types of gentlemen tend to get what they want." She grinned.

"The duke?"

"Indeed. The man didn't understand the meaning of *no*… unless he was telling it to himself," she amended. She glanced to the low-burning fire and furrowed her brow. "This isn't adding up. Something's amiss. Let me speak with Charles. I'll get to the bottom of this."

"What do you mean?" Bethanny asked, desperate for some sort of hope.

"Lord Graham isn't one to dally with—" She began quickly then stopped. "What I mean to say is if Lord Graham kissed you, then he wasn't simply playing with your affections. His friendship with the duke is far too important for him to entertain a flirtation with you. So there must have been a reason he left."

"But—"

"I watched him, you know." Carlotta leaned forward, her eyes dancing.

"What?"

"I watched him around you. And don't think you're pulling the wool over my eyes, young lady. I saw you leave the party at the Symores'. It wasn't long after that Charles... oh, dear heavens." Carlotta's green eyes widened.

"What?" Bethanny leaned forward, her heart pounding a staccato rhythm.

"I... I think... Bethanny, I need you to be honest with me, I'll not be upset. But did Lord Graham kiss you when you two left the ballroom at the Symores' rout?"

"Y-yes." Bethanny answered.

"And... forgive me, but I'm going to be blunt. Was it more of a passionate exchange than a simple chaste kiss?" Carlotta reached out and grasped Bethanny's hands.

"Er... yes." Bethanny felt her face color and heat with shame and embarrassment at admitting such a private affair to her former governess.

"Blast it all," Carlotta swore.

"Pardon?" Bethanny's eyes widened.

"I've got to talk with the duke." Carlotta stood.

"Excuse me?" Bethanny followed suit.

"Charles, the duke, he — botheration! He went searching for you after I saw you leave. I didn't think much of it; I was too happy about — never mind. The issue is that if he... *found* you in a particular situation with the earl..." Carlotta leaned forward and gestured with hand.

"Oh heavens."

"Exactly."

"Wh-what are you going to do?" Bethanny asked, her hands gripping the soft muslin of her day dress.

"I'm going to go and speak with my husband."

"About? What are you going to say?" Bethanny panicked. The very *last* thing she wanted was the duke to hear about her clandestine activities with his best friend.

Bloody hell.

Yes, swearing is fully acceptable in this situation, she told herself.

"Don't fret. I'll keep what you've said to me confidential, but if I suspect that it's not a necessity... I'm quite convinced he already knows, dear."

"What do you think this has to do with Graham leaving, then?" Bethanny asked, her heart pounding.

Carlotta paused mid-step. With a weighted sigh, she turned to face Bethanny. Her expression was shuttered, yet a determined light illuminated her green gaze. "Everything, dear. Everything," Carlotta spoke gravely then spun and left, the door remaining slightly ajar in her wake.

It was turning into the worst disaster.

And it wasn't even noon.

CHAPTER ELEVEN

"Did I miss anything?" Berty asked as she rushed into Bethanny's room. With a complete lack of grace, she sprang onto the bed, her impact jostling Bethanny and Beatrix who were reclining.

Fretting was more accurate.

Molly had been sent to fetch more chocolate.

Of course, this probably was the third time, but Bethanny refused to count.

"Yes, you did," Beatrix answered.

"I knew it," Berty whined. "I couldn't get here fast enough, blasted lessons."

"Berty!" Bethanny's brow furrowed. Goodness' sake, it would be a miracle if Berty ever turned out to be lady.

"It's true." Berty shrugged, nonplused by her sister's reprimand. She reached for the last bit of chocolate and quickly popped the decadent piece of bittersweet delight into her mouth.

Bethanny scowled.

"It's not as if you both haven't had your share," Berty took in her sister's glower.

"True," Beatrix amended, though she was eyeing the few small specks of chocolate remaining on the plate with acute longing etched on her features.

"So, what did I miss?" Berty asked after swallowing.

"This is a disaster," Bethanny fell back on the bed and closed her eyes.

"Why?" Berty asked impatiently.

Bethanny swore she could *hear* her younger sister's eyes roll — if that were possible.

"Carlotta affirmed her suspicions."

"Suspicions?" Berty asked, her tone lingering as she waiting for an answer.

"Suspicions that the duke... er... witnessed an amorous encounter taking place between our dear sister and Lord Graham."

Berty's eyes grew to the size of tea saucers. "Blast it all."

"I agree wholeheartedly," Bethanny murmured.

"So..." Berty shifted on the bed, causing Bethanny to shift her gaze from the ceiling to her youngest sister, "what are we going to do?"

"We?" Bethanny spoke at the same as Beatrix, disbelief coloring their tones.

"Yes, we! You love Lord Graham, do you not?" Berty asked, rising up on her knees and placing her hands on her hips.

"Yes," Bethanny affirmed.

"Then we can't just let this... setback... steal away your opportunity to snatch him up." Berty nodded.

"Snatch him up?" Beatrix repeated.

Berty shrugged. "Very well. Leg shackle him, marry him, give him the ol' parson's noose."

"What a lovely picture you paint of marriage," Beatrix drolled.

"That's what they all say," Berty answered succinctly.

Beatrix's eyes narrowed. "All? And who is all? Just who

have you been speaking with, Berty?"

"Very well, I read it."

"In a book?"

"In the gossip papers, if you *must* know," Berty huffed.

"Because *that* is a reputable source of information," Beatrix whispered quietly for Bethanny's ears only.

Bethanny nodded.

And rolled her eyes for good measure.

"We are digressing!" Berty slammed her fist into her hand, startling Bethanny. "What we need…" Berty bit her lower lip and slid off the bed. Her slippers made a muted sound as she paced the hardwood floor of Bethanny's room.

"We need a plan," Beatrix added, moving to stand as well.

Bethany smiled. "I believe we established that."

"What we need…" Berty paused and tapped her lip with her first finger. "I've got it!" she shouted, causing Beatrix to squeal and jump back slightly.

Bethanny scooted back on the bed, so devilish and mischievous was the glint in her younger sister's eyes.

"We need a house party!"

"Because?" Beatrix cocked her head to one side, casting a confused glance to Bethanny.

"Because then we can invite Lord Graham," Berty finished, with a tone that suggested she thought her older sister quite daft.

"Ah, yes! Because Lord Graham will *flee* Scotland at the first opportunity at visiting his dear old friend, the Duke of Clairmont, who, from what we understand, ran him off English soil!" Beatrix said with more than a hint of sarcasm.

Bethanny held her tongue. Her comment wouldn't have been as kind.

"No. We don't have him invited by the duke. You ninnies are daft! We have his *sister* invite him."

"And why would he come to the summons of his sister?

That hasn't exactly worked in the past," Bethanny asked, dubious.

"Oh, he'll come..." Berty nodded, her eyes dancing.

"Why?"

"Because we're going to tell him it's Bethanny's engagement party."

"I am not certain this will work," Bethanny heard herself say once again as she cast a dubious glance to Beatrix.

She shrugged, which wasn't any help whatsoever.

"Of course it will work!" Berty affirmed again. She was the only one with any conviction on the matter; of course, that could be because it *was* her idea.

Bethanny wondered why she hadn't protested.

No, she knew.

She was that desperate. It had been a full week since Lord Graham's sudden departure, and as each day passed, she'd felt his absence more acutely than the last.

"But what if word gets out—"

"It won't. Lady Southridge will be the sole of discretion." Berty nodded, her soft curls bouncing as if adding emphasis.

"That—" Beatrix started.

"Is what I'm concerned about," Bethanny finished.

"You need to give her more credit," Berty huffed quietly as they approached the salon door. "Now, you remember the plan?"

"It's not espionage, Berty." Bethanny rolled her eyes.

"But think of how much more fun it would be if—" Berty began.

"If this were over with?" Beatrix interrupted.

"You two are no longer any fun to be around," she said quietly then added. "If this is what falling in love does to you, I'm considering spinsterhood."

Beatrix glanced to Bethanny and rolled her eyes dramatically.

Bethanny shared the sentiment deeply.

As Berty opened the door to the blue salon, filtered sunlight spilled into the hall and illuminated the rich tone of the hardwood floors. The sound of skirts swishing accompanied their entrance a moment before Murray caught up in efforts to announce her.

Poor Murray. As if anyone could hope to keep up with Lady Southridge.

"Girls!" Lady Southridge stood and welcomed them with a bright grin.

"Good afternoon," Bethanny spoke for her sisters.

Lady Southridge's eyes skittered from Beatrix to Berty, not making eye contact with Bethanny.

Strange.

"I received your missive, Berty. I must say you have a wild flair for the dramatic, love." Lady Southridge grinned and raised an eyebrow.

"Berty?" Bethanny turned to her younger sister, her tone questioning.

"Er, thank you, Lady Southridge." Berty took a few steps away from Bethanny and sat, ignoring Bethanny's question.

"I'm not sure it was meant as a compliment," Beatrix whispered to Bethanny before she moved to sit on a chaise across from Lady Southridge.

"Indeed," Bethanny answered, eyeing her sister meaningfully.

"Now, what is this secret mission?" Lady Southridge leaned forward, her eyes dancing.

"Secret mission?" Bethanny repeated, then turned accusing eyes to Berty.

Berty had the wisdom to study her lap and not meet her sister's gaze.

"Yes! The note was quite cryptic! I was utterly impatient

to discover what needed such secrecy! Oh! And Berty, do not fret. I did not even disclose my whereabouts to my lady's maid. And you'll be impressed," she grinned wildly and held up her gloved hand next to her mouth as if to whisper, "I had my coachman drop me off at the Kensington Gardens, and I walked the rest of the way here, so absolutely no one knows where I am!" She lowered her hand and swept it with a grand flourish.

"Brilliant." Berty leaned forward, her manner delighted.

"Lady Southridge! No one knows where you are? And you walked? Alone? From Kensington Gardens?" Bethanny scolded, hanging her good manners and placing her hands on her hips.

"Psh, love. I'm nearly sixty — though you'll carry that information to your grave." She narrowed her eyes dangerously until Bethanny, along with her two sisters, nodded their agreement. "And being such, I am perfectly capable of taking care of myself."

"But what if thieves had assaulted you in the park?"

"At this hour?" Lady Southridge shook her head. "Besides, I always carry this," she pulled up her reticule and withdrew a pistol," when I'm alone."

Bethanny gasped.

Beatrix leaned back.

Berty reached for it.

"Ah, no." Lady Southridge smacked her hand. "When you're older," she amended then winked.

Berty's grin was wide enough to split her face.

"Heaven help us all, it's bad enough that you're carrying around a weapon. Don't promise that Berty might do the same. Goodness knows what trouble will follow!" Bethanny shook her head.

"And to think I said that Berty had a flair for the dramatic." Lady Southridge turned a slightly irritated gaze to Bethanny. "Now, are we going to cackle about like old hens, or are you going to let me in on your little secret?" Silently, she put the pistol away in her reticule and set it on the floor beside her.

Bethanny's gaze kept straying to it, the seemingly benign sky-blue reticule. She didn't know what was more dangerous: the pistol or Lady Southridge.

It was a tie.

"Well, you see there's been… a situation," Berty began, as she smoothed her lavender skirt and nodded slightly, causing her chestnut curls to spring.

"Oh heavens…" Lady Southridge leaned forward, her eyes widening, but her tone anything but delighted.

"You see." Berty cut a sidelong glance to Bethanny." My sister and *your* brother—"

"Berty, perhaps *I* should explain?" Bethanny cut in. Heaven only knew that with the current state of things, by the end of the conversation their original plans would be wildly overstated.

And absurd.

And utterly unhelpful. And right now, she *needed* help. Desperately.

"Very well." Berty pouted and leaned back.

"Ah, so this is about Edward." Lady Southridge turned knowing eyes to Bethanny.

"Yes." Bethanny swallowed the lump in her throat at the mention of his name. "You see, Lord Graham and I… that is, we…" She stumbled trying to, in some sort of ladylike fashion, disclose the nature of the situation.

"Blast it all. They kissed! And the duke saw the whole thing—"

"Not the *whole* thing," Beatrix cut in, her eyes darting between Bethanny and Beatrix with a worried crease to her brow.

"Berty!" Bethanny cried.

"It's true!"

"Yes, but—" Bethanny started.

"You didn't have to put it so—" Beatrix interjected.

"Honestly?" Berty finished.

"Girls?" Lady Southridge asked softly.

Bethanny turned her furious gaze from Berty to Lady Southridge.

"I'm quite certain that I have surmised the situation." She nodded confidently.

"Er, how?" Bethanny asked, her brow furrowing in confusion. It wasn't as if they'd stated, or interrupted each other, with much information.

"You see, I was actually going to contact *you*, Bethanny dear, to see if you knew the cause for my dear," she shook her head as if exasperated, "deluded brother's departure to Scotland. Especially when things were going so well."

"And?" Bethanny prodded, still not comprehending what exactly she was trying to explain.

"*And*, knowing that Edward was... more amorous than I anticipated, coupled with the information that the duke had caught your... shall we say, affection for one another? It simply all makes sense. The question is, what are we going to do to remedy the situation?" She placed her hands placidly on her lap as she warmly regarded Bethanny.

How in hades is the woman so calm about it all?

"I have a plan." Berty clapped, her expression overjoyed.

"Let's hear it."

"What we are assuming is that Lord Graham left after having a bit of a gentleman's argument with the duke."

"If I may ask, how are you aware of this... gentleman's argument?" Lady Southridge asked skeptically.

"Carlotta. She approached the duke."

"And who described it as a gentleman's argument?"

Berty glanced to Beatrix, who glanced to Bethanny.

"The duke, I believe," Bethanny answered, unsure as to why it was important.

"Ah."

"Ah?" Bethanny questioned.

"Yes, the very fact that he used the words, *gentleman's argument*, means that it was anything but, my dears. Or else he wouldn't have gone so far as to describe the nature of it."

"How are you so sure?" Bethanny asked, darting a glance to Beatrix.

"I know those two boys well, and even though they are men now, not so much has changed. And there's nothing that reverts a man back to his boyhood more than feeling scolded and wanting to defend himself."

"Noted." Berty nodded sagely.

Bethanny cast a longsuffering glance to her sister then turned her attention back to Lady Southridge. "So you're saying it wasn't a small argument."

"No, but it's beside the point. Berty, your plan? Please continue." She gestured to Berty, indicating for her to proceed.

Oddly enough, Bethanny fancied she looked very much like a queen as she did such.

"Since Lord Graham has left for Scotland, we decided we needed him to come back."

"Berty, I'm sure that is already understood," Beatrix murmured.

"I'm getting there," Berty huffed. "So we thought—"

"You. *You* thought." Bethanny felt the need to correct her sister.

"Very well, *I* thought that we needed to get him alone with the duke and my sister. Give him a chance to work out the issues with the duke and also make amends for being a nodcock to my sister. Garden Gate would be a lovely location for a house party. It would easily serve the purpose."

"Yes, indeed. I see the cunning of your proposal. However, what is your bait? How are we going to entice my brother from licking his proverbial wounds in Scotland and fight for the fair maiden?" Lady Southridge's eyes were dancing as she pointed to Bethanny.

"Because we're going to have *you* send him a missive stating that the house party is actually an engagement celebration... for Bethanny."

"Brilliant!" Lady Southridge clapped.

Berty stood and curtseyed.

Beatrix rolled her eyes but smiled softly at her sister.

"That will surely light a fire under his intentions. So, who am I to say is the lucky gentleman engaged to Miss Bethanny?"

"Er, I hadn't thought that far ahead." Berty bit her lower lip.

"Lord Neville," Beatrix spoke.

"Yes!" Bethanny grinned at her sister.

"Neville? That would work. Is there a specific reason why you chose him, Beatrix?" Lady Southridge asked while shifting her gaze from Bethanny to Beatrix.

"Didn't Lord Graham show particular jealousy that day you were accepting callers, Bethanny?"

"Indeed. I thought of that as soon as you mentioned his name." Bethanny raised an eyebrow.

This might just work.

"Delightful! Already there's a seed of jealousy. We'll simply water it."

"And let it grow?" Berty asked, a devious tone to her voice.

"Exactly."

"The question is, will he believe you?" Bethanny asked hesitantly.

"I can be quite convincing when I need to be." Lady Southridge winked. "The true question is, when are we going to have the party?"

"Bethanny?" the duke's voice called from behind his wide desk. His dark head was bowed over some missive he was finishing.

"Yes?" Bethanny replied, swallowing her trepidation.

The duke set aside the letter and met her gaze. Folding his hands, he furrowed his brows in a concerned expression. "Carlotta and Lady Southridge both spoke with me about your... ploy."

"Oh?" Bethanny tried to remain still; all she wanted to do was fidget.

"Indeed. Though I have to say, I cannot believe that one as such as yourself, a diamond of the first water, feels the need to resort to such measures to snare a gentleman... especially when the man in question is already in love with you." He sighed heavily.

"But—"

"No, let me finish. I'll agree to this scheme upon one condition." He speared her with a glance.

She nodded.

"No more moping, no more long face, no more tears behind closed doors, and absolutely no more lamenting. I accept the truth that I played a part in the departure of Lord Graham, but you must first also admit that such was my duty, my position and honor to do so, Bethanny. "He stood and walked around his desk then sat on the front of it.

Even though Bethanny held him as an older brother more than father figure, she could appreciate the handsome man before her.

Though none could compare with Lord Graham.

Blast the man.

"You behaved in an unladylike manner. You risked your reputation *and* Graham's. Naiveté is no excuse. I suspect you were fully aware of the implications of your actions if they were discovered by anyone but myself." He raised his eyebrows, awaiting her response.

"Yes, Your Grace."

He exhaled a sigh. "Why did you not speak with me? Why did you not confide in me? And why Lord Graham of all people? When you could have your choice of all the—"

"I love him, Your Grace. Pardon the interruption," she added belatedly, her face heating at her brash behavior.

"One kiss does not equal love."

"No. You're correct. But love can begin in the heart of a child and grow till it can be mature in the heart of a woman," she answered.

He twisted his lips and glanced at the fire before turning once again to her. "Indeed. But you still haven't answered my question."

"I didn't approach you, Your Grace, because Lord Graham is your friend. Already I knew this would be difficult for you to accept—"

"Because he's my friend?"

"Because of his... past reputation. One that you, at one time, shared, Your Grace."

Bethany held her breath. This was the only time she had admitted to knowing anything about the duke's past. Though it was odd that everyone expected her to be ignorant, since she was a full sixteen when she'd met him. Even at sixteen, a young lady can understand certain things.

"And it was because of this... reputation of Lord Graham you thought his pursuit would be unacceptable?"

"Yes. Because you seemed to imply that I deserved something... different."

"You mean *more*."

"To your perspective, yes."

The duke pushed up from his desk and paced about the room. "As I said, I'll agree to this... whatever it is you ladies have concocted. Personally, I'd rather simply go to Scotland myself and wring the bloo — er, my dear *friend's* neck. In the future, please pass along to your sisters that I'd like to be told everything up front and not find out the secret intentions of suitors after I find them in compromising situations and certainly not when I have them in an enclosed carriage where I can easily murder them and dispose of the body. I'm far too handsome for Newgate." The duke smiled then, implying he was joking.

But Bethanny wasn't fully convinced.

"Yes, Your Grace."

"You have two weeks till the house party. That should be enough time for Graham to get the invitation and for him to arrive. However, no one else is to find out our little... embellishment concerning Lord Neville. That will be kept in completely confidence. Lord knows, we don't need further drama." He wiped his hand down his face.

"Of course."

"You're excused, but remember when the time comes, this is all on my terms, my rules, and no exceptions. Understood?"

"Utterly, Your Grace." Bethanny curtseyed and turned to leave.

"Bethanny?"

"Yes?"

"For the record, yes. I would have had some trouble accepting Lord Graham as your suitor. However, that would have been quickly overcome had I known about your mutual attachment. You need to understand that I fully approve of the gentleman you've given your heart to," he nodded, "though I don't approve of his methods. I can't exactly call the kettle black now, can I?" He chuckled softly.

"Thank you, Your Grace," Bethanny whispered.

"And don't worry, if this ruse we've created doesn't work, I'm perfectly willing to go and collect him from Scotland for you. All he's doing is wallowing in his own misery." The duke spoke the words as if they gave him utterly glee. "Though I'd wait a little longer than necessary, just to make him suffer a bit."

"How kind."

"I thought as much. You're excused." The duke chuckled and walked back around to his desk and sat.

Bethanny left, expelling a long breath of relief as she walked down the hall. Two more weeks.

But it seemed like two years.

CHAPTER TWELVE

GRAHAM PACED HIS office like a caged animal. It had been four weeks. Four blasted, bloody, cursed weeks, and he was no closer to a moment of peace than the moment he'd set foot out of the duke's carriage.

Blasted bloody love.

He'd hated every moment of it, and conversely, he would hold on to it with his dying breath.

Edinburgh had always been his sanctuary, his safe harbor where he could weather the storms of life.

Or the storms of his sister.

But it wasn't that way any longer. Even though Bethanny had never been to his estate, she haunted the halls. He heard her laughter in the soft rustle of the leaves as the sea breeze teased them from their lofty perch.

Damn it all, he was even growing poetic.

Either that or pathetic. Perhaps it was both.

Lucky him.

In the past weeks he had made a supreme effort to continue his normal routine when in Scotland. He had attended a dignitary's ball that was held in the main hall of

Edinburgh castle.

Bloody drafty, that old place.

Of course, his good intentions fled once an elderly woman had caressed his thigh at dinner.

That, coupled with her missing teeth as she smiled lecherously at him, was enough to kill what little appetite he had summoned for the occasion.

He shivered.

One of his chums had invited him to a rout of Highland Games. Normally one of his favorite diversions when in Scotland, but even caber tossing didn't sound entertaining.

To be honest, he usually didn't participate; he simply watched in amazement as others did.

Caber tossing. He shook his head. Some Scot had to have been bloody daft to of thought up such a game.

Or desperate to impress a woman.

Now *that* he could understand.

And commiserate.

His lips drew down as he wondered if it had worked, impressing the woman as the poor bloke threw the ceremonial log, trying to land it upright.

He'd toss a caber for Bethanny.

Brandy, he needed it desperately. The good French kind, the very kind that was outlawed.

Bloody Bonaparte.

"Sir?" Selwyn's voice interrupted Graham's odd musings.

"Yes?" Graham turned to face his aged butler.

"This came for you. Since the sender is your sister, I took the liberty of bringing the post to you directly." The man extended a silver tray holding a square missive.

"Thank you, Selwyn."

"Will there be anything else, sir?" The butler's green eye studied him; concern etched the corner wrinkles of his face.

"Not at the moment, thank you." Graham dismissed the

man, guilt gnawing at him from his butler's expression. To Selwyn's credit, he hadn't pressed for information.

Another blessing for being in Scotland.

The butler nodded and left quietly, closing the study door behind him silently.

Graham studied the missive and withdrew his sharp opener from the wide mahogany desk. With a quick slit, the letter opened. Graham placed the family heirloom opener back on his desk and took a fortifying breath.

He had to give his sister some glory; she had waited two weeks to contact him.

Thank heavens for small miracles.

However his prayer was cut short by a string of swearing.

In German and Dutch.

Then he swore in Italian for good measure.

The thick paper missive slipped through his fingers and lightly tapped against the Aubusson rug.

Immediately, a thousand fragmented memories, ones he had been so determined to keep locked within, sprang to life, enveloping him in her smile, the tone of her laughter, and the warmth of her soft body pressed against his.

And mocked him.

He'd fled to Scotland to resist the temptation she presented.

He hadn't returned, hoping that she'd find a love worthy of her.

He was an utter fool.

Because in his sister's letter he learned that everything he'd tried to accomplish had succeeded.

Bethanny was engaged to — hell take him — Lord Neville.

His heart seized in his chest, each thumping beat painful, aching.

She was out of reach.

Unless...

Graham picked up the missive and studied it again, re-reading his sister's *words:*

> To celebrate, His Grace is hosting a house party at Greenford Waters. You've been invited as well, though I doubt you'll wish to attend.

He damn well was going to attend!

Bethanny was thankful that Lady Southridge had agreed to speak with the duke about the house party.

Of everyone she knew, Lady Southridge was the most difficult to refuse. She'd have to learn that particular trait.

In short work, the party was set up for the third week in June and would last for a full week. Carlotta had been thrilled with the idea and went out the very next day to select the stationary for the invitations.

The duke wasn't as thrilled. However, Bethanny felt it insufficient penance for him to simply be disgruntled. After all, it was because of his meddling that the house party was necessary at all!

With a long sigh, Bethanny leaned back against the chaise in the library and studied the tall ceiling. Carlotta had explained the duke's reason for intervention between her and Graham, but she continued to struggle to find the happy medium between forgiveness and anger.

She knew that his intention had been honorable and within his right. However, that didn't change the fact that because he had exercised that power, Lord Graham wasn't even in the same country as she.

Did he miss her? Was she haunting his dreams as he was haunting hers? Melancholy had been her companion since she had been made aware of his departure to Scotland. Thank the heavens for her sisters; they had been her source of comfort — and entertainment — since the awful occurrence.

Speaking of which, Bethanny tilted her head as she heard soft footsteps in the hall.

"Bethanny?" Carlotta's melodic voice called in a quiet grace.

"Yes?" Bethanny sat up straighter and smoothed the soft velvet of her light violet day gown.

"Ah, I — er—" Carlotta paused and glanced behind her in the hallway. A moment later she slipped in the door and closed it tightly.

Bethanny raised an eyebrow in question.

"I just spoke with the duke, and I wanted to inform you of the circumstances of his agreement."

"I was under the impression he already *had* agreed." Bethanny felt her brow furrow.

"He had. However, today he made known some... conditions." Carlotta smiled softly.

Her quiet grin gave Bethanny encouragement, soothing her initial concern.

"I imagine that these conditions aren't too trying, based on your expression." Bethanny grinned.

"Nothing too problematic, I assure you." Carlotta continued into the room and sat opposite of Bethanny. "However, these conditions are to be followed with all alacrity." Carlotta shot a meaningful gaze.

"Understood."

"Very well, the first condition is quite self-explanatory, and I think you'll understand it, based on the fact that the very reason we're in this predicament is that this social protocol was thoroughly breeched." She narrowed her eyes in a scolding manner. "You are not to be alone with Lord Graham."

"But—"

"Unless..." Carlotta waited as Bethanny halted her argument and practiced patience.

Extreme patience.

"Unless I am aware of your request and am at a suitable distance to chaperone."

"*That* is not the same as being alone."

"*That* is the best you're going to get." Carlotta raised an eyebrow as if daring her to argue.

Bethanny understood the social standards, the rules to follow that were proper protocol when dealing with sexes; however, that didn't mean she agreed or even liked them. After tasting the delicious flavor of freedom in a lover's embrace, she was more than reluctant to agree.

However she saw no other option.

And as much as she hated to admit it, perhaps it was for the best.

"Very well." Bethanny nodded.

"I suppose some leniency could be arranged..." Carlotta's tone drifted.

"Yes?" Bethanny leaned on the edge of her seat.

"If, *if*, a proposal is forthcoming."

"Oh." Bethanny's hopes felt flat. Of course she hoped, dreamed, desired above all things for that very thing to happen, but how did a lady provoke such a degree of sentiment if she were unable to be alone with her suitor?

"I know what you're thinking."

Bethanny shot her a curious glance.

"Just because the idea of falling in love is more fashionable than in the past is no reason to disregard our standards. There are reasons for the rules, Bethanny. They protect you. They also protect Lord Graham. Would you wish to enter a union as holy as marriage on any less of a footing than complete authenticity? Would you trap him? Or have him trap you? Pretend that it's not Lord Graham we're speaking of. What of Lord Neville, for example? Would you wish him to be forced to offer for your hand because you were foolish enough to be caught alone with him?"

"No, of course not, but—"

"No *buts*." Carlotta held firm.

At Bethanny's nod, she continued.

"Now the final condition His Grace required was that upon Lord Graham's arrival, he is to be unable to find you." Carlotta's grin widened.

"Pardon?" Bethanny tilted her head in confusion. It was customary for the gentleman to be out when the lady arrived. How was this any different?

"Allow me to explain further. For the first day of his arrival, you are to be hidden away. Unable to be found. The first time he shall see you will be at dinner."

"I'm not sure I fully understand—"

Carlotta waved her hand playfully. "His Grace is quite a romantic at heart, dear. You might not be able to see it. However, when I disclosed to him all the particulars concerning the party—"

"You what?" Bethanny was aghast! Never had she expected Carlotta to lay out all the true intentions behind the plan.

"Would you have me deceive my husband?" Carlotta asked softly.

"No, but... I would have preferred..." Bethanny trailed off, uncertain as to how to continue.

"As I said, my husband is a romantic at heart. Truth be told, he didn't expect the deep attachment Lord Graham had toward you, or you toward him. When it became apparent that Lord Graham's intentions were honorable, the duke tried to reason with Lord Graham, but the damage was done. And, I must admit that although it has taken him a bit to get over the idea of his friend offering for you, he has warmed considerably to it."

"I assume that I have you to thank for such a feat?"

Bethanny asked kindly.

"No, you may give credit to your guardian. He came to the conclusion himself." Carlotta smiled.

"Why, may I ask, does the duke wish for Lord Graham to not find me upon his arrival, assuming that he *does* in fact, arrive?"

"Oh, he'll attend, don't you worry about that." Carlotta gave a sly wink. "But, according to the duke, the fact that Lord Graham will not be able to find you will only twist his already prolific imagination and, given the nature of the party — as far as he's concerned — it will only progress the plan and accelerate the desired outcome."

"Diabolical." Bethanny breathed in awe.

"Indeed. I must say I was quite proud." Carlotta's grin widened.

"I'm quite impressed myself. Though, such a scheme truly smacks of Lady Southridge's influence — though I'd never tell him!" Bethanny giggled as Carlotta nodded.

"Undeniably! That was my very same thought. Though I wisely agree with you, he need not know where he gleaned his nefarious, scheming ideas." Carlotta bit her lower lip as if trying to restrain her mirth. She tilted her head, her green eyes studying Bethanny. "Soon, dear. I know the wait is torture, but I have all faith it will work out."

"How?" Bethanny asked in a small voice. "How can you be so sure? This is quite an elaborate scheme, and it might all be for naught. Yet my heart is bursting with fear and anticipation because… what if it *does* work? And what of love? Am I naïve in hoping for more than a match, but for devotion, love, and honor? Am I unwise in seeking those from Lord Graham? I… I simply am questioning—"

"Yes, you *are* questioning, because sometimes distance gives us the opportunity to evaluate. This can be both beneficial, yet also detrimental. You mustn't let all your thinking result in an acute lack of hope. That is not what God would have for you."

"I hadn't actually thought of this in the context of God, actually. Though admitting that seems quiet selfish." Bethanny glanced down to her lap, her brow furrowed. It wasn't that she didn't believe in God. After all, church was a monumental part of one's life. However, to think that God would be concerned with something as minimal as her life... she simply hadn't considered the thought.

"Remember the verse, 'Faith, hope and love, but the greatest of these is love'?" Carlotta asked.

"Of course." It was one of the first ones she'd memorized as a little girl.

"Love is coupled with faith and hope, yet it is declared as the greatest. Love is surrounded by faith — *believing* without seeing the evidence — and hope — *continuing* to believe even when you don't see the evidence — because love is consummation of both. Love serves, it lowers itself, love cannot exist apart from faith and hope, yet it is glorified above them because it's the fullness of faith and hope experienced. And, when you are questioning, as you are now, it is easy to lose sight of this truth, letting fear steal it away. Fear is the opposite of love. It's the antithesis of faith, and it always will steal your hope."

"Fear. That's truly what I believe plagues me. Because what if—"

"Indeed, what *if*, not what *will*," Carlotta finished, folding her hands in her lap.

"True."

"To get back to answering your question, the true question you should ask yourself is not if this whole scheme will work, but if you trust God enough to allow Him to do what is best for you, even if you don't understand it yourself."

"I—I'm not sure."

"Then *that* is the answer you must seek. Because it's the only one that will offer peace. But for the record, I can honestly say that while having faith and holding to hope are difficult, they never disappoint. After all, if God closes a door..." Carlotta let the old saying linger.

"He always opens a window?" Bethanny finished.

"And who knows what that window will be."

"How did you get so wise?" Bethanny asked, her heart softly melting into a relaxed state.

"Dear one, all you need to remember is where I've come from and where I am now. After all, one needs to be exceedingly wise to be married to a duke... especially one such as mine." She grinned and nudged Bethanny's shoulder.

Bethanny laughed, her heart feeling lighter than it had in so long.

Hope.

CHAPTER THIRTEEN

LORD GRAHAM SAT on the very edge of his luxurious carriage as it progressed into the countryside around Bath. Every clip-clop of the matched bays' hooves meant that he was one step closer to seeing her.

To setting his plan into action.

Though to be fair, he hadn't come up with much more than to break up the engagement.

But that was enough. The particulars would come later, once he evaluated the situation.

Once he evaluated *her.*

His thoughts veered toward the dramatic as he sighed and wondered — not for the first, or the twentieth time — if Bethanny had missed him even a fraction of what he had missed her.

Was her engagement a foolhardy way to try and mend the broken heart his departure had caused? Shaking his head, he knew it was wishful thinking that her attachment to him had been so firm.

Though in his next thought, he questioned the validity of such an argument. After all, if she were attached to him, how could her loyalties switch so quickly?

Which brought him to his worst fears: that the emotion, the passion, and loyalty was one-sided.

His.

But then he remembered their last kiss, her forward manner — good heavens! Was she *that* forward with Neville.

Graham saw red; not till he heard a distinctive ripping noise did he glance down. In his distracted anger, his grip had tightened to the point where he had pierced through the padding below the carriage seat cushion.

Blast it all.

He needed to calm himself. Because all he was doing was speculating. Nothing was known for sure.

Except the most damning of all: that Bethanny wasn't his.

And nothing could have been worse.

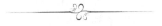

Bethanny was strolling in the gardens with Carlotta when a footman made determined strides toward them. Glancing at Carlotta, Bethanny paused and waited, holding her breath.

Could it be?

"Pardon, my ladies. But His Grace dispatched me directly to inform you that Lord Graham's carriage has been sighted." He bowed smartly. "Do you have a reply?"

Carlotta reached out and squeezed Bethanny's gloved fingers, a smile spilling over her lips. "No, simply tell His Grace we appreciate the information."

The footman bowed and strode away to deliver the message to the duke.

"Did I not say that he would attend?" Carlotta's grin grew unchecked.

"Yes, I scarcely let myself believe—"

"We haven't a moment to waste! Let's get you to your room... and let the afternoon take its course." Carlotta lifted an eyebrow, her gaze seeming to take wicked delight.

Bethanny bit her lip and stared at the large stone structure of Greenford Waters. The next few days would likely determine her future. How she wished she could simply know what the end result would be.

But that wouldn't be faith.

And if there was one thing she had learned, it's that with faith and trust come peace. And that peace was worth its weight in gold.

With a deep breath she exhaled her anxiety and said a silent prayer.

The peace returned, and a smile teased her lips.

Carlotta led them to the servants' entrance to make sure they wouldn't be seen. The large wooden door creaked as Carlotta pushed it open. Still tugging on Bethanny's hand, she glanced back with a saucy grin as they rounded a corner to take the stairs.

"Oh my! What'er you—" A scullery maid was rounding the corner at the same time. With a leap and startled shout, the maid began to berate them only to gasp, cast her eyes downward, and apologized. "A thousand pardons, my lady. I wasn't payin' proper attention—"

"No need." Carlotta held up her gloved hand, her cheeks a light dusting of pink. "If anyone should apologize, it is I."

The maid seemed quite discomfited as her eyes widened slightly at the apology of her betters.

Bethanny hid a smile. The poor maid must be new, for almost everyone was accustomed to Carlotta's unconventionality in dealing with the servants.

After all, she had practically *been* one a few years ago.

"Beggin' your pardon, miss." The maid curtseyed to Bethanny, and she nodded in return as Carlotta tugged her hand and they ascended the stone stairs that would lead them to the hall so she could slip, unnoticed, into her room.

Bethanny trotted down the hall with Carlotta, her bonnet

strings bouncing against her arms as she made her way to the room assigned to her. Swiftly slipping in, she drew in rapid breaths against the tight corset.

"I'll leave you now, but I'll return post haste once he has arrived. And don't fret. I take my role as chaperone very seriously." She wagged her eyebrows. "And I'll monitor Lord Graham's every move and report back."

"Perfect." Bethanny exhaled in gleeful expectation.

"Now, try to relax. It's likely to be a long afternoon. Did you gather the books you wished?"

"Yes."

"Brilliant. Now, if you'll excuse me." Carlotta spun around and slipped through the door.

Bethanny sighed deeply and walked to the window. Carlotta had purposefully given her a window that faced the back wood, eliminating the danger of Lord Graham seeing her upon his arrival from her window perch.

When Carlotta had passed the guest room arrangement by the duke, he had agreed with her choice of location, murmuring something about being thankful for the room's location on the third floor.

Carlotta had giggled as she had explained his strange comment.

Lord Graham had been quite the expert at climbing... and the duke wasn't about to give him an opportunity to exercise his prowess.

So as Bethanny glanced down at the vivid green grass below, she shivered slightly, thinking that it was indeed a fair way to fall. Though there was something utterly romantic about a suitor being so desperate to attempt such a feat.

She glanced back down.

Perhaps not.

If anything was *not* romantic, it was the suitor plunging to his death.

With a slight shake of her head, she rose and evaluated

the teetering piles of books on the table next to her small sitting area. After scanning their titles, she selected *The History of Edinburgh.*

As she opened the first page, a knock sounded on the door.

"Yes?"

Lady Southridge bustled into the room, closing the door silently behind her. Her green eyes were illuminated with a mischievous sparkle, and her hands were clapping. "He is here! In my haste to find you, I almost knocked over a footman. Poor dear, I think I scared a few years from his life."

"Carlotta and I had a similar instance with a scullery maid," Bethanny confided, her tone light.

"Ha-ha!" Lady Southridge laughed. "Now, I can only stay a moment, I want to be there to assist my brother—"

"Torment, you mean?" Bethanny grinned as she teased.

"What cheek! How can you accuse me — ah, very well. Yes. I want to torture him. I still haven't forgiven him for his utter stupidity in fleeing to Scotland." She exhaled an exasperated sigh. "Don't you tell me you don't think he deserves it." Lady Southridge narrowed her eyes and pursed her lips a she studied Bethanny.

"Indeed he does." She nodded.

"Good girl. Now, I'll report back directly, but I have a little brother to... welcome." Lady Southridge giggled and turned to open the door.

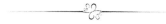

Lord Graham shot out of his seat the moment the carriage wheels ceased their movement. Without waiting for the footman's assistance in opening the carriage door, he lifted the latch and descended the single step till his Hessian boots crunched the gravel beneath them. Taking a fortifying breath, he narrowed his eyes at the large estate. Built before the

Tudors, the stone structure was not only imposing, but old and grand in a fashion that couldn't be replicated, though many had tried.

Sometimes age only made things more beautiful, stronger, more secure.

There was a definite undertone to his thoughts, but he didn't pause to evaluate them; he strode toward the grand entrance and took the stairs two at a time till he reached the entrance.

The house party would be in full swing by now, since he was a day late, so hopefully he'd catch them unaware and be able to see Bethanny immediately.

He should have known that wouldn't have been the case.

Rather, as soon as he entered the foyer, he removed his hat and was greeted by none other than his sister.

"You're late." She arched an eyebrow and regarded him coolly.

"It's a pleasure to see you as well. Nice to know I was missed," Graham replied quickly, a tense grin lifting his lips only slightly.

"Nonsense. Of course you were missed." She waved dismissively. "However, that has nothing to do with the fact that the party started yesterday, dear."

"I thought it was fashionable to arrive late, to make a flamboyant entrance." He bowed mockingly, a bit of the tension releasing from his shoulders as he settled into comfortable banter with his sister.

He rose just in time to see the end of his sister's eye-roll.

"Is this any way to greet a guest?"

"You're not my guest," she retorted.

"Forgive me. I thought you had rather forcibly instigated yourself in this family."

"I was invited."

"As was I."

"Yes, but I'm not here to start a ruckus," she shot back,

daring him to refute her statement.

"And why do you believe that I'm here on such an errand?" He narrowed his eyes. Was his cause already doomed before it had a chance?

"Because I'm—" His sister paused. "This is no place to carry on this type of conversation. Besides, you must be exhausted from the journey."

"Ah, you do have a heart. I had rather thought that hospitality was only a Scottish custom."

"Bah." Lady Southridge swatted at him playfully and directed him up the stairs, then continued on the first landing.

Graham glanced up at the second flight of stairs and furrowed his brow. Normally the guests were given rooms on the third floor. Odd.

"Er, sister dear, where are you taking me?" he asked as he jogged slightly to catch up with her.

"As I said earlier, you are late. I assured His Grace that though you are one of the higher-ranking gentlemen in attendance, you forfeited your right to one of the grander rooms through your tardiness. So naturally, Neville received your customary room, he, being the guest of honor, and you will need to establish your lodgings here." She paused before a plain door.

"I knew this was a bad idea," Graham grumbled.

"No, rather, this is the best idea you've had in some time. I must confess, I was concerned that you wouldn't show up at all... but you know..." she leaned in slightly till her flowery fragrance floated around him, reminding him of his childhood, "some things are worth fighting for." She offered him a kind smile then opened the door.

Graham cleared his throat, and glanced inside. The room was small but clean, with a small bed to the side and a window that overlooked the front of the estate. It could have been worse.

Though it did boil his blood to know that Neville was

established in *his* room. Blasted blackguard! Not only did he have to steal his woman, but his room? It went beyond the pale! With a grunt, Graham strode purposefully into the room and stared out the window, praying for a glimpse of Bethanny.

All he saw were ducks.

"I meant what I said, you know. And I must offer a word of caution." His sister's voice softly echoed in the room.

"Oh?" Graham asked without turning.

"Yes, you see, I might have... rather, I *did* offer privileged information in my letter to you. Lord Neville has spoken with the duke about his intentions toward Bethanny, but His Grace has left the final decision to Bethanny."

"Pardon?" Graham felt his brow furrow as he gazed intently at his sister.

Could it be?

"Miss Lamont, Bethanny, isn't aware of his intentions as of yet. Carlotta thought it a wise idea to have a house party where she and Lord Neville could come to know one another and help Bethanny with such a decision as marriage. That being the case, you are not to mention such... sensitive information... at any point during your stay. Are we in accord?"

"I see. So Beth — Miss Lamont is not spoken for?"

"Not at the moment." His sister leaned forward, a devilish smile playing across her lips.

Graham felt his own spread into a wide grin, and he quickly pulled his sister in a tight hug. "You know, sometimes you're not so bad."

"I shall take that as a compliment," came her lighthearted reply.

"Now, I assume you will need to speak with His Grace?" Lady Southridge asked as soon as Graham released her.

"I — yes," Graham answered, his voice crackling slightly as he fought the urge to loosen his cravat.

"Graham, I'm not aware of the full situation, but he is your best friend, a brother. You must speak with him. You must work this out. I know enough of what happened to know that it was why you left for Scotland. You must work this out between you two." His sister spoke with thick compassion, her green eyes soft with love and loyalty.

"You are correct." Graham took a deep breath. "Do you know where I might find him?"

"In fact, I do. He was in his study, but I suggest you hurry. The men were to hunt this afternoon, provided it did not rain."

"Very well." Graham cleared his throat. Might as well get this part over and done with.

"It's good to have you here." She paused as she lingered at the doorway.

"Thank you… for letting me know," Graham spoke with heartfelt emotion.

"It's what family is for." She smiled softly. "I'll leave you now."

He watched his sister silently close the door. With a deep sigh, he closed his eyes and prayed a simple plea.

It had been a while since he'd spoken with God… but some things were too important to *not* include the Almighty.

And right now he could really use some assistance.

So with a determined stride, Graham left his room and headed to his friend's study.

The very room he had snuck into more than once when a boy, in order to steal brandy. The room in which he and Clairmont had mourned the passing of the late duke… and now the room where he would press his suit for his best friend's ward's hand.

How he wished it were as simple as stealing brandy.

But it wouldn't be; rather, it would likely be one of the most difficult things he'd ever do, but Graham wasn't about to let anything stand in the way of love. Some things were worth any cost.

Any fight.

Any price.

So with a solid knock, he awaited fate.

"Enter!" Clairmont's voice boomed, his irritation obvious in the single word.

Good heavens, this was not a promising start.

Graham opened the door slightly, feeling like a boy caught with something precious and forbidden... who had just been discovered.

Clairmont was bent over his desk, writing forcefully. Several missives were scattered on the wide expanse of rich wood, and one slipped to the floor as Clairmont violently pulled up the paper on which he was writing and crumped it.

As Graham took a step into the room, the duke paused and glanced up, his clear blue eyes piercing, evaluating.

Graham held his breath.

"It's about bloody time you got here," Clairmont grumbled then stood, taking great strides toward his friend.

"Pardon?" Graham asked, unsure as to what the duke meant by such a salutation.

"You're a bloody idiot, but I'm glad you're here." The duke held out his hand, and Graham took it, shaking it.

"Thank you?" Graham responded, still not sure as to what exactly was happening.

"You can wipe that damned look from your face, Graham. I'm not going to name my seconds. You bloody well look like you're watching a ghost," Clairmont grumbled, though a smile teased his lips.

"I — that is—"

"Stuttering is never a good sign. I take it you've spoken with your sister."

"Er — yes."

"Very well. Then you're aware of the situation?"

"Situation?"

"With Bethanny, you nodcock! That *is* the reason you hauled your bloody arse from Scotland, isn't it? Because if it's not—"

"It is," Graham assured the duke, still wanting to pinch himself to see if perhaps he had fallen asleep in the carriage and was dreaming this whole scene. Was it possible that his friend was actually *welcoming* his suit?

"Then I suggest you bloody well get started. You have some steep competition, with you leaving like a blasted French coward, only to return in the final hour."

"I—I was under the impression—"

"You drew your own conclusions, Graham. I'll admit I was enraged at your behavior, and let me say that if I ever hear of such an... example of lack of self-control around my ward..." he cleared his throat, "there *will* be no need for a duel because I'll shoot you in your sleep. Understood?"

"Quite." Graham nodded. "I—"

"I'm not finished." Clairmont paced before the low-burning fire. "I was enraged, and justifiably so. But when it became apparent that your intentions were honorable — though I must say your actions were not necessarily a clear example of that fact — I amended my opinion. But you and your bloody pride wouldn't hear of it! You left, and *that* is why you are at a severe disadvantage, my friend. If you truly want to win Bethanny's heart, her affections, then you must prove that you are sincerely more of a man than you have shown yourself to be thus far. And frankly, I don't know if you can do it. Now, I have been honest about my stance and my reservations. What have you to say for yourself?" The duke rocked back on his heels, his gaze intent as he studied Graham.

Gone was any semblance of his friend; rather, Graham knew he must plead his case as if he were facing Bethanny's father unknown and needing proper assurances.

Assurances that Graham didn't know how to express,

other than bleed out his bloody heart.

Pride be damned. It was the whole reason he was in this mess to begin with.

"I love her," Graham spoke softly, his words raw with unrestrained emotion. "I left hoping, foolishly, that she'd forget about me and find one more worthy. As much as you berated me for my actions, I berated myself far more. We, the two of us, are quite alike." Graham shrugged self-deprecatingly and took a few steps toward the fire. Staring into the orange embers, he continued. "As much as I hate to remind you, my past is far less pristine than I wish to admit. And to know that Bethanny is so… pure, perfect and undefiled. My unworthiness, as well as my pride," Graham conceded, "propelled my actions." He turned to match the duke's frank gaze. "Please understand, that while they could be misconstrued as a lack of loyalty, rather, I left because I know, above all things, that she deserves far better than me. And I'm only proving my lesser character by showing up, praying for a chance at stealing back her affections, because while she is strong enough to survive without me, I doubt my ability to survive without her," Graham finished then glanced to the fire, watching the orange flamed lick the wood hungrily.

"Well," Clairmont cleared his throat, "I must say… for coming in here like a stuttering fool, you surely waxed poetic when describing Bethanny."

"To do any less would be a gross disservice, Your Grace." Graham answered, taking the further step and showing deference by using the customary title.

"Graham, if you start *Your Gracing* me, I'll turn you out on your ear," Clairmont grumbled.

Graham nodded.

"Damn, the girl has you in knots, doesn't she? Not a grin or sarcastic remark? I feel as if I should be concerned for you, rather than her. Apparently I'm taking this becoming a fath—" Clairmont stopped mid-word, his eyes widening before glancing down at the Aubussan rug.

"Pardon? Do you mean to say...?" Graham's eyes widened as he noticed his friend's posture and the slight reddening of his ears, the telltale sign that he was trying to conceal something important. "Forgive me. It is none of my affair." Graham nodded.

"Actually, it will be a relief to tell someone. But first," Clairmont straightened his shoulders, "you have my permission to pursue Bethanny, provided that you remain within the proper bounds of propriety concerning courtship. My dear wife will take over all chaperone duties and..." the duke took a warning step toward Graham, "I purposefully placed Bethanny on the third floor, in a room I will not disclose. So, there will be no climbing in efforts to secure a private audience with her... unless you wish to pummel to your death and bruise your pretty head."

"I do believe this is the second time in less than a quarter hour that I've been given a death threat," Graham remarked with slight sarcasm, his tension beginning to recede.

"They are not empty threats, my friend." The duke raised a challenging eyebrow.

"Noted."

"Now," Clairmont strode to his desk, "have a seat."

Graham walked to a wingback chair opposite the duke and sat in the plush red velvet.

"Here." A box of sweet-smelling cigars was opened before Graham. "Take one, for we, my friend, have a reason to celebrate." Clairmont grinned, his own cigar tipping from his lips as he held it in his teeth.

"Would there be an heir on the way, by chance?" Graham asked, his grin wide as he sniffed the tobacco and sweet spicy scent before clipping off the end and taking the offered light.

"Indeed," Clairmont affirmed, his grin widening till he withdrew the cigar from his mouth.

"Brilliant! I'm thrilled for you ol' chap! This does call for a grand celebration! I assume that Carlotta is not within her confinement as of yet?"

"No, but soon. She was practically racing across town getting this house party together before she began to... er... display her condition."

"Many felicitations to you!" Graham raised his cigar.

"Yes, well, see that we have another reason to celebrate soon. Hmm?" The duke issued a challenge to Graham, his intent clear.

"Believe me, I shall do my best."

"See that you do."

CHAPTER FOURTEEN

BETHANNY FLIPPED THE page of her book and let out an impatient sigh.

Botheration.

Where *was* everyone! Didn't they know she was sitting on pins and needles waiting to hear about what was taking place with Lord Graham? With more than a little irritation, Bethanny strode to the window — pointless as it was — and searched the grounds for any sign of him.

A knock interrupted her futile searching.

"Yes?" Bethanny responded instantly, her heart's rhythm increasing its pace as she waited.

"Climbing the walls yet?" Lady Southridge asked with a wide grin as she let herself into the room.

"Practically," Bethanny admitted.

"No need. I have spoken with your swain, and I must assure you, there is nothing to worry about, save the sanity of my younger brother. Surely you are driving him mad! It is delightful! I never thought I'd see the day when my — er, shall I say — free-spirited brother fell in love!" She clapped her hands and bit her lower lip.

"Truly? What happened? I've been going mad myself up here as I waited!" Bethanny strode forward and grasped the older woman's hands.

"You mustn't worry, dear. If I'm correct — and I always am." She winked. "Then your Lord Graham is speaking with the duke right now."

"About?"

"About the weather." Lady Southridge rolled her eyes. "You, you ninny! Of course they're talking about you!"

"I deducted as much, thank you kindly. However, what *about* me in particular are they discussing?" Bethanny asked archly as she released Lady Southridge and sat in the wingback chair by the fire.

"You'll simply have to wait and see," Lady Southridge shot back as she followed Bethanny's example and sat in the chaise.

"Pardon?" Bethanny felt her eyebrows shoot up in surprise.

"Don't you think it's quite unfair that you are up here, knowing all that happens below pertaining to my brother with no mystery involved at all? No! I cry foul. Therefore, you must also wait in some suspense, my dear. After all, anticipation is part of the fun." Lady Southridge hitched a shoulder, a gleaming smile of innocent intent teasing her lips.

"Cruel," Bethanny replied.

"No. Simply being fair."

"Very well," Bethanny conceded. "Must I still wait till supper?"

"Indeed. Because while I'm certain the gentlemen are conversing about you, I also know the duke has no intention of doing Lord Graham any favors. If he wishes to win your hand and heart, he must do so without any assistance."

"But—"

"I know you think he's already won both, dear. But let me give you some wise advice from an old lady."

"Old?" Bethanny asked with a smirk.

"If you ever disclose that I called myself thus, I shall smite thee!" Lady Southridge stood and struck a dramatic pose.

"Understood," Bethanny answered through her laugh.

"Now then, listen closely, my dear. These are pearls of wisdom you must keep. String them together and wear them around your neck, close to your heart." Lady Southridge touched the neckline of her gown to emphasize her point as she took her seat. "There is something to be said about courtship. Is there anything more romantic, anything closer to your heart than to remember your lover's actions as he pursued you relentlessly?" She paused. "As women, we need to be wanted, loved, cherished. The process of courtship is a beautiful opportunity for a gentleman to display his affection, his loyalty to you. When you're my age, you'll be grateful that you took this opportunity to let my brother pursue you properly, adding to the wonderful memories you're sure to create in your future. Let this be a wonderful beginning, where you are able to see his heart, and in that, carry that precious view into your future together. Let him chase you, my dear, for as much as we women love to be pursued…" she leaned forward, spearing Bethanny with a direct gaze, "men love to take part in the chase."

Bethanny grinned, warmed by the idea of memories that would keep her company when she got older. Truly was there anything more endearing than to recollect those past stolen moments with Lord Graham? Nothing was dearer to her heart. How much more would the upcoming memories be when combined with an honest pursuit of her affections without the hindrance of her guardian's lack of approval?

Provided the duke *gave* his approval.

"Er, Lady Southridge, the duke *was* intending on giving his approval to Graham to press his suit, was he not? I believe it was implied earlier, but I didn't ask the direct question—"

"Dear, if he wasn't welcome, he wouldn't have made it to the front step." She nodded decisively.

Bethanny took in a relieved breath. "Then I shall simply... wait."

"You're not simply waiting, dear." Lady Southridge stood and walked to the door. "You're setting the stage. After all, each epic romance has its hurdle, does it not? You're simply making the obstacle clearer for him to see and dismantle."

"What obstacle?" Bethanny asked, curious, since the only obstacle she'd considered was the duke's approval.

"Fear, my love. Fear."

"Of me?"

"No, fear of failure, fear unworthiness, lack of faith." Lady Southridge's tone was soft.

"I'm well-versed in fear, it seems. I've lived in its shadow for some time. Strange that I didn't even realize it at first," Bethanny confessed.

"That is why it's so dangerous. But have no fear, for if there is one weapon against fear that is always sure to emerge the victor... it is love." Lady Southridge offered Bethanny a warm smile and slipped out the door.

Love indeed.

Graham strode purposefully to the library, cursing under his breath. Damn the man! When he had asked where he might find Bethanny, the duke simply grinned.

Grinned!

As if Graham's entire future didn't depend on the woman's forthcoming decision. He could have strangled the man had he not been utterly grateful that the duke was not trying to strangle *him* for his affection toward Bethanny.

Affection? If what he *felt* was affection, then the English

Channel was a small pond. No this was love, pure and menacing, that was slowly driving him mad.

Because love unrequited, or on the verge of being unrequited, was worse than any torture Napoleon could invent.

So he found himself searching high and low, the gardens and grounds, the parlors and dining rooms, the sitting rooms and finally now the library. He *almost* thought the duke was *hiding* the girl! But why?

Unless…

Was she out with Lord Neville? He hadn't seen the man since arriving.

But he hadn't seen Bethanny either.

The whole party *was* set up to promote a courtship. Could he be too late? Was Neville proposing right now? A cold chill of fear caused perspiration to dampen the nape of his neck. *No!* He couldn't allow it!

Lost in his own fears, he opened the door the library with far too much force, and the heavy wooden door swung open only to hit the wall behind it, creating a loud thud.

"My heavens!" Beatrix stood, clasping her heart. Her eyes were wide as she glanced from the door to Lord Graham.

Graham felt his face heat with humility as he cleared his throat. "A thousand apologies, Miss Lamont." He adjusted his coat nervously. As he did he noticed another person in the room.

Neville.

He narrowed his eyes at the gentleman. Rather than hold the gaze, Lord Neville glanced away then slid his gaze to Beatrix, then back to Lord Graham as he cleared his throat.

"I thank you, Miss Lamont for your… assistance. Good day." He bowed smartly and left.

Graham had the intense urge to trip the man as he walked by; rather, he simply glared at him.

However, Neville simply murmured a soft, "Pardon," as

he slipped by.

Hardly the response Graham was expecting.

Especially from a rival.

Confused, Lord Graham turned back to Beatrix. She was tucking a stray lock of chestnut hair behind her ear, her cheeks blooming with color. Upon closer examination, Graham noticed her hair was slightly disheveled, and her lips rather... pink.

As if they'd been assaulted by a man's kiss.

But the only man in the room was...

Neville!

Could it be? Were his affections changing to the younger sister? It would be a scandal for sure! And what of Bethanny! Immediately, righteous anger swelled within Graham, ironically, on behalf of Bethanny. She didn't deserve such treatment!

"I... am trying not to assume—" he began.

"No, no, my lord. It..." she took a deep breath and strode forward, "it isn't as you think. Truly," she pleaded, her brown eyes so like Bethanny's it made his heart ache.

"I'll not press you, Miss Lamont, but I must urge you to use caution—"

"As I said, you are mistaken, it — I wasn't — he..."

"Stuttering is never a good sign, Miss Lamont," Graham teased softly, hoping to relieve some of the tension radiating from her.

"Indeed. It is not. Have..." she delicately cleared her throat, "have you seen my older sister?"

The minx surely knew how to steer the attention away from herself!

"In fact, no, I have not," he answered, his tone wary as he studied the innocent expression in her eyes.

"Ah." She nodded.

Graham waited.

She shrugged her shoulders and made an effort to pass

him.

He stepped in front of her. "Miss Lamont, I get the feeling you know something that I do not."

"Indeed. I would think that I know a few things that you do not, my lord," she challenged back and took a step to the side, quickly passing him.

"Miss Lamont, may I remind you that I just caught you in what could easily be deemed a compromising situation—"

"There's not need to be threatening," Beatrix ground out as she turned to glare at him.

"Where is your sister?"

"Here."

"In the library?" Graham turned to glance about the room.

"No, *here* at the manor. I'm sure you'll run into her at supper." The girl gave him an arch grin and all but fled.

"Bloody hell," Graham swore softly. Well, if there was one good thing that came out of his searching, at least he knew that wherever Bethanny was, she wasn't keeping company with Lord Neville.

Rather, the younger sister was.

Interesting.

CHAPTER FIFTEEN

BETHANNY TOSSED HER book on the side table as soon as she heard someone twist the knob of her door. It was torture, waiting, not knowing, and yet *knowing* that he was there.

It was going to drive her mad.

"Bethanny?" Beatrix called softly as she entered the room and closed the door softly behind her. Her brown eyes were twinkling as she bit her lower lip and hurried into room with a whisper of her skirt.

"Yes? Please, in the name of all that is merciful, tell me you have *some* sort of news. I'm dying up here waiting!" Bethanny spoke earnestly, her desperation evident.

"I saw him." Beatrix's grin widened. "And he was asking about you. He was most insistent! In fact he tried to block my escape, so desperate was he to find out your whereabouts!"

"Truly?" Bethanny asked, her lips spreading into a wide grin.

"Indeed." Beatrix's eyes danced with delight.

"So... what is he doing now? And where did you see him?" Bethanny asked as she bit her lower lip.

"Uh..." Beatrix began then shifted uneasily.

Bethanny felt her brow furrow as she studied the sudden bloom of color that highlighted Beatrix's face, along with the downward glance of her gaze.

"I saw him in the library," she replied, then cleared her throat delicately and strode to the window.

"And? Please, tell me everything!" Bethanny asked.

"And he cornered me and tried to find out where you were. That is simply all." Beatrix shrugged, but she wouldn't make eye contact.

Odd.

"Very well. What did *you* say then?" Bethanny tried a different approach.

"Ah, well." Beatrix turned to face her then, her eyebrow arching with mischief. "I simply told him that you were here, at the manor. He didn't appreciate my information."

"Ha! I should think not! But it was very clever of you. What did he say then?"

"He wanted to know *where* at the manor, and I simply said that he'd surely see you at supper. Then I fled before he could question me further!"

Bethanny took a deep breath of delight. "Evening cannot come soon enough. I'm quite certain that today has been the slowest day I've ever endured!"

"Lord Graham surely shares that sentiment!" Beatrix teased.

"Serves him right."

"Indeed it does."

Bethanny glanced to the window and was lost in her own thoughts when she heard her sister's soft question.

"Bethanny... how... that is... you've always been so sure about Lord Graham. There was never another. How did you know that your heart belonged with his? Was there something that happened that offered that insight? Was it simply a feeling?" Beatrix asked tentatively, her hands smoothing her light blue skirt.

Bethanny regarded her sister. "I'm not certain. But I do know that from the first time we met, though I was still quite young, I knew that I wanted him to see me as more than a silly little girl. When I had that opportunity, I took it and ran." Bethanny giggled softly, remembering her flirtation with Lord Graham before he was certain of her identity.

"Oh," Beatrix said, her brow slightly furrowed as if frustrated.

"Why do you ask?" Bethanny placed a soft hand on her sister's shoulder.

"I—"

"Bethanny?" Carlotta's voice came through the door as she softly knocked.

Bethanny offered an apologetic smile to her sister. "Yes," she answered Carlotta.

Carlotta opened the door and entered, followed by Berty. "Ah, good. You are indeed here, Beatrix. I have news, and I wish to tell you all at once." Carlotta's face glowed with joy.

Beatrix and Bethanny shared a glance.

"Indeed? What do you wish to tell us?" Beatrix asked.

"Yes, what's the big secret? She wouldn't tell me till we found the two of you!" Berty placed her hands on her hips.

"Well…" Carlotta gestured to the settee and chairs by the fire, burning low in the grate and then waited for Bethanny and her sisters to sit.

"Now, I have some news to tell you, and I wanted you to hear it from me rather than the gossips of the *ton*."

"Yes?" Bethanny asked, her suspicions growing.

Carlotta took a deep breath and placed a delicate hand to her abdomen. "You are going to be aunts."

It took a moment for the news to register with Bethanny. With a delighted clap, she stood and moved to embrace her beloved guardian. "Truly? How wonderful! When can we expect to have a little one to spoil? Because you should know now that we intend to do just that!"

Carlotta hugged her back tightly, the scent of lavender gently floating from her skin and offering the comfort of memories to Bethanny. Soon Beatrix and Berty were squealing and offering congratulations as well.

"This is the best news! You must answer Bethanny's question! When? How long must we wait till we can hold the little dear?" Beatrix asked, her face lit up with enchantment.

"I believe very late winter. February," Carlotta answered.

"How long till your confinement?" Berty asked.

"I have a couple months left. So…" Carlotta shifted her gaze to Bethanny, "*when* this engagement happens between you and Lord Graham, it must be a short one." Carlotta smiled.

"I do not think that will be an issue." Beatrix cut a grin to Bethanny. "He already tried to block my departure from the library, so desperate was he to find her."

"Truly? How wonderful! The duke did indeed have a good plan in keeping you away, dear. He's likely going mad!" Carlotta clapped her hands.

"Bloodthirsty lot. Poor man." Berty shook her head. When Bethanny glared at her, she amended. "I didn't say he didn't deserve it. I quite like the torture he's enduring. It's about time!"

"There's still hours left till evening. What lengths do you think he'll go to in his determination to find Bethanny?" Beatrix asked, a wicked grin teasing her lips.

"One thing is for certain. Whatever lengths he attempts will not be nearly enough. We've ensured that. Supper should prove to be quite entertaining. Don't you agree?" Carlotta grinned.

"Indeed," Bethanny agreed. Though the wait might kill her in the process.

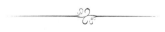

Truly, he felt as if a year had passed in only one day. His impatient nature was making him overly dramatic.

Bloody hell.

When he saw the damnable woman, he was going to snatch her away in front of God and everyone. To hell with the consequences! After all, the consequences were exactly what he was trying to create! Marriage!

A half-mad bark of laughter escaped. To think that no more than few months ago, marriage was the last thing on his mind. Then, as the idea had become more of a necessity, he'd looked upon the blessed union as more of a chore. To think he had come to the point of contemplating compromising the girl in front of her guardian to simply ensure that she'd be his. It was madness. Not to mention suicidal. The duke had made it clear that it was to be Bethanny's choice. So regardless of his impatience or his desire, his love, he couldn't do a damn thing unless the girl wanted him.

Please, Lord, let her want him.

Beatrix had made it clear that Bethanny wouldn't be found till supper, so Graham had gone out to the grounds of Greenford Waters, removing himself from scaring the servants and starting fisticuffs with the other guests. He surely wasn't good company at the moment.

But at least he realized this; surely that must redeem him somewhat.

He paused in his walk and glanced at the regal wood that edged the property. The tall, majestic trees pointed upward, and he followed their direction till his gaze settled on the pale blue sky, dotted with creamy clouds. With a deep breath, he felt his tension recede. Forcing Bethanny's hand, or anyone's hand, for that matter, wouldn't work. And truth be told, he didn't want Bethanny because he'd made sure she didn't have choice; he wanted her to want him, to need him like air.

Like he needed her.

He considered their past and felt ashamed. Either he had

taken brazen liberties with her, when his self-control was lacking and his desire had overcome his sane judgment, or he'd pushed her away.

She deserved more.

Hadn't he always said as much. But what she deserved was more *from him.*

She deserved to be pursued, chased, shown that he would ride to the end of the world to save her, to have her belong to him and him alone.

Or simply ride at breakneck speed from Scotland to Bath.

She needed to see that his desire was far more than simply attraction; it was attachment, a weaving of the fabric of his very soul intertwined with hers. It was knowing that her breath was as vital to him as it was to her, each heartbeat the same. It was telling her that she was beautiful, but not just on the surface, but the deep beauty of a rare woman who has the purity and splendor of a lovely heart. It was the way her smile lit up a room, the way her laugh haunted him, even when she wasn't around.

It was the hope of having daughters who looked exactly like their mother, with decadent brown eyes and silky, coffee-colored hair.

All calling *him* father.

Now, if only there was some way to communicate that in a few hours, in a few conversations that had to take place in the company of a proper chaperone.

Not likely.

Graham sighed.

There was only one way.

Carlotta.

With a determined stride, Graham made his way back to the house. It was now or never.

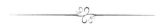

Supper had finally arrived. And, of course, Bethanny had spent the past two hours preparing for it. With the utmost care, she had selected her soft yellow dress with the pale blue belt. Molly had gone to great lengths in styling her hair for the evening. The decadent locks were pinned gently around the crown of her head, the candlelight causing a shimmering golden hue to highlight the rich color. Bethanny sighed as she tilted her head slightly in studying her reflection. Indeed, she looked beautiful, but more importantly, she *felt* beautiful, from the anticipation glowing in her dark brown eyes, to the sky blue slippers she wore. Biting her lip in nervous anxiety for the last few moments to hurry on their way so that she could leave the prison of her room and face her future, she closed her eyes and willed her heart to slow its excited cadence.

Glancing to the door, she debated whether she should arrive early or late. There were other guests in the house, not that she had seen much of them, but surely they would be milling about conversing. That decided, she stood and strode to the door. With a final glance at the mirror, she saw her reflection gazing back at her, a light dancing in her eyes that was born of anticipation and wonder.

Tonight would define her future.

With a fortifying breath, Bethanny strode into the hall. The candlelight danced off the walls, frolicking with the shadows it created. Glancing to Beatrix's door, she paused to listen, curious if her sister was already downstairs or still preparing.

Through the heavy wooden door, she could hear her sister's maid answering her question, and so she continued on.

Would Lord Graham be there already? Waiting for her? Her heart leapt with hope. Hurrying her steps, she took the stairs quicker than usual and was practically running once she hit the marbled floor of the main level hall. Her slippers skidded slightly, and a grin teased her lips. How many times had she and her sisters skated across the highly polished floor in just their stockings? It was tempting, but now was not the time.

"Miss Lamont." A rich voice caressed her name.

Spinning to her left, she watched as Lord Graham strode toward her with the lithe strength that had haunted her memories and invaded her dreams.

"Lord Graham." She forced her voice to be calm, level, unaffected. Her heart was an entirely different matter. It pounded wildly, racing.

His tawny eyes roamed her features, settling on her lips for a fraction of a second longer than the rest of her face. A pained expression lurked in his eyes. "Beautiful as always. You are quite a difficult lady to locate," he added lightly, though his expression was one of deep emotion.

Good.

Let him linger in the unknown as she had for the past weeks. Yet another quiet voice reminded her that he'd had his own demons to fight during that time, as well.

"I would think that I should be exceedingly easy to locate, my lord." She raised a daring eyebrow. "This *is* my guardian's estate, and it is a house party. And before that, I hadn't strayed further than the occasional ballroom in London."

Lord Graham paused as if weighing his words, his eyebrows darting upward in recognition of her jab. "Indeed. Rather I was referring to locating you *this* day."

"And I believe that my guardian explained to you that I was... indisposed till supper." It went against her nature to be crisp and coolly polite, yet she needed, with a desperation she couldn't put into words, for him to pursue her. From day one, she had made her affection known, pursued *him.* Now the tables were turned. For as much as she wanted him, she wanted him to need her just as desperately. If he did, then a little cool aloofness wouldn't hinder him.

"That is true." He nodded. "Since we have a few

moments till supper is served, would you do the honor of accompanying me on a short walk?"

More than anything, she wanted to agree, to throw her arms around him and pull him into a kiss that would melt any restraint he might possess, but she remembered the duke's terms and Carlotta's words.

"I'm afraid I cannot, at least not without—"

"Right on time," Lord Graham interrupted, his face lighting up a wide grin that caused his dimples to surface.

Bethanny swallowed hard. As much as his smile had haunted her, nothing was more potent than gazing upon it face to face. He was beautiful, a picture of masculine glory that took her breath away. She startled as Carlotta placed a gentle hand on her shoulder.

"Lord Graham asked for permission to take a walk with you. I went by your room just a moment ago, and upon discovering you had already left, I assumed you'd be here." She smiled encouragingly.

"Yes, thank you," Bethanny murmured to Carlotta.

Lord Graham held out his arm, and Bethanny placed her gloved hand over it, immediately warmed by the simple fact that she was touching him.

"A turn in the back garden would be ideal for such a short walk. Dinner should be served in less than a half hour," Carlotta added helpfully.

"Delightful. Don't you agree, Miss Lamont?" Lord Graham turned to her, his smile soft.

"Indeed." Bethanny nodded, her heart still hammering. The whole situation felt... awkward. Not necessarily in a bad way, simply because she knew that they needed to talk, and nothing could be said, aside from idle chatter about the weather and nonsense, until they had worked through what had happened.

And what the future held.

And *that* conversation was surely not going to take place

in the small back garden with Carlotta at their heels.

So she remained in purgatory, heaven only a breath away but utterly out of reach. "Are you enjoying your time here at Greenford Waters, Lord Graham?" Bethanny asked, hating the bland topic, but needing desperately for something to speak about, even if to only hear his voice.

"Each moment continues to be better than the last," Lord Graham spoke softly, as if whispering a secret.

Gooseflesh prickled across her skin as she delighted in the soft caress of his voice.

"That is good. What did you do this afternoon?" she asked, her voice slightly higher in pitch, revealing her tension.

"Waited," he answered succinctly.

Bethanny turned her head toward him. "For?" she asked, though she suspected the answer.

"You," he replied quickly, as if any other answer would be utterly ridiculous.

"I see," she replied, not sure how to continue on that topic without going into other things... that shouldn't be said with a chaperone.

"Tell me, Miss Lamont, what did you do this afternoon?" Lord Graham asked after a few moments of silence.

Bethanny glanced about at the small hedge of boxwoods that created a small garden inside of the larger one. "I read, spent time with my sisters. Nothing too terribly exciting." She shrugged.

Lord Graham nodded and continued to lead them on in silence. Carlotta's echoing footsteps were the only noise in the deserted area.

Forget awkward, this is miserable! Bethanny lamented. In all her dreams, in all the hopes she had over the past weeks and especially today, this was *not* how she'd imagined their reunion. Stilted conversation, silence, and an eagle-eyed chaperone.

This is what she was counting the hours for? Yet there

was a bright star in the sky, radiating hope. He had said he had been waiting for her all day; surely he wouldn't let this pathetic conversation be the end of it all.

Surely he'd do something... more.

Because it would have to be him. He would need to initiate it; he would have to chase.

And Bethanny would make sure she was easy to catch.

Just not *too* easy.

CHAPTER SIXTEEN

LORD GRAHAM WAS close to his breaking point. It was sheer willpower that kept him from growling in frustration.

With his luck, Bethanny would think he was growling at *her*.

That would be bloody brilliant.

And the perfect end to a miserable day.

She was so beautiful, so tempting. From the top of her glorious mane of hair to the pale blue slippers peeking from her gown, she was a lethal threat to his self-control.

Damn Carlotta for insisting on chaperoning.

Though it was probably her presence that was saving his life. Goodness only knew how he'd stop short of ruining the girl if he had her alone. And only hell knew what torture he'd endure at the duke's hand if he were to do such a thing.

Also, he was assuming she was half as in love with him as he was mad for her.

A chill ran down his spine. She *did* hold affection for him, didn't she? It was hard to tell, her normally warm demeanor was cooler, aloof.

Distrusting.

He hated that he was the cause. He had many sins to make up for.

And he'd start making up for them now.

It just would be hell of lot easier if he didn't have to proper about it.

He shifted his gaze toward her. The graceful arch of her neck invited is kiss; he could almost taste the soft creamy texture of her skin. Her form was intoxicating, alluring in its perfection, and his hands nearly trembled with restraint as he wanted to pull her into a tight embrace.

And more.

So much more.

Clenching his teeth against his raging desire, he glanced back to her face, to find her watching him with an openly curious expression. Unable to hide his emotions, he knew that his expression was one of fierce desire.

Of passionate love.

The dawn of understanding illuminated her bottomless eyes, and her gaze widened as her lips parted, then a slight smile began at her lips, traveling upward till it was reflected in her eyes. The guarded expression that had prevented him from reading her expression fell away, giving light to the desire mirrored in his own.

"I don't mean to interrupt…" Carlotta spoke, her tone hesitant.

Graham refused to glance away from Bethanny, even for a moment.

"Supper will be served momentarily. We should return," Carlotta finished, her tone more resolute.

Bethanny was first to break their gaze, her brown eyes turning to her beloved guardian, her head nodding in understanding.

Bethanny began following Carlotta to the house but paused when Graham placed his hand atop of hers. Gently, he removed her hand and held it within both of his. Without breaking his gaze, he lifted it and kissed it softly. He closed his eyes, inhaling the rich alluring scent of her skin to overwhelm his senses, and teased her gloved flesh with the end of his nose, before placing another lingering kiss, this one on her wrist.

Her sharp intake of breath caused him to glance back up. Her eyes were wide and excited as she bit her lower lip.

"Bethanny," Carlotta warned.

Bethanny glanced heavenward, as if praying for deliverance... or for Carlotta to disappear, and waited as Graham straightened and pulled her in closer as they walked toward the house.

To think, all day he'd been waiting for supper.

Now all he wanted was for the bloody thing to be over with so he could steal her away.

Because that's exactly what he was going to do. If he could only think of a way to go about it without risking his life.

Supper was an acute form of torture, Bethanny decided. Lord Graham was seated beside the duke, and thus was across the table and up three spaces from where she was seated. Upon seeing the seating assignments, her eyes narrowed at the duke, not certain if he had placed Lord Graham beside him simply to keep him away from her, and in agony longer, or if he was placing him there because of his rank and connection with the family.

She rather suspected it was the first reason.

Miserable man.

Lord Neville was seated to her left, and Lord Bruxton to her right. Lord Bruxton was nearing fifty and was a business associate of the duke's from Bath. The only conversation he offered was the occasional "This is delightful!" as he continued to feed himself with a little too much enthusiasm.

"Lord Neville, have you had a pleasant day?" Bethanny asked, trying to start up any semblance of conversation in efforts to move the night along quicker than the snail's pace it seemed to be currently.

"Er, yes," he answered with a slight smile.

Bethanny felt her brow furrow. Was Lord Neville *blushing?* It certainly seemed so!

He cleared his throat awkwardly and cast a furtive glance down to the end of the table.

Bethanny followed his gaze.

Beatrix?

Acting on an instinct, Bethanny turned back to Lord Neville. "Tell me, Lord Neville, have you seen our library here at Greenford Waters?"

Lord Neville paled slightly but nodded, reaching for his wine glass.

"It's quite extensive. I'd show you myself, but I'll not have a spare moment tomorrow." Or so she hoped! "My dear sister, Beatrix, loves the library. She would be a wonderful candidate to show you." Bethanny offered her most innocent smile.

Lord Neville gave her his full attention, his eyes narrowing slightly as he seemed to debate whether she was innocent or simply fishing for information.

Bethanny held her guiltless smile firmly, adding a slight arch to her brow as she waited.

"I believe I'm leaving in the morning," he replied after a moment.

"Oh? Why so soon?"

"I... am needed elsewhere." He gave her a curt smile and turned his attention to his food.

Throughout the rest of the course, Bethanny watched his gaze continually falter as it would shift toward Beatrix.

Could it be? Had Beatrix somehow captured the interest

of the reclusive lord?

Bethanny moved the roast pigeon about on her plate, her mind wandering, till she felt a slight prickle of awareness on the back of her neck. Immediately she glanced up toward Lord Graham, instinctively knowing it was he who'd caused the tingling sensation. Indeed he was gazing at her, boldly, not caring that the other guests could easily see his intentions.

It was delicious.

And Bethanny allowed herself to return the gaze, basking in the glow.

His lips twitched, softening the desire on his face and phasing into an expression of amusement, one of secret delight as he glanced at the duke, who then cleared his throat meaningfully.

Bethanny felt a soft smile tease her lips; then she gasped as Lord Graham winked scandalously at her. Glancing about, she wondered if anyone had seen it. Beatrix met her gaze with a knowing grin and a raised eyebrow, her expression one of mischief and delight.

Thankfully, it seemed as if Beatrix was the only one who'd noticed.

And Carlotta, but she was glancing down at her plate, her face pinched as if trying to restrain a giggle at Bethanny's expense.

All too slowly, the final course was cleared. Blessedly, the duke stood and asked the gentlemen to accompany him to the retiring room for a brandy.

Like sheep, the other two gentlemen followed, but Lord Graham lingered last. He glanced to where the duke had exited, and back to Bethanny, but in truth, his hands were tied in such matters. With a reluctant grin, he bowed and left, following the other gentlemen.

"Ladies? Shall we retire as well for sherry? Then I have some lovely games planned for later, once the gentlemen join us." Carlotta spoke brightly as she stood and led them into the light blue sitting room, the one with the pianoforte. However the room was arranged differently than usual. The furniture lined the walls, allowing a wide-open space in the center of the large room. Curious, Bethanny glanced to Carlotta.

Carlotta simply winked and sat along the wall.

Bethanny followed suit, choosing a seat beside her sister, and waited.

The gentlemen hopefully would finish their brandy quickly.

One could pray at least.

One day, the Duke of Clairmont was going to pay dearly for his misdeeds.

Dearly.

Perhaps he'd have an heir that was just as stubborn as he, causing him to want to pull out his legendary black-as-sin hair.

Better yet, he'd go grey all at once.

Or lose his hair.

Yes! Graham thought. And gain weight. Like a potbellied stallion. Truly it would be glorious.

Damn the man, he was playing Graham like a concerto violin, and Graham wasn't appreciating it, especially since he had to play by the duke's rules.

Wanting to preserve his life and all.

But most importantly, have Bethanny.

Assuming she was amicable to the idea... but he was quite certain she would be; if her earlier behavior was any indication.

But who could understand the mind of a woman?

Not he, and he'd grown up with one constantly bossing him around.

Granted, he should put his sister in an entirely different

category… but still. She was a woman.

As he considered it, he realized that he hadn't seen his sister at dinner.

She was never one to miss out on food.

This couldn't be good.

To think that she once thought that *he* was the one who should never be left unattended.

Ha!

Nervous, Graham had the intense desire to begin checking behind curtains or around corners for her.

Women like Lady Southridge could never be underestimated.

He'd have to check on her whereabouts later.

"Gentlemen, I believe my lovely wife has a few diverting games for us to take part in. Shall we join the ladies?" The duke rose with his crystal brandy glass still in hand, raising it highly as if toasting his own brilliant idea.

"About bloody time," Graham spoke softly.

"Yes, Graham?" The duke turned toward him, his eyebrow arched in challenge.

"Ah, just affirming the validity of your decision, Your Grace." Graham replied with a hint of sarcasm.

To his left, Lord Neville snickered, trying to cover up his amusement with a cough.

Graham shot him a glare, but he couldn't seem to muster any venom for the expression, not after he had determined that Neville wasn't a threat to his pursuit of Bethanny.

The younger sister, however, was a different matter. One he'd keep in the back of his mind for later.

"You always were smarter than your looked, Graham," the duke shot back, pulling him from his thoughts.

"Indeed." He nodded and waited as the gentlemen filed out of the room, the duke lingering behind. Graham approached him quietly. "Being I'm so intelligent and all, I had hoped I might have some sort of semblance of privacy for

Bethanny that I might..." he glanced to the final gentleman as he left the room, "ask her an important question."

"Perhaps. Although a truly intelligent gentleman wouldn't need privacy." The duke speared him with a meaningful expression.

"You've got to be joking." Graham took a step back. Had Clairmont lost his mind?

"Graham, once you hit the point of desperation, privacy will not matter. All that will matter is that you find a way to secure her heart to yours. You'll not care if you have an audience of one, or three hundred. Because all you'll see... is her. All you'll hear... is her answer. You could be in the presence of the Regent and Napoleon having tea, and you wouldn't care a whit. Because all you'd be aware of is *her*."

"I bloody am only aware of her. I'm only thinking of her comfort..."

"You, my dear boy..." The duke patted Lord Graham's head.

Like a dog.

And Graham affirmed his earlier curse of the potbellied stallion.

Only this time, he was a gelding,

"Know nothing about how women think. There's nothing more romantic than an overt expression of love. There is a time for candlelight, romance, and whispered love, but there is also a time to throw caution to the wind and to go with your heart, your very impatient, demanding, and lonely heart. And when you do, your actions become the very stories they can't wait to tell the lovely children you'll undoubtedly have. Remember that."

The duke nodded and strode away, leaving Graham alone with his very loud, very demanding, and lonely heart.

And at once, he knew exactly what he'd do.

He only hoped that the duke knew what he was talking about. Or else it was going to be a disaster.

CHAPTER SEVENTEEN

"CHARADES!" CARLOTTA ANNOUNCED to the group as the gentleman settled themselves from their arrival. Lord Graham was last, his gaze meeting hers immediately, a fierce light of determination causing goose bumps to prickle on her arms.

A few ladies clapped, bringing Bethanny's attention back to the group, their gloved hands causing the sound to be a muted thump. A few gentleman bit back groans.

Bethanny glanced at the array of guests, amused. Lady Whitehead and her daughter seemed overly eager, and Lord Neville looked as if he wished he could blend in with the rug on the floor.

Apparently charades wasn't the first selection of diverting games for the reclusive bachelor.

Bethanny bit back a laugh at the poor man's expense, but before she could fight it too terribly, it was lost to a sense of curiosity. Lord Neville, as uncomfortable as he appeared, cast his gaze toward Beatrix.

And lingered.

Beatrix seemed utterly unaware, and Bethanny had the sisterly urge to inconspicuously sidle up to her and pinch her till she noticed.

There was far more going on than either would admit.

Very well, she'd simply watch and, when the moment came, she'd pounce and figure out what exactly was going on between her sister and the reclusive lord.

"You suspect something as well," a low voice murmured softly to her left.

Only a fraction of a moment later, her body sensed the warmth coming from his nearness, sending her into a state of provocative desire.

And the parlor was *not* the place to have such emotions.

"Indeed. Have you also noticed something?" Bethanny asked, her tone slightly breathless, though she was desperately trying to control it.

"I have my own suspicions... though I must admit I've been far too distracted by someone else to pay proper attention to the amorous intentions of others," he answered.

Bethanny met his gaze. The intensity of it was deep and comforting, like steaming chocolate on a dreary day, inviting and uplifting, yet secretive and alluring.

The man could cause more emotions than a Shakespearian play.

And all it had taken were a few moments, a few seconds of conversation, and she was in knots.

"Are you enjoying your evening?" Bethanny asked, trying to steer the conversation into safer waters.

"I can think of ways I'd enjoy it more," Graham replied, his gaze dancing as he lingered on her face and settled on her lips.

Involuntarily, Bethanny moistened them, trying to quell the intense desire to bridge the short foot of space and take him up on his implied offer.

Lord Graham groaned softly, closing his eyes as if in agony. "Clairmont is a master of torture," he whispered softly, more to himself than anyone.

But Bethanny heard and couldn't help the small laugh that escaped.

His eyes shot open. "You're just as bad, minx. But don't worry. I'll even the score… someday," he promised.

"I certainly hope so," Bethanny heard herself reply before she could stop herself. A deep blush was painful across her face.

"I always make good on my word, love. Always," he whispered, reaching for her hand, and placing a smoldering kiss to the back of it. "Please excuse me. I have to speak with our hostess." With a fiery, lingering gaze, he spun and left Bethanny with her heart hammering and her belly warm with anticipation.

She watched as Graham approached Carlotta and spoke softly to her. Carlotta's eyes widened, and she glanced to Bethanny then back to Graham before excusing herself from a few other guests and conversing privately with him a few feet away from the group.

Bethanny grew suspicious.

Eyes narrowed, she watched as Graham spoke and Carlotta nodded.

Drat.

Neither gave away any indication as to what they were planning.

With a reluctant sigh, she glanced to the duke, who was conversing with Neville. He met her gaze and raised his glass as if toasting her.

Something was underfoot.

A moment later, Carlotta clapped, calling the attention back to herself. "Shall we begin? I've had a volunteer to begin the game! Lord Graham, if you please?"

Lord Graham smiled tensely and strode to the middle of the room. The twenty or so guests backed away, giving him room to proceed. Bethanny walked over to her sister, Beatrix, and waited, her brow furrowed, curiosity eating at her attention.

Lord Graham bowed and crossed the room toward her. With a smart bow, he paused, pointed to her, then backed away. Smoothly, he began to waltz with an imaginary partner.

Bethanny held back a giggle as she watched the dashing gentleman waltz across the floor... alone.

Suddenly he paused and took a startled step back, placing a hand to his heart. He raised his hand as if judging the height of a person, then placed the hand much lower as if judging the height of a child. Shaking his head, he backed away and ran to the other side of the room. With a determined stride, he approached Clairmont. He pointed to the duke, held up his hands, then purposefully placed them over his throat.

As if he were being strangled.

Bethanny lost it and began to laugh, covering up the sound with her hand as Graham made silent choking noises. By now, she was following the story and couldn't help but watch in utter excitement and disbelief as the very masculine, very rakish Lord Graham, proceeded to tread the boards like he were at Drury Lane! She glanced to Carlotta, who appeared just as amused, though her eyes lingered longer on her husband than the actor.

Lord Graham had stopped strangling himself and ran toward a table across the room. With a quick glance about it, he pulled up a napkin and placed it around his waist and held up a silent instrument.

Surely he was implying Scotland, with the makeshift kilt and imaginary bagpipes. Suddenly, his expression was one of sorrow, as he pretended to wipe his eyes and dab his nose with the napkin that he'd just used as his kilt.

Then he picked up something invisible from the table and slit the top with a letter opener. He mimed the motions of opening up a letter and made quite a show of reading it. He threw it to the ground and stomped on it! But that wasn't dramatic enough apparently, because he began jumping on it, grinding into the floor with his boot!

Bethanny watched with wide-eyed wonder. Was that what he'd done when he received the letter? What *that* his reaction? How glorious! It was as if she were watching from afar all that had happened during that dreadful time when he left. As much as it was entertaining, it was also a gift.

A very public gift.

The other guests were watching with expressions ranging from confusion to rapt entertainment.

Lord Graham dusted off his hands and acted as if he were mounting a horse. Granted, he'd ridden in a carriage, but she wasn't going to be picky. With loping strides, he galloped around the room a full circle and paused, dismounting. He strode toward a bare wall. Standing back a few feet, he placed his hand to his heart and patted in a quick rhythm.

The fast beating of his heart.

With an over-exaggerated deep breath, he pretended to enter a house. Striding across the room, he approached the duke again; only this time, he knelt.

The duke chuckled approvingly and winked at Carlotta.

Lord Graham lifted his humble gaze and folded his hands.

Begging.

Bethanny's heart pinched then swelled with love and adoration for the gentleman who was laying his heart out for all to see.

Such a display couldn't be easy, but it was clearly done in love.

Love that was pouring off Bethanny in waves, resisting any kind of restraint.

Lord Graham then took it a step further and began bowing as if worshipping at the duke's feet.

Bethanny laughed loudly, along with the rest of the group, as the duke pretended to kick Lord Graham.

Smiling, Lord Graham bowed and pretended profuse

gratitude and then began to search. With his hand placed at his forehead, he pretended to be looking for something.

Someone. *Her*.

He picked up books and looked under them, picked up pillows to glance beneath them, and then paused to scratch his head in consternation.

Finally, he pulled out his pocket watch and waited. Then, he smiled grandly and placed his timepiece away and patted his belly.

Supper.

He paced the floor, his gaze shooting upward as if watching a stairway. He paused, his expression changing into wonderment. Without further delay, he strode toward Bethanny.

Her heart hammered in her chest, knowing this whole scene was for her, was an overt display of what was in his heart. She was certain that there was no way for him to speak with her about their pained past and their uncertain future in the company of chaperones and guests.

Yet, he had vaulted that wall and created his own path to her heart.

Nothing was more wonderful, more beautiful.

One day, she'd tell their children this story over and over, never tiring of it.

Lord Graham's gaze was hot with desire and intensity, heating her from the inside out and sending the silent message that he was no longer playing a game.

He stood before her, grasping her hands. He kissed each of them and knelt slowly, never taking his gaze from hers. Tenderly, he took her hands and placed them at his heart, smiling softly, moving them slightly, as if mimicking his heartbeat.

"You," he whispered, continuing to move her hands in the rhythm of his heart.

Bethanny took a deep breath.

It was her turn.

He had risked much. The least she could do would be to offer a small token as well. With a deep breath, she followed his example, kneeling before him as an example of her own affection. After all, he had humbled himself before the cream of the *ton*, the least she could do was meet him halfway.

Lord Graham's brow furrowed, and she offered him an indulgent smile. Pulling her hands slightly from his, he released her immediately, but she gasped his hands and pulled them toward her. Slowly, she placed them on her heart, mimicking the same rhythm he had begun.

"You," she whispered.

Lord Graham smiled then, a glorious and wonder-filled expression that stole her breath.

"No," he leaned forward, "mine." With the last word, he closed the distance and kissed her, a chaste kiss by most standards, but utterly scandalous in the aspect that it was in front of God and every one of their guests.

It was a good thing she was going to marry him.

After that display, she had no other option.

Nothing could have pleased her more.

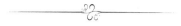

He did it! Truly, at first he thought he might expire from the weight of the implication of his actions, not to mention he wasn't an exhibitionist, but after seeing the wonder in Bethanny's eyes as he continued his charade, he was bolstered with courage. The crippling fear of rejection was no longer an issue. Further, he found himself not caring that he'd likely be the source of the sweetest gossip once they returned to London. He didn't care that he'd acted like a lovesick fool for the girl.

Because all that mattered was that she'd seen his heart, and that she returned his love.

As he watched her eyes brimming with unshed tears, he couldn't help but reach out and kiss her once more, not caring that everyone was watching. It was scandalous, but perfect. Releasing her lips and kissing her cheek, he tasted the salty trail of a tear that had finally spilled over.

Someone cleared his throat, and Graham reluctantly backed away, though his gaze never left Bethanny's. Her eyes were shining pools of love and delight, of hope and forgiveness.

Thank the Lord. Forgiveness.

"I'm assuming there is more to your extended version of charades than an unrealized desire to moonlight as an actor?" Clairmont asked, his tone amused yet with a slight edge.

Though Graham couldn't fault him; he *had* kissed his ward publically.

Couldn't blame him, but couldn't exactly regret his behavior either.

"Indeed. I'd like to announce my engagement to Miss Bethanny Lamont." Graham spoke with excited wonder, his tone almost foreign to his own ears.

Bethanny glowed, her face radiating the joy that echoed in his own heart.

"Then I shall not call you out," Clairmont announced.

Graham shot him a dark look but was beaten to the punch, so to say, by Carlotta, who had done the same then swatted her husband with her fan.

Clairmont simply chuckled and winked at his wife, who blushed.

It was most assuredly time for those two to retire to their bedroom.

"I'm sorry, but I didn't hear a proposal." Beatrix took a step forward, her tone assertive and challenging. "Did you?" She turned to Lord Neville.

"Er, actually... no." He shrugged and then shared a smile with her.

Graham exhaled an impatient breath. "It seems I forgot something, Miss Lamont." Standing, he pulled Bethanny up as well. "Miss Lamont, will you do me the intense honor of being my wife, and thereby putting me out of the acute misery of living without you, since you are my heartbeat, my breath, my very life?"

He didn't think Bethanny's smile could grow any brighter, yet it did. It was like trying to stare at the sun. It was too bright, too beautiful, only something heaven could contain.

"Yes. Finally!" she answered and threw her arms around his neck and pulled him into a tight embrace, before leaning back and placing an enthusiastic kiss, far less chaste than the one he had initiated earlier.

"Bethanny!" Clairmont scolded.

She ignored him

Bless the woman, she was perfection.

"Bethanny, dear," Carlotta whispered softly.

Reluctantly, Bethanny pulled away, but not before she whispered a soft, "I love you."

Graham felt his heart swell with gratitude. "Not as much as I love you, but I'll give you the rest of your life to try."

"Agreed."

CHAPTER EIGHTEEN

LONDON HAD NEVER felt so free. Of course that was likely because Graham had spent the remainder of the house party under guard.

For pity sake, they were engaged! Yet Clairmont insisted some footman dog him at all hours of the day... and night.

The day wasn't so terrible.

The night, however, was an entirely different story.

In truth, knowledge that a guard was posted outside of his door and, also, Bethanny's door had given him pause before he acted rashly.

But as soon as he kissed the soft skin of her hand and bid her goodnight, losing himself in the blatant desire in her expression, he'd go to his room... and stare at the door.

Then walk to the window, gaze down at the two-story drop, and calculate just how painful a broken ankle or leg would be. After all, any injury would be worth the reward of capturing a secluded moment — or entire night — with Bethanny.

Truthfully, he might have jumped if the result wouldn't have been a broken bone that would have inhibited the activities he wished to engage in to begin with. One cannot... please... if unable to even walk.

And then there was the guard at her door.

Blast.

That plan thwarted — and after an uttered curse toward the duke — he would sit on his very large and lonely bed and pray that the guard would fall asleep.

He never did.

And so, each morning Graham awoke in an awkward mess, sprawled out on top of his bed and with a worse disposition than the day before.

Until he saw her, and then it was as if the sun shone after months of rain, and he'd continue on — like the lovesick swain that he was — till night fell again.

Thankfully. the party had lasted only three additional days past his epic performance at charades; otherwise it might have killed him.

That *epic* performance was currently the most *on dit*, gossip, much to his chagrin. Granted, it had only been a week since the house party; A week where each of those seven days passed with the speed of frozen molasses. Though thankful to be home, he couldn't contain his anticipation for when it was not just his home... but Bethanny's as well. Graham smiled to himself and double-checked for the special license tucked carefully within his desk.

Two days.

Truly it couldn't soar by fast enough. Especially with Clairmont *still* insisting on Bethanny being shadowed by a chaperone *and* a hulking footman.

A footman that had far too many scars and far too little teeth.

Graham shivered.

No, Clairmont had won that round. It was clear he wasn't getting anywhere near Bethanny until she was safely married to him.

Graham bit back a groan of frustration at the conclusion that he hadn't kissed her since their very public engagement, and *that* wasn't very much of a kiss.

Yet, if he were to truly kiss her now… yes. He understood Clairmont's angle.

A kiss would *not* simply be a kiss. It would turn into something much more at a rapid pace.

Two days. He could make it. Graham sat behind the desk in his study and leaned back. Closing his eyes, he placed his hands behind his head and willed his tight body to relax.

The effort was futile.

Even in the soft crackling of the fire, he could hear the gentle swish of her skirt. The air seemed to carry her cloying fragrance of lemon and soft jasmine that captivated his senses. He even fancied he could hear the soft tinkle of her laughter.

His nose tickled, and, without opening his eyes, he swatted the pesky fly that had undoubtedly landed on his person.

Sighing deeply, he tried to relax once more, only this time the fly landed on his cheek.

Irritated, Graham slapped the offending insect and was greeted by feminine laughter drenched in amusement.

His eyes shot open as he turned to face… *Bethanny*?

"I…" He paused, narrowing his eyes. At first he was quite certain that all the madness of desire had finally caught up with him, and he was hallucinating.

There was no other plausible explanation.

"Hello to you as well… though I had anticipated a different sort of welcome." His eyebrow arched in challenge, and she held up a small feather and grinned unapologetically.

Slowly, Graham reached out and plucked the feather from her hand, his wits slowly restored. "Life will certainly be interesting with you, wont it?" he teased, before pulling her until she tumbled onto his lap.

Without hesitation, Graham placed his hands on her

shoulders and guided her into an immediately scorching kiss. His lips caressed hers, each sense overwhelming him, pulling him in deeper, causing him to thirst for more, to need to satisfy his desire for the woman he loved so deeply.

Breaking the seal of their lips, Graham gently tilted her head to expose the flesh of her neck. It was soft and inviting, begging to be ravished.

"How did you..." he spoke between kisses trailing down her jawline to the graceful curve of her neck, "get away?"

"I, er... good heavens." Bethanny made a soft moan of pleasure that caused Graham to smile in delight that he was rendering her senseless.

"Hmm?" he asked, toying with her buttons at the back of her dress to expose her shoulder.

"I, er..."

"I believe you said that," Graham teased.

Abruptly, she pulled away and narrowed her eyes slightly, though they danced with passionate delight. "Do you want to sit and have a chat with tea, or are you going to be quiet and kiss me?"

"Kiss you," Graham answered succinctly and proceeded to taste her mouth once more. His arms, far too long empty, were now full of her sweet body pressed against him. His hands roamed her back, traced the line of her waist, till resting on her hips. He gloried in her perfect shape, the delight of her form adding to the intense pleasure of her enthusiastic kiss. He trailed kisses down to her now-exposed shoulder and tasted her soft flesh, committing the scent and flavor to memory.

"Besides, it doesn't matter... I'm here, aren't I?" She breathed.

Graham paused.

His body demanded he continue his sweet exploration of their long-desired freedom, but he also wanted to live past the evening and long enough to marry the sweet temptress before him.

And Clairmont had warned him one too many times for his threats to not be valid.

Graham reached up and trailed a soft touch over her face before he let his fingers explore the softness of her rich hair. "Love... are you certain that—"

"If she is compromised—" Clairmont's voice boomed from the other side of the study door.

"Thank the Lord I had the good sense to lock it!" Bethanny scrambled from Graham's lap and righted her dress.

Which was, fortunately, only slightly askew.

Graham lamented the fact that their secret encounter was already at an end.

But oh, had it been deliciously sweet.

Two days, he reminded himself.

With a longsuffering sigh, he shared a glance with Bethanny as Clairmont proceeded to bang on his study door.

"Heaven help him when he has daughters... and you know the Almighty will give him a dozen as penance," Graham murmured to Bethanny as he went to unlock the study door.

"Yes?" Graham asked as he opened the door wide and was met with an angry duke.

"Bethanny," he ground out, his gaze slipping past Graham and landing on his previously missing ward.

"Yes, Your Grace." Bethanny curtseyed, her smile wide and utterly unapologetic.

"We're leaving... now. And I'm tying you up till you're officially married," he threatened, though Graham could see the bluster leaving, a sincere light of affection coloring his gaze.

"Perhaps if you granted a small amount of freedom to spend time with my betrothed, I wouldn't resort to such measures," Bethanny offered back, her arms crossed and her gaze leveled.

Graham wanted to kiss her so desperately his body ached

with the denial.

Turning, he watched Clairmont.

"You'll be lucky if you're allowed to leave your room after this incident," Clairmont shot back. "But perhaps I've been a bit..."

"Overbearing?" Bethanny finished just as Graham said, "Demented."

Clairmont shot a glare toward Graham.

To which Graham shrugged.

"Two days... and she is all yours... and your problem," Clairmont threatened with narrowed eyes.

"Believe me, I'm counting the hours."

Clairmont chuckled. "I do not doubt it." He then turned to Bethanny." If you're finished enjoying your measure of freedom with your fiancé, may we now return home? You may see Graham tomorrow, and I'll even allow five minutes alone."

"Alone without you... or alone without anyone at all?" Bethanny challenged.

"Without anyone... as apt as Graham is in the rakish talents... five minutes wouldn't be a very gracious start to your marriage." Clairmont shot a dark-humored glace to Graham.

To which Graham narrowed his eyes.

Bloody hell... the blackguard had him.

But he wasn't planning on compromising Bethanny before their wedding.

No, he wanted to be sure to take every consideration and make their lovemaking far more than a simple tumble brought on by overheated passion.

He wanted to give her more.

But more importantly, she deserved more.

"Very well." Bethanny nodded and began to walk toward the door.

"Just out of curiosity... how *did* you escape?" Graham

asked as he caught her hand and lifted it to his lips, inhaling the sweet fragrance one more time.

"She wasn't a prisoner." Clairmont rolled his eyes impatiently.

Graham arched a sarcastic brow as he glanced to the duke.

"It turns out my bodyguard has a fondness for the parlor maid…" She winked at Graham. "When I invited Molly to read with me… and then engaged the two into conversation… all that was left was for me to excuse myself to gather a book from my room, and the rest is not important."

"I believe it's very important," Clairmont challenged. "You were traveling alone, at night—"

"I never said I was alone… but a lady doesn't reveal all her secrets. Just know this. I was indeed safe."

"If you weren't alone, who was with you and where are they now?" Clairmont challenged.

Graham's gaze continued to dart between Bethanny and the duke, his amusement growing as he watched the two interact. It was a battle of stubborn will.

"That is none—"

"Indeed it is! I'm your guardian! How am I to guard you if you are out gallivanting—"

"We were not gallivanting—"

"Who is we?" Graham asked, his anxiety growing.

"Oh, for the love of all that is holy, will you two just be quiet?"

A shadowed figure eased his way from the hall. "Upon seeing Miss Lamont escaping your home, Your Grace, I offered to take her wherever she was trying to go. Forgive me this trespass, but I was more concerned about the lady's safety than social stigma," Lord Neville replied succinctly.

Graham felt his jaw drop.

Neville?

Graham glanced to Clairmont. His jaw, too, was

clenched.

"And just how do you plan to explain that your carriage was seen picking up Miss Lamont after dark and bringing her to a—"

"I wasn't in my carriage. I had hired a hack. And no one saw us," Lord Neville interrupted, his tone clipped.

"How can you be so certain?"

"It's my profession to know such things. I assumed that Miss Lamont was trying to make her way to Lord Graham's residence, which coincided with my own plans for the evening." Lord Neville adjusted his great coat. "To make a long story short, Miss Lamont was quite… determined. Once she was aware of my intentions, I had no choice but to take her with me to Lord Graham's residence. I didn't doubt her threat to walk alone at night, and I wasn't about to let her be in danger. Miss Lamont understood that I would give them a few moments of privacy." He glanced to the duke. "Not long enough to do permanent damage, I assure you." He then turned to Lord Graham. "And then I was going to make my presence known."

"Thank you for your consideration." Graham nodded appreciatively to Lord Neville. His curiosity piqued, he asked "Me? You were on your way to pay me a visit… at this hour?"

"Indeed. Now, since we have worked out all the sordid details of Miss Lamont's escapade, may I have a private audience with you, Lord Graham?" Neville asked, his dark eyes serious.

Graham nodded, and, after bidding a far-too-formal farewell to Bethanny and the duke, he ushered Neville into his office.

And bloody hell, if that office didn't still carry her scent…

"Graham, I have some distressing yet very important news I must share with you." Lord Neville seated himself.

Graham strode to this desk and sat, his brow furrowed. "Proceed."

"It has come to our attention—"

"Our?" Graham asked.

"Indeed. That's all you need to know at this point," Neville replied curtly.

"Very well."

"It has come to our attention that the deaths of the Baron and Baroness Lamont were not accidental."

"Pardon?" Graham felt his blood chill as he leaned forward, placing his hands on the cool wood of his desk.

"The deaths of Miss Lamont's parents appear to be intentional. And until we are able to lay to rest this suspicion, we must take care with the living relations."

"And you're just discovering this now?" Graham asked angrily.

"Indeed. We recently came upon incriminating evidence... of a sensitive nature."

"So Bethanny? Beatrix? Berty? They are all in danger?" Graham asked, leaning back in his chair, his heart hammering with resolution that not a hair on Bethanny's head would be harmed by any threat.

"Possibly, and until we have evidence, we are going to need to keep a sharp eye on the ladies," Neville paused and leaned forward, "especially Bethanny, being the oldest. That is why I'm approaching you first. I will call on Clairmont in the morrow."

"This is greatly disturbing news." Graham exhaled, his heart constricting with anger over someone threatening the one he loved.

"Indeed. Now you understand why I found myself outside of the Clairmont's residence."

"Yes, it makes sense now. Do you work for the war office?" Graham questioned.

"No," Neville replied, but offered no additional details. "I'll leave you to your evening. Don't worry, I shall see myself out."

"Much like you saw yourself in?" Graham arched an eyebrow.

"Indeed." Neville lips bent into an almost-smile, and then he disappeared into the hall.

Graham stood and walked to the fire.

As the flamed licked the wood, he considered his evening. The heat of desire had been quenched with a sickening dread.

But one thing was for certain, no harm would come to Bethanny as long as he still drew breath.

And with that final thought, Graham found peace.

CHAPTER NINETEEN

Bᴇᴛʜᴀɴɴʏ ꜱᴛᴀʀᴇᴅ ᴏᴜᴛ the carriage window, the dim streetlights blurring as she considered Lord Neville's purpose in seeking out Graham. Obviously, she wasn't privy to hearing their private conversation, but she couldn't help but be intensely curious. Narrowing her eyes, she turned to the duke. She inhaled, opening her mouth to speak, but upon catching the leveled glare the duke was sending in her direction, she closed her mouth and sighed instead.

Drat.

She had rather hoped her courageous statement of opinion earlier and the verbal sparring that had resulted were the end of the issue.

No such luck.

Truthfully, she should have known better.

"Whatever you do, please do not turn out Molly and Douglas on their ear. Truly, it wasn't their fault," Bethanny pleaded softly.

"Oh, believe me, I lay the entire situation's blame at your feet, and your feet alone." The duke spoke curtly, his blue eyes narrowing.

Bethanny felt the distinct desire to shrink under his scrutiny. Immediately, she felt as if she were five and being scolded by her father. True, the duke was far younger, but the expression was one and the same. She glanced down. Thankfully, the usual pain at remembering her parents had dimmed with time and, much as Carlotta had said so long ago, the memories were ones of joy, rather than an unending source of pain.

With a soft sigh, she raised her gaze to the duke, only to be speared with the same expression of *just you wait till we get home, young lady*. With such a perfected fatherly glare, the duke was sure to be a wonderful parent.

At once, the amusing curse Graham had spoken just before he had allowed the duke entrance into his study caused a bubble of laughter to escape her lips.

She raised a gloved hand to stifle the mirth, but it was too late.

"Please, don't control your amusement for my benefit. I'm deeply curious as to what you find amusing in this situation, especially since I can't think of a damn thing," the duke spoke darkly.

Bethanny should have been scandalized at his foul language, but rather she supposed it was accurate for the emotional turmoil she had put him through, so with a reluctant sigh — and a brimming smile that wouldn't remain hidden — she explained, "Well, Your Grace. It would seem that your good friend said something earlier that I simply found all too... accurate."

"I'm assuming the *good friend* you're referring to is Graham, though I'm struggling with that title at the current moment." He leaned forward and placed his hands on his knees. "What is this *accurate* thing that he spoke of?" He let out a beleaguered sigh. Clearly irritated, he took off his tall, dark hat, setting it to the side of him on the bench.

For good measure, he smoothed the soft felt. Satisfied

with its state, he turned to Bethanny, a question in his expression.

His impatient expression.

"I believe you're aware that Carlotta confided in us that soon we shall all have a lovely little one to spoil." Bethanny grinned widely, her hands refused to stay prim and proper on her lap; rather, they excitedly fidgeted on her lap.

"Indeed." He nodded slowly. "And I must make certain you understand that spoiling is perfectly fine. However, you mustn't *teach* my heir anything. Heaven only knows the poor child will be born with enough mischief in his blood simply being mine." The duke shook his head as if concerned already.

"Actually, what Lord Graham said was of the same variety." Bethanny shrugged.

"I doubt it was that exactly." He narrowed his eyes.

Bethanny simply smiled in return.

"Must I remind you that—"

"Very well, I do believe I've been threatened enough for one evening. Goodness, is this what it feels like to be Graham? It's a wonder he still likes you!" Bethanny shook her head as she studied her guardian.

"He has to. I'm allowing him to marry *you*," the duke shot back, his eyebrows raised.

"You do have a point."

"Yes. I rather do." He nodded then wiped his face with his hands, as if reaching the end of his rope. "Good Lord, as much as I want a daughter who is the image of her mother, I truly hope she is less work than the lot of you."

"I feel rather slighted," Bethanny huffed, an amused smile on her lips.

"If you had endured what I have, at your hand, in the past few hours, you'd not be offended. You'd saint me for my patience."

"Yes, sainthood is most assuredly in your future," Bethanny replied with a hint of sarcasm.

"Since when did you get so... bold. I do believe I must lay the blame at Lady Southridge's feet," he mumbled.

"Or Carlotta's." Bethanny smiled sweetly.

"Blast it all, I'm surrounded."

"Speaking of Lady Southridge, where is she? I heard she left the day after Graham's proposal, but I didn't even remember seeing her at supper," Bethanny asked.

"She had some important business that couldn't wait. That's all she told me as she took her leave. I'm quite certain she wasn't concerned about the outcome of Graham's intentions, knowing both of you as she does."

"Indeed." Bethanny nodded, still slightly confused, but she was accustomed to feeling that particular emotion when in conjunction with Lady Southridge, so she shrugged it away.

"At least Beatrix is a bit quieter," Bethanny offered.

"Berty will more than make up for that," the duke shot back. "By the time I have you three married off and settled, with my luck, I'll have a little girl parading around and mimicking her aunts' every move and... good Lord, I'm too old for this." He leaned his head back against the seat and closed his eyes.

"I have a feeling that we all will have quite the opposite effect, especially your expected heir." Bethanny leaned forward slightly till the duke gave her his attention. "Rather, Your Grace, we keep you young." She smiled and braced herself slightly as the carriage halted. Without another word, she waited for the footman to open the door. Soundlessly, she exited and walked into the house.

Thankfully, the duke hadn't lectured her further, and she'd been able to ready herself for bed. With a soft sigh, she lay down on the soft mattress and inhaled the familiar scent of lavender. As she rubbed her feet together and listened for the sweet song of the chirping crickets, the last coherent memory was a simple number.

Two days.

Two days, and she'd no longer be sleeping alone.

Graham studied his reflection as his valet continued to brush his fine wool coat, pausing only to tug on a sleeve or adjust a dimple in his cravat. He stared at the mirror, but wasn't seeing himself; he was imagining Bethanny.

His soon-to-be wife.

The past two days had been an eternity wrapped into a mocking forty-eight hours.

But blessedly, he had only two hours left till the ceremony.

Already, guests had arrived to St. George's. The chapel had become quite the rage for *ton* marriages; thankfully, they were accustomed to accommodating the impatient requests of the local gentry.

Lord Graham included.

And so, at precisely eleven in the morning, the priest would join them together in marriage.

How unfortunate that it was only nine.

"Sir, if you insist on moving, this will regrettably take much longer to do," Simmons, his valet, scolded gently.

"Very well." Graham tried to remain still.

And apparently failed, as Simmons shot him an imploring expression.

"I do believe this is as good as I can do at the moment." Simmons took a step back and regarded him, his trained eyes taking in every line, stitch, and fold in Graham's appearance.

"Thank you," Graham offered.

"It is an absolute pleasure, my lord." Simmons bowed and left silently, leaving him alone with his thoughts.

Graham exhaled an anxious breath. As impatient as he was, another part of him could hardly believe that the moment was almost upon him. A wonder-filled smile teased his lips.

Bethanny

Passionate love and a protective instinct roared to life within him at just the thought of her name. To think he had wasted so much time running from the gift that was standing before him.

He was simply thankful he had amended his way of thinking before it was too late.

Before he lost the only woman who would ever own his very heartbeat.

As much as he had seen love, experienced aspects of it from various points of view, nothing could have ever prepared him for the all-encompassing drive it created within, the utter sacrifice of self and the complete exaltation of another.

Not that Bethanny was perfect. He wouldn't do such a disservice to her as to put her on a pedestal she'd only topple from. No one deserved the pressure of being worshiped.

Even one such as he knew that belonged only to God.

Besides, it was her imperfections, the specific ones that set her apart as the perfectly flawed one that completed him.

That drove him to distraction.

That somehow combined into the most beautiful, mysterious creation God had fashioned.

And he was to be her husband.

The enormity of the situation hit Graham hard. It was now his responsibility — no — his *honor* to protect her, love her selflessly, love her *only*. She would be his to serve, to stand by, to support.

His.

No one else's.

Closing his eyes, he pictured her face, the soft curl of her mahogany mane, the dancing light in her bottomless brown eyes, and the sensual curve of her neck.

Two hours.

One ceremony.

One celebration.

And then there would be nothing left to separate them.

Literally.

With a rakish grin, Graham turned to the fire.

Two hours.

And she'd be his.

"She's perfect. Would you *stop* fussing with her?" Berty's impatient voice clipped.

"I *know* she's perfect," Beatrix ground out, shooting a glare in Berty's direction. "She's breathtaking. I'm simply adjusting her dress slightly—"

"No, you're going to wrinkle it," Berty interrupted.

"I. Will. Not." Beatrix bit the words and then took a step back. Expelling a frustrated sigh, she relaxed her shoulders and regarded her sister.

"Bethanny, you truly are a vision. Lord Graham is going to swallow his tongue."

"Beatrix!" Bethanny cried, though she was delighted that Beatrix thought her *that* beautiful.

"He won't do such a thing." Berty rolled her eyes. "It's practically impossible to do."

"He won't take his eyes off of you," Beatrix asserted.

"That is for certain." Berty nodded.

"Oh, dear Lord, am I too late?" Lady Southridge rushed into the room, her dress slightly disheveled and her hat askew, as if she had been running.

"Lady Southridge!" Bethanny cried, her sisters echoing her words a moment after her. "Where have you been? We've been worried though Carlotta assured us—"

"Oh, my darlings! I'm perfectly well. Simply had to rush off. So sorry I didn't pause to say goodbye. It was rather a pressing matter, however. All is well, though. No need to fuss." She swatted the air delicately and then pulled Berty —

who was closest in proximity — into an embrace. Beatrix stepped over and wrapped her arms around the two, laying her head on Lady Southridge's back.

Bethanny waited, her heart swelling with joy and relief. When Carlotta had said that Lady Southridge had been called away upon urgent business, Bethanny had despaired whether she was well, or injured, and if she'd return in time for the wedding.

"I'm here, I'm here, my dears," she cooed and pressed a soft kiss to Berty's cheek.

"Thank heavens. What in creation had you leaving without so much as saying goodbye?" Beatrix asked, releasing her.

"All in good time, my loves. Now," she turned to face Bethanny, "I do believe I'm gaining a sister today." She beamed delightedly.

"You know," Bethanny tilted her head and studied Lady Southridge with a grin, "I had never thought of it that way. It's true, isn't it?" Bethanny grinned widely.

"Indeed, however, since I've already asserted myself as your grandmother, I'll retain the position. I've always felt more of a mother to Graham than a sister. He'll tell you I've been bossy enough to be one as well!" She giggled.

"What matters," Bethanny stepped forward and grasped her hands, "is that we are family."

"Indeed. And I must say, my brother has delightful taste. Not only are you stunningly beautiful to behold, dear one, but..." she leaned forward, a twinkle in her eye, "you are even more breathtakingly beautiful inside." Softly she reached out and touched toward Bethanny's heart.

Tears stung Bethanny's eyes at the soft gesture. "Thank you."

"Girls! Are we ready? It's about time to depart." Carlotta swept into the room and paused. "Lady Southridge! Thank Heavens! I got your missive that you were trying to be here, but when I didn't hear anything further, I began to worry!" Carlotta rushed forward and embraced her.

"All's well. I'm the least of your worries. Keep your concerns for these ones and the new little one you'll be handing over to me shortly to spoil." She winked.

"Between you and the girls…" Carlotta smiled indulgently, as she placed a hand to her belly, "there's no hope for this one. He or she will be rotten to the core."

"Spoiled with love." Lady Southridge amended with a firm nod and a bright smile. She turned and glanced past Bethanny. "Good heavens! Why didn't anyone tell me I looked such a fright! 'Take the curricle,' he said… my foot," she mumbled

"Curricle?"

"Long story. I'll explain later… however, I must say they are indeed fast." A wild light entered her gaze as she fixed her appearance and nodded as she finished.

"Shall we depart? I believe Bethanny has an appointment with a priest."

"Indeed I do." Bethanny grinned.

"Indeed you do, sweet one." Carlotta grinned. "Will you three give us a moment?" she asked.

"Of course. Girls?" Lady Southridge ushered the girls out of the room and left with a quick wink then closed the door.

Carlotta took a deep breath.

Bethanny began to feel slightly uneasy.

"Sweet one… let us sit for a moment." Carlotta led Bethanny to the chairs situated by the fire.

"Bethanny, tonight is a very important night, and I want to make sure that you are… prepared." Carlotta visibly swallowed.

"For… er…" Bethanny blushed painfully, unable to finish the sentence.

Carlotta cleared her throat. "Yes." She smoothed the already-pressed lines in her skirt.

"I… may I ask you a question?" Bethanny asked after an awkward moment.

"That is why I'm here. I'm sure you have quite a few." Carlotta smiled bravely, but it didn't reach her eyes; she was clearly as uncomfortable as Bethanny.

In fact, the only person she *wouldn't* be uncomfortable with in addressing this topic was her soon-to-be husband.

Graham.

Immediately the tension that had risen within her melted away.

"Actually… would you think it incredibly foolish of me to simply *not* ask any questions and discover more about this topic… with my husband?" Bethanny felt her cheeks heat with color in embarrassment.

Carlotta tilted her head, a grin taking root in her lips and then flourishing in her expression. "Sweet one, I believe that is brilliant. Not," she tilted her chin down and speared Bethanny with a glance, "because I'm uncomfortable with this topic and do not wish to address it with you." She paused, waiting for her words to sink in. "But because I have no doubt that your husband will be far and away the best educator. After all, it is apparent that you trust him deeply."

Bethanny nodded. "With my life… my heart."

"Then your body will easily follow. Simply know this. There is no reason to fear, because perfect love casts out all fear. This includes fear of the unknown, fear of inadequacy, fear of inability. Physical love can lay bare every insecurity you possess, yet the perfect love it consummates destroys that fear, because it's there where love was created to be its strongest. And that strength comes from the knowledge that it isn't for the night, it isn't for the next week… it's for a lifetime."

Bethanny nodded, her heartbeat loud in her ears as she considered Carlotta's words.

Hid them in her heart to remember at all times.

"Now." Carlotta stood and held out her hand. "Shall we go and get you married?"

At last.

Graham struggled to remain still as he waited at the front of the St. George's chapel. The music had begun; it would be only seconds until—

Bethanny.

Resplendent in sky blue silk, she began toward him, her gate graceful yet slightly stilted — much like the way she waltzed.

Graham would have smiled at the correlation had his heart not been beating furiously or his lungs stopped taking in air at the sight of her. She was beautiful, in every classical way a woman would surely wish to be beautiful for her wedding, but it was deeper, a glow that emanated from within that gave her a heavenly radiance almost too brilliant to behold.

Her hair was loosely tucked into soft curls that framed her delicate features, the heavy mane simply waiting for him to explore it thoroughly.

But not yet.

Graham finally took in air, practically gasping as he felt the burning in his lungs. However, it was the stinging in his eyes that demanded his attention.

Though he was never one to be overly emotional, he couldn't help himself and the passionate response her very presence provoked.

The last few steps toward him were torturous, till at last, she placed her dainty hand within his, her eyes alight with tears and joy, with promises and hope.

The rest of the ceremony was simply a blur. He spoke when prompted, turned when nudged, yet all he saw was the lovely face of the woman becoming his wife.

As the ceremony came to a close, he couldn't fight it any longer.

"Before God, let me now present—" the priest began.

But Graham didn't wait for him to finish his declaration. Rather, he reached forward and pulled Bethanny into his embrace, finding the softness of her lips and filling himself on their flavor. After the initial shock — and slight gasp — Bethanny met his passionate response with an equal one of her own, as if she were just as impatient as he!

The priest coughed.

Graham ignored him.

Rather, he teased Bethanny's lower lip with his tongue, pressing his lean body into her soft one, savoring the sensation and memorizing the fragrance of rosewater as he inhaled her sweetness.

The priest cleared his throat.

Twice.

And it was Bethanny who gentled the kiss and eventually released him, her face blushing a vermillion that only heightened her beauty.

The cathedral hummed with the amused chuckles of the guests and a few indignant huffs of disgust.

But Graham didn't care. He already was the source of gossip with his dramatic proposal; this would only add to his legend.

And he rather liked to think his actions as legendary rather than simply hopelessly romantic.

Although *romantically legendary* had a certain ring to it.

The priest took in a breath as if preparing to speak, but then he shrugged, an amused grin taking over his features. With a gesture to the organist, the music began, and Graham ushered out his bride, squeezing her hand tightly within his.

And, thank the Lord, he'd never have to let go.

CHAPTER TWENTY

DAMN THE MAN or woman who decided wedding breakfasts were necessary.

All Graham could do was pray for mercy as the seconds ticked away with painful, unhurried method. Yet each time he'd glanced at his pocket watch, Bethanny's grip had tightened on his arm. Each time her grip had tightened, he'd glanced back to her and remembered the moment he'd first seen her walking down the aisle toward him.

She was beautiful, a vision from every dream he had ever been creative or poetic enough to imagine. The beauty of St. George's arched ceilings, the pillars and molded wood seemed ragged against the breathtaking beauty now standing beside him. As she'd walked down the aisle, it was as if his body had revolted against him, not allowing breath into his lungs and his heart pounding so hard its cadence drowned out the organ music.

The rest was a blur; all he remembered was when she'd said yes.

And the warm sensation of her hand within his.

Much like the warmth of her hand placed upon his arm.

Right now, he wanted that warmth on far more than his arm.

And, in the seemingly never-ending cycle, he'd reached down for his pocket watch and realized that only two minutes had passed since the last time he'd checked.

"I do believe it's time to depart," Graham spoke suddenly, interrupting Lord Neville's congratulatory words.

Bethanny shot him a surprised and slightly panicked expression.

Hopefully, she was only concerned about his lack of social grace, and not his impatience to begin other... activities.

Yet, as he remembered their clandestine meeting and the kiss that had scorched his very soul, he was quite certain she was only scandalized at his social skills.

But he was a desperate man.

And desperate men didn't hold to convention.

No, they simply didn't give a damn anymore.

So, with a knowing look from Lord Neville, Graham excused himself and his stuttering bride and made his way out of the entrance of the duke's residence, where the breakfast had been held.

And God was smiling on them, for behold, his carriage stood waiting.

"I rather thought your impulsive nature might get the best of you," Clairmont called out behind them.

"I can't imagine your meaning," Graham shot back as he helped a beaming Bethanny into the carriage.

"Let's just say I've been in your shoes... and they are hell itself."

"You do have a heart in there." Graham grinned as he glanced to the duke's chest.

"So I've been told." Clairmont shrugged. "I don't expect to see you soon." He smirked and turned back to enter the house.

"Please remind me to thank your guardian profusely...

much later." Graham murmured as he gathered his bride into his arms and settled her onto his lap.

Good Lord, if I thought the breakfast was torture, the carriage ride will be even worse!

"I'm surprised you lasted *this* long." Bethanny grinned and leaned down, tracing her tongue along his lips before passionately assaulting him.

Graham groaned in pleasure as her sweet tongue danced with his, her body shifting slightly to press into his frame.

Her soft fragrance driving him mad.

With herculean self-control, Graham continued to kiss her, *only* kiss her as they made their way to his townhome. Her lips were soft delights that caused the fire of desire to burn and smolder till his self-control held on by a slight thread. Only the knowledge of her innocence held him in check.

He wanted to be perfect for her, each time, every time, but especially the first.

The carriage rocked to a halt, and Graham gently set Bethanny from his lap, his body demanding that he return her to the previous position, yet he resisted the urge to ravage her in the carriage and exited, holding out his hand for her to alight as well.

Then, without warning, he bent and swept her into his arms. Bounding up the stairs, he sent up a silent prayer of thanks when Watkins immediately opened the door and bowed, a knowing grin on his face.

"We are not to be disturbed," Graham shot over his shoulder as he made his way to the stairs.

"Of course." Watkins bowed, but Graham only caught the first hint of the gesture; rather, he was focusing on taking the stairs, two at a time, savoring the sweet tingling laughter coming from his wife as she held tightly to his neck.

She *knew* she should be scandalized, first with the presumptive and overly passionate kiss interrupting the priest, and *then* with leaving their own celebration far too early, yet Bethanny couldn't find it within her heart to give a fig.

Rather, she was lost entirely in the bliss of knowing she was loved by the man who had utterly captured her heart. Graham's strong arms held her tightly as he bounded up the stairs, as if almost afraid to let her go.

She understood the desperation. It had been too long since they had been afforded any measure of privacy.

The five minutes the duke had given them over the past two days didn't signify.

She ached, *needed* to have him to herself, uninterrupted and unhurried.

And, thank the good Lord, she was finally able to have that time.

And it was only the beginning. Because she was his wife, of all the women in the world, only *she* would carry his last name, his title... his children. Unable to restrain her delight, she leaned forward and pressed her lips against his neck. His flesh was scented with a sweet spice that sent her senses to reeling as her body warmed further with desire. She nipped his skin slightly with her teeth, earning a groan of delight mixed with frustration from her husband.

Husband.

She'd never get tired of saying it.

"You will be the death of me," Graham swore as he shifted her weight so he could open the door to his rooms with one hand, while balancing her weight with his other.

Bethanny raised an eyebrow to show her approval.

"Love, I appreciate that you are easily impressed... but it's not necessary," Graham teased and carried her over the threshold. Kicking the door closed, he promptly deposited her on the bed, not allowing even a breath of time before his lips covered hers. Gently pressing into her, she reclined on the bed, relishing the intoxicating sensation of her husband's weight atop of her. He teased her lips with his own before darting his tongue along hers, the beautiful expression of give and take that sent her body to humming with a need she didn't understand.

"I do believe we are finally alone, countess," he whispered along her lips as he moved to nip teasingly at her jawline.

"Indeed," Bethanny whispered back, arching her neck to give him greater access.

"I love the curve of your neck. I swear you taste like heaven just here." Graham swirled his tongue just where her shoulder and neck met, causing her to gasp. "I'll remember that." He chuckled and proceeded to nudge the fabric of her dress with his nose. "However, I do believe we must do something about this." He pulled at the fabric with his teeth.

Bethanny gasped slightly as she glanced down to watch him. His eyes were dark and smoldering embers that promised to set her aflame.

Though she could have sworn she was already burning.

Gathering her courage, she ran her hands over his chest and under his coat, loosening it from his frame. "The same could be said of you, my lord." She teased as she tugged on his cravat, loosening it and pulling till the silk was removed from his neck entirely. She tossed it to the floor, not waiting for the soft garment to float downward; rather impatiently, she leaned forward and began to kiss the small opening at the base of his neck.

"Good Lord, Bethanny," Graham spoke hoarsely.

She smiled against his skin, savoring the millions of pleasurable sensations all surrounding her, creating a fog of desire.

"Enough." Graham pulled himself from the bed, his eyes dark with something mysteriously delicious. He made quick work of removing his coat entirely and began on the buttons of his blindingly white shirt. Groaning after impatiently unbuttoning three, he swore under his breath and removed the garment over his head.

Bethanny gasped.

His movement had tightened the hardened muscles in his abdomen, causing a rippling effect, which captivated her. He was beautiful. As he tossed the shirt to the floor, his shoulders bunched with the gesture, and her gaze traveled upward, taking in the firm lines of his chest and the smooth texture of his skin.

When she moved her gaze to meet his, she grinned as he winked at her. "I'm delighted you approve." He smiled, showing off his dimples.

Bethanny sighed in appreciation.

"If you've finished enjoying the view, I believe it's my turn," he whispered softly as he lithely stepped toward her, his amber eyes never leaving hers.

"For?" Bethanny asked, her attention arrested by the way his shoulders swayed when he walked, the way his stomach tensed when she reached out and touched the smooth and firm, warm skin.

"To enjoy the view." He pulled her from her sitting position on the bed. Without a word, he tugged on the sash behind her, loosening the fabric so that it was no longer tight, but flowing around her waist. At first, he slid each button through with unhurried motions. "I hate buttons." He swore after a moment. "You're never to wear them again," he pleaded impatiently before tugging on the fabric and sending the offending objects scattering along the floor.

Bethanny shot him an irritated glare. She had rather liked that dress.

"I'll make up for it, I promise," Graham assured with a wicked grin as he removed her gown from her shoulders and let it pool to the ground in a whisper of silk.

"Bethanny," he whispered as he bent and kissed her bare shoulder. His breath tickled her flesh all while sending shivers of desire along her body. Silently, he tugged on the strings of her corset, and quicker than her maid had ever accomplished the task, had it loosened enough to be removed.

"Don't be afraid," he assured her as she clung to the French-designed garment.

Taking a deep breath, she raised her arms and allowed Graham to pull it over her head.

His Adam's apple bobbed as he took in the sight of her, fierce emotion clouding his gaze as he placed a delicate kiss at her heart.

She lifted her hands and placed them at his head, tugging at his dark hair and exhaling softly as he turned so that his ear was placed against her heart.

Graham lifted his head and all but attacked her lips, his hands immediately going to her hair, loosening it from its bindings.

She heard the clatter of pins hitting the floor.

Joining the buttons.

However, that was the last coherent thought she was able to pull from her mind as Graham's hands roamed her back, deftly eliminating the remaining clothing that separated them.

With a grace she'd never be able to attain, Graham had expertly laid her out on the mattress, joining her and warming her, all while overwhelming her senses.

And as the night wore on, Bethanny discovered all the knowledge she had lacked, and, by far, experience was the best teacher.

Especially when one's teacher was her husband.

Graham awoke with the sweet scent of rosewater tickling his senses.

And his nose.

Opening his eyes, he turned slightly, only to encounter his wife's unclad form pressed against him in the most provocative manner imaginable.

And Graham had always had a very active imagination.

His nose twitched again as he gently brushed away a few strands of her glorious mane that were tickling his face.

Biting back a groan of desire, he relaxed and simply gazed at his sleeping beauty.

Heaven knew, after last night she needed her rest.

He needed his rest.

After all, no one would disturb them for days, weeks even.

He might be able to stretch it for a few months, if luck were on his side.

There was no need to be impatient or hurried.

Bethanny stirred and pressed into him further.

However, this time he wasn't able to stifle the groan, and it came out as a hoarse croak.

"Good morning," she murmured, her eyes far too bright for one to have just awakened.

"Minx. But I must say your choice of torture is quite persuasive," he mumbled as he kissed her deeply.

"Is that so?" she purred against his lips.

"Hmm."

Hang rest, Graham thought as he once again sought the intensely captivating pleasure found in his wife's arms.

Afterward, Graham caressed the soft, inviting skin of her shoulder. "I almost feel as though I'm in danger of waking up."

Bethanny shifted so that she met his gaze. "I understand entirely." Her gaze was so perfectly clear, so full of love it was almost blinding to behold.

"It seems so inadequate... but, I love you. Utterly, completely love you." He leaned forward and kissed her nose.

"I think I love you more," she replied softly.

"I highly doubt that." Graham chuckled and pulled her in closer.

"It's true. You know why?" Bethanny glanced up at him, a twinkle in her eye.

"Why then? Though I must add that I will not agree to the validity of your argument."

"Very well. But I love you more because I loved you *first.*" She raised a daring eyebrow for emphasis.

Graham chuckled, tickling her ribs and earning a squeal.

He was going to enjoy teasing her for the rest of their lives.

Teasing and tasting.

It was a beautiful combination.

"You might have loved me first…" Graham growled as he leaned into ravage her mouth, "but I most assuredly love you the most," he murmured as he trailed kisses down to her navel and paused, glancing up at her.

"And why is that?" She grinned, though he could see the passion building in her eyes.

Graham shifted so that he was facing her once more. Tenderly touching her face, he trailed his fingers down her brow and over her cheeks to the sweet temptation of her lips. "You know… how about I simply show you… for the next fifty or so years?" He grinned.

"Fifty at least," Bethanny agreed and pulled him into her embrace.

At least fifty.

EPILOGUE

"WHAT DO YOU mean, it's Beatrix?" Graham narrowed his eyes as he studied Neville as the gentleman swirled brandy around the crystal glass, staring at it.

"I cannot say… other than our first assumption was that the threat was aimed at the eldest — your wife. It seems that after her marriage to you, she was no longer a threat, or threatened, however you look at it." Neville exhaled tightly, his body a ridged pose of tension. "We are taking every effort to assure that Miss Lamont is completely safe."

"I'm sure you are," Graham ground out. This wasn't good. Heaven only knew what his wife would do when she found out her sister was the prime target in such danger. As it was, the duke hadn't informed her or her sisters of the possible threat.

Unfortunately, Graham hadn't known that when he addressed the topic with Bethanny. His poor wife had gone white; then as the news apparently settled, she'd turned a rather fetching and dangerous shade of red.

And after her display of temper — aimed the unnamed persons providing the threat — he'd decided that his wife just might be able to take care of herself as well. And he'd assumed that Beatrix and Berty were more like their sister than Neville imagined. However, that didn't mean that they should take the threat lightly; no, it simply gave Graham a small amount of peace, knowing that his wife wasn't as helpless as he'd originally thought.

"I simply wanted you to be aware of the situation." Neville stood. Striding to the sideboard, he placed his half-empty glass upon it and made his way to the door.

"Pardon me, my Lord, but—"Whitaker began but was interrupted by the roar of the Duke of Clairmont.

"Graham! For pity sake, move, old man." Clairmont blustered through the door, practically knocking Whitaker over in the process. "You!" Clairmont paused and narrowed his eyes at Neville. Slowly, he took menacing steps toward him. "You said it was a threat, you didn't say—" Clairmont didn't finish his sentence; rather, he swung and hit Neville directly in the jaw, sending the man stumbling backward.

To Neville's credit, he didn't let the powerful impact level him; reasonably, he rolled his shoulders and wiped the blood from his mouth.

"She's gone," Clairmont spat, his voice shaking with a fury born of fear.

"Who?" Neville whispered, though his face turned white, and his fists clenched.

"Beatrix, you bloody bastard! She's been taken!"

Graham felt his blood run cold.

"No," Neville whispered, the sound hoarse.

"Yes," Clairmont responded, his voice just as hoarse and broken.

"Good Lord, tell me you have something to go on, some lead to find her," Graham spoke up, striding toward them.

At his question, Neville eyes snapped from their horrorstricken expression and transformed him into a man with a vendetta, with a mission he'd not fail. "I have my suspicions… but know this. I *will* find her." He swore, his dark eyes resolute, his voice cold with purpose.

"See that you do, or do not come back at all," Clairmont threatened and turned to leave. "I have a family that needs me, and you…" he turned back to Neville, "fail this and I'll make sure you have nothing."

Graham watched as his friend left with a dark scowl, his very steps threatening.

"If she's lost, I'll have nothing regardless." Graham heard Neville whisper a moment before he left the room, his form engulfed in shadows before his footsteps down the hall.

Graham exhaled a tired breath.

He had to tell Bethanny.

ABOUT THE AUTHOR

KRISTIN VAYDEN'S inspiration for the romance she writes comes from her tall, dark and handsome husband with killer blue eyes. With five children to chase, she is never at a loss for someone to kiss, something to cook or some mess to clean but she loves every moment of it! She loves to make soap, sauerkraut, sourdough bread and gluten-free muffins. Life is full of blessings and she praises God for the blessed and abundant life He's given her.

BLUE TULIP

PUBLISHING

www.bluetulippublishing.com

21375302R10162

Made in the USA
Middletown, DE
27 June 2015